Praise for Emma Wildes
An Indecent Proposition

"Regency fans will thrill to this superbly sensual tale of an icy widow and two decadent rakes. . . . Balancing deliciously erotic encounters with compelling romantic tension and populating a convincing historical setting with a strong cast of well-developed characters, prolific romance author Wildes provides a spectacular and skillfully handled story that stands head and shoulders above the average historical romance." —*Publishers Weekly* (starred review)

"Wickedly delicious and daring, Wildes's tale tantalizes with an erotic fantasy that is also a well-crafted Regency romance. She delivers a page-turner that captures the era, the mores, and the scandalous behavior that lurks beneath the surface."
—*Romantic Times* (4½ stars, top pick)

"A luxurious and sensual read. Both deliciously wicked and tenderly romantic . . . I didn't want it to end!"
—*New York Times* bestselling author Celeste Bradley

"[A] gem of an author . . . Ms. Wildes tells this story with plenty of compassion, humor, and even a bit of suspense to keep readers riveted to each scandalous scene—and everything in between."
—Romance Junkies

"A historical gem. . . . Don't expect a cookie-cutter romance in *An Indecent Proposition*. Ms. Wildes places enough twists and turns in the story as more than one character finds everlasting love."
—TwoLips Reviews

continued . . .

More Praise for Emma Wildes

"Of all the authors I've read, I believe Emma Wildes to be my hands-down favorite. . . . Ms. Wildes has once again shown her ability to present new variations of romance in all of its infinite forms. Be prepared to feel your passions grow as you read the beautifully written love scenes." —Just Erotic Romance Reviews (5 stars)

"Emma Wildes has an amazing flair for taking what could be considered controversial subject matter and turning it into a beautiful love story that has the reader cheering for the characters. . . . It is a truly rare and remarkable talent." —Euro-Reviews

"Unique, masterfully written, and engaging story lines coupled with fascinating characters are what every reader can expect from Emma Wildes. For fans of historical and Regency romance, look no further. Ms. Wildes possesses a beautiful, flowing writing style that transports her readers to another time as the sights and sounds come to life around them. My expectations are exceeded every time I read one of her books!" —TwoLips Reviews

"Chock-full of mysteries, torrid romances, unforgettable characters . . . delightfully fun and wicked." —Romance Junkies

"'Sexy' and 'enchanting' aptly describe Wildes's latest. . . . This is delightful reading from beginning to end."
—*Romantic Times* (4 stars)

"Emma Wildes is a rising star who writes incredible historical romance." —Fallen Angel Reviews

Also by Emma Wildes

An Indecent Proposition

Lessons from a Scarlet Lady

EMMA WILDES

Seducing the Highlander

A SIGNET ECLIPSE BOOK

SIGNET ECLIPSE
Published by New American Library, a division of
Penguin Group (USA) Inc., 375 Hudson Street,
New York, New York 10014, USA
Penguin Group (Canada), 90 Eglinton Avenue East, Suite 700, Toronto,
Ontario M4P 2Y3, Canada (a division of Pearson Penguin Canada Inc.)
Penguin Books Ltd., 80 Strand, London WC2R 0RL, England
Penguin Ireland, 25 St. Stephen's Green, Dublin 2,
Ireland (a division of Penguin Books Ltd.)
Penguin Group (Australia), 250 Camberwell Road, Camberwell, Victoria 3124,
Australia (a division of Pearson Australia Group Pty. Ltd.)
Penguin Books India Pvt. Ltd., 11 Community Centre, Panchsheel Park,
New Delhi - 110 017, India
Penguin Group (NZ), 67 Apollo Drive, Rosedale, North Shore 0632,
New Zealand (a division of Pearson New Zealand Ltd.)
Penguin Books (South Africa) (Pty.) Ltd., 24 Sturdee Avenue,
Rosebank, Johannesburg 2196, South Africa

Penguin Books Ltd., Registered Offices:
80 Strand, London WC2R 0RL, England

First published by Signet Eclipse, an imprint of New American Library,
a division of Penguin Group (USA) Inc.

First Printing, May 2010
10 9 8 7 6 5 4 3 2 1

Library of Congress Cataloging-in-Publication Data
Wildes, Emma.
Seducing the highlander/Emma Wildes.
    p. cm.
"A Signet Eclipse book."
ISBN 978-0-451-22982-3
1. Scotland—Fiction. I. Title.
PS3623.I5415S43 2010
813'.6—dc22   2009046982

Set in Goudy
Designed by Alissa Amell

Printed in the United States of America

For Ashley, Lauren, and Michelle.
Because I love you three beautiful ladies,
I thought you each needed a wild Scottish hero.
Doesn't every girl?

Acknowledgments

As always, my lovely and talented agent, Barbara Poelle, is a fabulous rudder in the storm-tossed seas of the publishing world. My editor, Becky Vinter, has the insight to tap me on the shoulder when I go astray, and the talent to gently suggest just the right direction. It is a pleasure to work with you both.

I'd be remiss if I didn't mention my very patient family. Your unfailing support allows me to have the best job in the world. Thank you for such a wonderful gift.

Contents

Book One

Seducing Ian

Prologue

The night was hot and close, the moon blazing, and the horses raced forward with thundering speed.

"Damn," Ian McCray said quietly for the hundredth time. *Damn and damnation and hellfire . . .* This was now his fight, his task.

Eye for an eye . . .

Luckily, his clansmen were skilled after generations of riding in just such raids under a glowing reiver's moon like the one above them. Despite the unusual heat, Ian shivered in anticipation as they crossed the border.

It was best if they took the girl without a fight.

However, he was spoiling for one. The term *bloodlust* had taken on a whole new meaning in his life.

English bastard. *He* would pay in kind.

If he thought a McCray would sit idle, the Sassenach was mistaken.

Chapter 1

The intruders entered through her window, high as it was above the waters of the lake. Not understanding what was happening at first, Leanna Arlington blinked, realizing with a start her bedchamber was filling with dark forms and that what had actually woken her was a gloved hand pressed firmly across her mouth.

"Don't." The order was firm, terse.

And she fully understood, as something in that masculine warning told her that the man bending over her in the darkness meant what he said. Eyes widening, she obediently fought the urge to scream, her heart beginning to race, her body rigid beneath the thin sheet. It was very warm and she was wearing her sheerest nightdress, which had seemed logical when she prepared for bed, but not such a good choice now, especially when the sheet covering her body was ripped back and she was unceremoniously lifted and bound. Her arms were pulled behind her back, the unrelenting hand still over her mouth, and she felt bonds wrapped tight around her ankles and wrists, several men working at once. A piece of cloth was shoved into her mouth and secured with a strip around her head.

To her horror, the tall man who had awakened her tossed her over his shoulder and headed back for the window. Outside, the velvet dark sky showed vague stars.

Lord help her, it was hundreds of feet to the water. Her heart, already slamming against her ribs, began to hurt and she started to struggle for the first time, whimpering through the gag.

"No noise, my lady." His words were lethally soft. "Relax; I won't drop you."

Relax . . . Well, yes, that is easy to do under the circumstances, she thought hysterically, almost wanting to laugh. When he slid over the sill, she realized they had stepped into some sort of basket—wide enough for the two of them—that suddenly began a jerky but secure descent on a system of ropes and pulleys. All around them, men on ropes rappelled downward like flitting shadows in a stealthy and well-managed operation.

When Baron Frankton found her gone, he would be livid.

Once they were almost to the lake, Leanna saw a giant skiff waiting, undoubtedly the one used to cross the water. She was swiftly removed from the basket, laid in one corner of the boat like so much firewood, and with impressive precision her abductors propelled the craft forward. The night was as eerily silent as her captors were efficient. Cooperating, the clouds obscured the light, floating in, making the summer air close and even more oppressive.

Feeling the tip and sway of the clumsy vessel, seeing the gleam of firearms and swords in the hands of the men around her, Leanna silently counted the company, coming up with at least fifteen in her line of vision. But when they reached the opposite end of the lake what felt like hours later, she observed with terrified amazement a host of horses and men waiting—a hundred strong, maybe more.

What had happened, she wondered numbly, to precipitate such a contrived and well-planned kidnapping?

"Got her?" a soft voice called from the gathered force. One man, large and burly, urged his horse forward a pace. "No trouble?"

"The stupid Sassenach slept like the dead. We had no trouble."

The boat touched shore, rocking lightly. Uncomfortable, bewildered, Leanna tilted her head, straining against the hazy light, watching the ensuing activity. The burly man said, "Aye, well, is what they say true? Is she worth it?"

The tall man—the one who had carried her out the window—said, "How do I know? It was dark and I could barely see the lass. But then again, they are all the same in the dark, aren't they?"

"Don't say that in front of my wife." A gruff laugh rang out, quickly smothered. "Come, we need to ride. Bring her, Ian."

Ian tried to ignore the imploring eyes of the girl in his arms, the river of her loose, pale hair streaming over his chest and face as they rode, the curls like stray silk as they brushed his cheek. Bound and gagged, she could hardly be comfortable, and the soft weight of her body against his elicited a predictable physical reaction. In fact, his shaft was rigid inside his breeches, the sensation of her rounded bottom pressed against his crotch invoking a sexual response that had him shifting in the saddle.

She was the betrothed of his most hated enemy, Ian reminded himself. Pledged to a man without honor and bereft of any moral fiber or code. Her beauty aside, she was now simply an instrument of revenge and he intended to use her as such.

However, he acknowledged wryly, despite the warmth of the night, it would have been better if he had wrapped her in a cloak or a blanket before carrying her off on his horse and racing through the countryside. As it was, she wore nothing but a thin gown. In fact, in the moonlight, he could see not only the fear in her wide dark eyes, but the tempting thrust of her nipples through the sheer fabric, the fullness of her breasts apparent, as was the graceful curve of her throat and the pale perfection of her skin. Their speed whipped her filmy skirts up to her knees, showing her slim, shapely ankles, bound together with a sturdy cord.

No wonder the lascivious Frankton wanted her. With her long, fair hair and delicate features, she was exquisite. Ian speculated on just what kind of hold the baron had over her father to persuade him to pledge the most beautiful woman in northern England to such a ruthless and power-hungry bastard. The stories were varied, but almost all of them intimated Frankton had done no less than purchase his bride-to-be.

They rode on, the noise of more than a hundred horses filling the road, the company not stopping until they were certain there were enough miles between them and any rescue attempt. Trotting into a clearing next to a rushing stream, Ian pulled up his horse and told his men, "Rest your mounts for a few minutes. We aren't camping until we set foot on Scottish soil, but I think we're safe enough to stop."

He slid to the ground, carried the girl to where a fallen log lay next to the stream, set her on it, and squatted down on his haunches to look into her eyes. He said with lethal sincerity, "If I remove the gag, you will not scream, you will not beg or cry, or cause trouble of any kind. I am already furious, tired, and hungry. I haven't slept in two days or had more than a single shot of whiskey. My patience does not even exist at this point. Do not test me, lass. Understand?"

The girl managed a nod, her lush lashes lowering a fraction.

Obligingly, he reached behind her head and loosened the knot on the gag, pulling the cloth from her mouth. Her chest heaved as she took a shuddering breath, her breasts, uplifted and high from having her hands bound behind her back, quivering in a tantalizing display. "Thank you," she whispered.

"I imagine you would like a drink of water." Ian tore his gaze away from the outline of those full mounds only barely shielded by thin linen, and went to get a cup from his pack, filling it from the cool stream and bringing it back to where she sat. "I'll untie you, but if you annoy me in any way, you'll be trussed like a chicken for the rest of the journey."

"I understand." Her voice was submissive, but her gaze straightforward.

Loosening the bonds on her ankles first, he couldn't help but notice how dainty and feminine her feet were, and how warm and smooth her skin. He untied her hands, slipped the cords from her fragile wrists, and handed her the cup. She drank with obvious thirst, and he felt a little guilty at his less than humane treatment of such a lovely, delicate creature. He then squelched that unwanted emotion easily enough when he thought of his uncle, already infirm and suffering from gout, locked in some squalid pile of rock that passed for an English jail. Uncle Thomas should have known better than to venture into business with anyone who lived on English soil, for the vermin were not to be trusted. Had he been consulted, Ian would have warned him about the despicable baron.

"Damn Frankton to hell," he said out loud, staring down at her graceful drooping form.

Her head came up at the sound of the baron's name, the cup suspended in her fingers, her eyes dark and wide.

"You can thank your future husband for your little Scottish sojourn, my lovely captive," he told her with a humorless smile. "His habit of having people arrested on ridiculous charges so he can take possession of their property has been a thorn in my side for a long time, but I have done nothing because he has left me and mine alone. Did you realize your intended bribes officials and claims fraud on a regular basis? There *is* fraud in all the cases he drags into court, but he fails to mention it is on his side. Since he coerces the magistrates and makes the charge first, his victims are all too often taken unawares."

She shook her head, golden hair brushing her shoulders.

"I am afraid he recently stepped over the line I tolerate and I can no longer ignore his venal dishonesty. 'Tis a fact," he added truthfully, "I cannot ever remember being quite so . . . irritated."

Whether she was responding to his warning to remain silent, or just horrified to learn of her betrothed's immoral activities, he wasn't sure, but she still said nothing. Ian told her, "You may get up and stretch your limbs a little, lass, but stay right here."

Turning and walking back to the circle of horses and men, he saw that he wasn't the only man there to notice the considerable charms of their female guest. Most of them openly stared, and when she stood up and the dappled moonlight flowed over the shimmering, almost transparent gown, he heard someone groan out loud.

"Now, that," an amused voice spoke at his elbow, "is a bonny, bonny lass, boy."

With a glance at his friend Angus, Ian lifted a brow as he pulled a flask from his saddlebag. "Aye, I certainly hope so, considering the trouble we've gone to take her. I wish I could be there when that greedy, lustful bastard realizes his enticing bride-to-be is no longer locked in her tower, waiting for the wedding, but is instead enjoying a protracted stay at my castle."

"He'll be livid." Sounding delighted, Angus chuckled. "Here, give me a drink and let me just imagine it. What a delight to foil the English rodent. When do we send the ransom note demanding the charges be dropped?"

Ian passed the flask after a deep drink, wiping his mouth and narrowing his eyes. "I've changed my mind. I have thought it over. He might agree, take back the girl, and then protest duress in court, reinstating the charges, the treacherous bastard. Anyone else would honor the agreement, but since he has no honor . . . he needs killing, really. Even from our distance, his antics have become too much to be tolerated."

Angus lifted his bushy brows. "Then why don't you simply hunt him down and kill him, boy? We took the girl for nothing."

"Nay." Looking over at where she stood, like a ghostly promise of paradise, all warm curves and alluring beauty, Ian said softly, "Her abduction has a twofold purpose. The first, of course, is that I will not have to hunt him down. He will come to me to retrieve his prize."

"And the second?" Angus asked, taking another swig, his black eyes bright with interest.

Ian's smile was dark and dangerous. "The second is that when he realizes where she is, and who has her, he can torture himself as he imagines me between those lovely legs, fucking her whenever I wish, enjoying her delectable body."

Angus roared with laughter, clapping him on the shoulder so hard, Ian almost winced. "Excellent, my friend, excellent. I have never met a woman yet who could resist your pretty face."

"It isn't my face," Ian countered dryly, "that they can't resist."

Chapter 2

They had stopped. Leanna realized she must have been dozing, for she came suddenly back into an awareness of her surroundings.

After incessant hours of movement, after being jostled and windblown for what seemed like a lifetime, the relief from that awful jarring pace was like waking from a dream. Leanna blinked. Her face rested on a hard surface, the steely muscles moving under her cheek telling her it was indeed the chest of the tall, dark man called Ian by some, laird by others. He had seemed to be not only in charge of the troop of men who had so efficiently plucked her from what was supposed to be an impenetrable tower, but had solely cared for her on the journey to this place, the only one who had even touched her. The others had watched her; she had felt the steady and interested male appraisal, but no one had as much as said anything but a polite word.

She would remember his scent, she thought, still half in a groggy sleep state. It was elusive but intriguing, a mixture of smoky liquor,

horses, and clean linen. Being lifted in strong arms now felt normal—
she had endured it the whole journey, had been enveloped for all
those hours in the saddle in that strength and that scent.

And yet her tall, handsome captor had not once bothered to
tell her his name.

When she opened her eyes fully, she realized that they were in
a courtyard, the ring of the hooves of more than a hundred horses
deafening. Stamping and whinnying, the animals snorted, and she
fearfully tightened her arms around the neck of the man holding her
as he slid off his mount into the melee of restless, sweating beasts.
He whispered softly in her ear, "You're safe, lass; don't panic."

Through the veil of her lashes, she saw his face, his eyes dark,
his cheekbones high and arrogant, his mouth modeled by what
surely must have been the gods, it was so masculine, so firm. "We're
here. All is well," he assured her.

Still a little confused and not fully awake, she clung to him as
he carried her toward a huge arched entrance, the massive door
thrown open to the warm night, well lit and inviting despite the
immense dimensions. Once inside, she could see they had entered
a large hall, hung with tapestries and well furnished, dominated by
a long table with enough chairs to seat thirty people. The floors
were polished stone and gleamed, the air perfumed with the scent
of roasting meat, and the soft sound of a lute being played was arrested by their entrance.

"My heavens, who is this waif? Is she injured?" demanded an
authoritarian female voice.

"She's exhausted," Leanna heard the man say, his arms still easily holding her body. "We rode hard."

"Who is she . . . ? My lord, what a beautiful child." A soft finger stroked her cheek. The woman touching her was very short, much shorter than the tall man holding her, so all Leanna could really see was a halo of dark graying hair.

"I'll explain later, Rossie. Right now I'll take her upstairs. Could you care for her yourself?"

Rossie, whoever she was, said crisply, "I insist on both, you young rogue. I'll care for her, the sweet young thing, and you will explain this all to me once you've washed and fed."

"I promise."

The humble boyish note in his voice was a surprise, Leanna thought wearily, as he carried her up a winding staircase built close to a high wall. With her head on his chest she heard the strong beat of his heart as he effortlessly climbed the steps, and she wondered—not for the first time—who and what this man was who had gone to such lengths to abduct her.

He shouldered his way through a doorway and stalked across the room to deposit her on the softness of a mattress.

It took her less than a second to fall back to sleep.

Rolling the loosened muscles in his shoulders, Ian toweled his hair, drying it briskly, his bath helping a great measure in making him feel normal again. So had the plate of food he had ravenously devoured. The pint of whiskey, he thought cheerfully, didn't hurt either. It was no wonder, after such a grueling pace on their journey back, that Lady Leanna had fallen asleep so quickly.

The knock on his door was brisk and merely a formality.

He frowned and hurriedly buttoned his breeches before his visitor burst on in, then said with resignation, "Aye?"

His old nurse, Rossie, was more mother to him than servant. When she flung open the door she fairly charged into his bedroom, fire in her faded blue eyes. She demanded with very little respect for his rank, "What are you going to do with that lovely lassie, Ian? I saw the way you looked at her, like a wolf circling a rabbit."

Towering over her by more than a foot, Ian simply lifted a brow.

Plump, with formidable dignity, Rossie glared up at him. "Men are impossible. Angus told me what is going on, and how you could bed a helpless girl as a part of your wicked scheme—"

"I have never forced myself on an unwilling female," he interrupted mildly.

"No, you handsome devil, I'm sure you never have." She sniffed disapprovingly. "That wee bairn won't be a match for you, at a guess."

"Lady Leanna is a woman fully grown." He could vouch for it personally, because there was nothing childlike about her voluptuous body, and he knew from the information he received when he plotted the abduction that the lass was nearly twenty years old.

Rossie waved a dismissive hand. "She's an innocent lamb. I saw it in her eyes."

"I don't see how. She was half-asleep," he argued, crossing his arms over his chest.

"She'll be spreading her legs for you before she even realizes what she's doing. Is this truly necessary?"

Killing Frankton was necessary. Seducing the woman the Sassenach bastard desired so much, well . . . that would simply be very satisfying. Ian gave his old nurse an innocent grin. "I promise you she'll enjoy it, if that will make you feel better."

"It does *not* make me feel better," she replied tartly, and then sighed. "However, ridding this earth of Baron Frankton would be a blessing for us all. Be careful, Ian. He is legendary for his evil treachery, and though I know you are the finest swordsman in Scotland, he knows it too. The cowardly devil won't face you directly."

"He wants the lass, and, from all reports, badly. Having seen her, I understand why. When he comes to demand her release, I intend to make the blackguard agree to tell the truth, free Uncle Thomas, and return his confiscated property. Once that is done, I will challenge him in front of witnesses, so even a crawling English worm like him will have to pick up a weapon."

Rossie's blue eyes were troubled. "I don't like it."

He reached out and touched her plump cheek reassuringly. "I don't really like it either, mother hen. I've killed men before in battle or self-defense, but I have never contemplated killing someone with relish. However, don't worry; I can take care of myself." Then he added with a wicked wink, "And the delectable Lady Leanna."

"You scamp, she's too tired to pleasure you tonight. I had to rouse her, and the poor child could barely stay awake long enough to bathe and eat."

"I think I can wait until tomorrow," Ian said serenely.

"Men," Rossie muttered.

Leanna paced across the room, the hem of the dressing gown she had been given trailing on the floor. Bright sunlight fell in squares from one of the tall windows, warming the thick rug under her bare feet. Restless, unnerved, she paused to stare at a portrait of a young woman with dark windblown hair that hung over the mantel, her observation distracted.

She knew her captor's identity.

McCray.

The young maid who had brought her hot water and breakfast this morning had willingly answered her tentative questions.

Good heavens, she was in the hands of Ian McCray, laird of what was reputed to be one of the fiercest Scottish clans, a powerful lord with a reputation as a talented swordsman and an even more talented lover. Even with her sheltered upbringing, Leanna had heard of McCray. It was obvious from the things he'd said that her fiancé, Baron Frankton, had done something to one of the laird's own family and, in turn, brought swift retaliation from a formidable foe.

The greedy fool, she thought with exaltation.

She was free!

Well, not precisely free, but she was never going back into that tower to be locked away like some exotic bird. *Never*. It was a vow, a pledge to herself. Being confined for weeks on end had been the worst torture imaginable, and the prospect of having to give her body to her loathsome groom-to-be had loomed like a poisonous cloud on the horizon. Were it not for the knowledge that the baron's wedding settlement would help her impoverished father properly present her sisters—four of them, all younger—into society so they might make respectable marriages, she could not have borne the dread she felt for her upcoming wedding night.

"What would you do now, if you were in my place?" she asked the woman in the portrait, musing aloud. "It seems to me I have been rescued by a dubious knight, it is true, but rescued still. The marriage settlement was paid when Baron Frankton escorted me from my home to his holding. It cannot be taken back, not when this is not my father's fault."

Quite naturally the painted image on the canvas offered no advice, but it didn't matter. Crossing to the window, Leanna stared out, seeing sunshine pour over the unfamiliar rolling hills, the sea glimmering in the distance like some jeweled beast. It was a rugged, harsh land, she mused, but beautiful. Rather like McCray himself. She remembered his tall, well-muscled body, that broad chest, his classically handsome features and thick dark hair worn loose like a warrior, brushing his shoulders.

The very first thing she needed to do was get rid of her virginity.

Baron Frankton had valued that as much as her beauty, going so far as to insist she be examined by a physician to confirm her purity. Every time she recalled the look that crossed his face when he mentioned their upcoming wedding night, she felt sick. He wanted a terrified virgin because he reveled in the idea. She had realized it even with her lack of sexual experience. The fact she despised him and was marrying him only to save her family aroused him.

The door behind her opened. "You demand an audience, I understand, lass."

The sound of the deep voice sent a small tremor through her body. Leanna whirled around, her heart beginning to race. Framed in the doorway, Ian McCray looked taller than ever, his long legs hugged by black breeches, a full-sleeved white shirt spanning his wide shoulders. The laird's booted feet were apart, and one ebony brow slowly eased upward in open amusement as she stared at him. His eyes were as dark as his glossy hair, the corner of his well-shaped mouth lifting slightly as he stared back.

"G-good morning," she stammered ridiculously. Her palms were suddenly damp and warm.

He laughed, showing white teeth. "I am pleased to be greeted with such polite friendliness. Since I snatched you from your bed and carried you halfway across Scotland against your will, I thought you might be a little perturbed with me."

"You did me the most enormous favor imaginable," Leanna told him honestly, recovering a measure of her poise.

His face registered a shade of surprise, his eyes narrowing slightly in sudden comprehension. "I see."

"I take it you wish to trade me back to the baron for his assurance he will repair whatever damage he has done to your family."

Ian McCray murmured, "Aye, something like that, lass."

Wondering just how much she would have to do to persuade him, she cleared her throat. "Can we strike a bargain between *us*, my lord?"

"Are you in a position to bargain, my lady?" The amusement was back in his voice.

"I think," she said coolly, looking him in the eyes, "I have something you want." Summoning her courage, she untied the sash at her waist and let her robe fall open, shrugging it from her shoulders so it pooled at her feet. It was a little daunting to stand there completely nude in front of the notorious chieftain, but she lifted her chin and watched his breathing change slightly as he examined her naked body with a compelling dark stare. "I noticed on our journey here that you were not physically indifferent to me, unless"—she managed a nervous smile—"you are that way all the time, which I would think would be most uncomfortable."

He said nothing for a moment, his heated gaze fastened on her breasts so intently, she could almost feel the warmth singe her skin. "What's your bargain?" he asked finally.

"Bed me," she told him, trying to keep her voice even. "Often. Whenever you like. Use me while I am here for your pleasure in any way you wish. In return, I promise to accommodate you at any time, without protest, to please you as best I can. If you do not desire me, pick one of your men—"

"No one will touch you but me," he interrupted, his voice curt. "I take it Frankton values your virginity and you seek to thwart him."

"I agreed to the marriage for the sake of my family, but now that I know the man better, I realize my mistake. My purity is important to him."

"Is it now?" McCray's dark eyes gleamed and he took a slow, long step closer.

A small surge of triumph rippled through her. Leanna smiled, slightly lowering her lashes. "Will you help me, my lord?"

His smile was full of sensual masculine promise. "I intended to all along, my lady."

Ian closed the door and turned the key in the lock. God knew Rossie might decide to check on her lovely charge, and he hardly wanted a lecture while he was in the middle of the intimate exploration of Miss Arlington's gorgeous body.

By the gods, he was already hard, so stiff he could feel the pulse of his cock strain against the material of his breeches. He had bedded scores of beautiful ladies, but he couldn't recall ever being more intrigued than he was by this young woman who was begging him to do with her whatever he wished, and promising complete capitulation.

It was infinitely arousing.

In the golden light of the summer morning coming through the window, Lady Leanna was bathed in gold and ivory, her nude body perfect and just as he had imagined as he held her in his arms on their journey. Her long hair, gloriously blond, tumbled over her slim shoulders and fell to her waist. Her breasts were high, firm, not overly large but full and tipped with pink nipples. The triangle of soft gold at the apex of her white thighs gleamed, and he imagined himself delving into that intriguing spot with his fingers, his mouth, his cock. . . .

"I think we can start right now," he said, his voice a trifle thick with arousal. "If you wish to please me, come here."

Her gaze lowered slightly, but she was as good as her word, coming forward obediently. When she was close enough, Ian pulled her nude body into his arms. Her soft scent was bewitching, and as he found her mouth with his own, he wondered if she had ever been kissed.

She hadn't, he discovered, his hands caressing her smooth back as he coaxed her lips apart and eased his tongue into her mouth. She tasted sweet, like the chocolate she had drunk with breakfast, a personal indulgence of his that the household had adopted. He felt her stiffen slightly as he rubbed his tongue against hers, the sensation obviously new. He felt those same muscles relax as he continued and she began to respond hesitantly, her small hands clutching his shirt, her long lashes fanned against her porcelain cheeks.

Patience, which was what he needed with an untried innocent, was not his strong suit normally, but when it came to lovemaking, he had plenty of experience in bringing a woman to full arousal. He took his time, leisurely exploring her sweet mouth, tasting the sensitive spot behind her ear, kissing her neck, her mouth again, until she breathed unevenly and was lax against him.

"The bed," he said, sweeping her up in his arms. He was still fully clothed himself, and her enticing curves were already familiar after all those hours in the saddle with only her thin nightdress between them. Shoving back the tumbled linens, he laid her down and started to undress, watching her face as he unlaced and pulled off his shirt, her eyes opening wide as he unfastened his breeches and exposed his rampant erection.

"Oh." She stared, lying quietly, her arms at her sides, her splendid bare breasts lifting quickly.

"Don't be frightened. It might look big," he assured her softly, "but it will fit inside you."

"I hope so," she answered unexpectedly, closing her eyes. "I feel so strange, hot, yet cold—"

"Spread your legs," he ordered hoarsely. "I want to look at you."

She did as she was told, slowly opening her thighs, giving him a glimpse of her cleft, the lips of her labia soft and partially shielded by that downy thatch. As he lay down next to her, Ian fought the uncharacteristic urge to simply mount her at once and ease his impatient need. He was an experienced man—an extremely experienced man, in fact—and renowned for his ability to leisurely and skillfully make love. Perhaps it was her poignant beauty and innocent appeal, but he was hot and oddly overeager. He forced himself to control, stroking her silken hair, kissing her again. As he fondled her breasts and enjoyed the sight of her compliant and open for him, the texture and weight of her flesh exquisite in his hands, he felt her nipples tighten in response under his touch.

Excellent. She might be giving him a virgin sacrifice, but she was also passionate under that cool, golden exterior.

She sighed when he bent his head and took the straining, flawless pink crest of her right breast in his mouth. He felt it harden as he sucked it deeper, her hands flying to his hair, sifting through in arousing urgency. Moving to her other breast, he murmured, "Keep your legs apart. I'll get there soon, my sweet hostage."

And she moaned out loud this time when he began to nuzzle and lick her nipple, her obvious enjoyment escalating his own desire. He stayed there until he could hear her pant, pleased with how responsive she was, her vow to acquiesce to his every sexual demand foremost in his mind. Moving lower, he kissed her soft stomach, her smooth inner thighs, pushing her legs wider until he settled, his mouth grazing her sex, inhaling the heady fragrance of female arousal.

"I've never tasted a virgin," he murmured, running his tongue along the intriguing line of those soft, damp folds. "Will you be different?"

"My lord," she said in obvious breathless shock, "what are you doing?"

You are so astoundingly beautiful, he thought, poised between her legs. Her long blond hair was spread over the linens, her pearly body a little flushed and so very feminine and beguiling. The delicate perfection of her face was highlighted by her heightened color, a deep blush flooding her cheeks. "There is no embarrassment in bed," he told her, lightly biting her inner thigh with just a teasing abrasion of his teeth, "and you will love what I am about to do. Trust me."

Her lashes fluttered slightly. "I can't think you would want to . . . to—"

"Then you'd be wrong, my lady," he said in a growl, and pressed his mouth to her heated center, plunging his tongue into those moist folds, delving between them and relishing the velvet feel of that acutely sensitive flesh, finding the tiny swollen bud of her desire and swirling his tongue around it.

She cried out instantly, arching. "Oh."

Her hips in his hands, keeping her in place for his tender assault, Ian continued to feast at her sweet cleft, sometimes stroking boldly, other times nibbling gently, until the tension in her body grew and he could taste the rush of her imminent orgasm, the small sounds she made at each movement of his tongue signaling her intense pleasure. When she went over the edge, she convulsed and twisted in orgasmic abandon, eyes closed tightly, her small scream of release echoing into the pleasant quiet of the bedchamber.

Considering how wet and hot Lady Leanna was, Ian thought with a grin as he lifted himself up, she was as ready as any untried female could be, in his opinion. And ready or not, he was dying to take her.

Leanna wasn't sure whether she had perished, but she certainly was no longer on this earth. It wasn't until she realized that the notorious laird had ceased pleasuring her with his tongue between her legs, and instead something large and hard was poised there, prodding her female opening, beginning to stretch it with insistent penetration, that she knew the moment had come and he was going to deflower her.

This was, after all, she thought hazily, what she had asked for, wasn't it?

Of course, she'd gotten a little more than her bargain entailed. What Laird McCray had *just* done to her was outrageous, but she had never guessed such sensation could be possible.

"I'll try to be gentle," he promised, his face dark above her, his smile slight, belying the fire in his eyes. "But you are damned tight, my sweet."

She must be, considering it felt as if he were forcing her incredibly wide, filling her burning passage as he invaded her body with his formidably large sex. Trying to relax and accept him as she had promised she would do, Leanna exhaled and opened her thighs wider to accommodate his size. It didn't feel unpleasant, she found, but was only slightly uncomfortable, and even when he suddenly pushed forward and she felt the tearing sensation as her maidenhead ruptured, the pain was negligible and she did nothing more than let out a small gasp.

"Is it terrible?" he asked through his teeth, poised above her, the muscles in his upper arms impressive and defined as he braced himself. "I have no desire to hurt you."

She actually lifted her hips a fraction, liking the friction as he inched forward. "It isn't terrible at all. Should it be?"

"You are very aroused from your climax. It helps," he said with a low, tense laugh. "I may not have tasted a virgin before, but I have bedded one and want to make this as easy as possible for you, lass. Here, put your feet flat on the bed and keep your knees as wide apart as you can."

She complied, finding he could push deeper when she was in that position, amazed when she finally realized he was embedded to the hilt, and her vaginal passage was actually able to absorb his entire erection.

He began to move very slowly, pulling almost completely out before he sank back in, and she found after a few repetitions that she enjoyed the slide of his sex within hers, her lashes drifting shut as carnal enjoyment built, all discomfort forgotten as her breasts tightened and her breathing became choppy.

"You feel like heaven," he whispered, his mouth grazing hers, "wet and snug and female."

"You feel . . . very large and hard, my lord, but not unpleasant," she answered in breathless agreement, opening her eyes.

"You like this?" he asked, holding her gaze with his dark one, deliberately pushing back inside her, the hard length of his cock filling her completely.

"Yes," she admitted, all thoughts of her revenge on the repulsive baron banished by the unexpected glory of what this Scottish lord was doing to her body. She said breathlessly, "I like it."

"God in heaven," he muttered, "for a virginal maid, you have the instincts of a born siren."

"Do I?"

He began to thrust quickly all of a sudden, and she could see the faint sheen of sweat on his forehead, his long lashes shielding his half-closed eyes, his breath brushing her cheek. Her own pleasure increased with his urgent movements, her nerve endings beginning to tingle, to pulse around his surging flesh. Leanna let the wash of sexual excitement take her away, rolling her helplessly in a sea of sensation until she felt again that exquisite tide of pleasure build and burst. This time her hands flew to his broad shoulders, her nails digging in as she threw back her head and cried out, her inner muscles tightening around that potent, insistent penetration.

The man above her went rigid all at once, buried impossibly deep and hard, a liquid heat flooding her as he groaned, the ripples from his body flowing into hers. He stayed there for what seemed like an eternity while she drifted in that blissful ocean of pleasure, until she could feel he was softening, no longer so rigid. When he eased out from between her legs, she actually had to stifle a sigh of loss.

Then he gathered her into his arms at once, pulling her damp body to his broad chest. A chuckle rippled through him and she glanced up curiously, seeing a twinkle in those seductive dark eyes. "I believe," he said, laughing, "this might be the best bargain I have ever made, lass."

Chapter 3

*H*is face livid, Baron Dartmus Frankton slammed his hand onto the table. "Who took her?" He breathed with such agitation he could hardly speak because of the fight for air.

"We don't know. They left ropes dangling from the roof. Someone had to have let them in." Impassively, the other man watched him, as if he carefully held back any emotion. "I rode here to tell you as soon as we discovered she was gone."

"The servants know nothing? I don't believe that." Frankton strode across the room and dashed liquid into a fat glass, taking a quick bracing gulp. *It can't be*, he thought incredulously. How *could* his prize be gone, especially since he had plotted so carefully to attain her, not taking her to bed before now because he wanted to savor the superb joy of the anticipation of the moment when he plucked her carefully guarded innocence? She would sob in fear and reluctance, he'd always gleefully imagined, and beg him to leave her alone even as he forced those lovely pale legs apart and plundered her luscious body. . . .

"The servants," his man—the stupid fool who had already failed him—was saying, "are being questioned one by one." Then, after a palpable hesitation, he ventured, "Your enemies, my lord, are many. A large party rode north that same night."

"All successful men have enemies," Frankton muttered, thinking furiously. Could, even now, some other man be enjoying his prize? "Find out everything you can. I want answers. Question everyone in the countryside surrounding the castle. Someone will know something."

"Perhaps a ransom note will come, asking for money for Lady Leanna."

That notion made him even more irate, and blood pounded in his ears. He'd paid for her once already and he'd be damned if he'd do so again. "If so," he rasped out, "keep the man delivering it. Messengers can be tortured, and I want answers."

His henchman paled at the open venom in his master's voice and bowed, licking his dry lips. "Yes, my lord."

"Lassie?"

Leanna rolled over and blinked, her gaze focusing on a small figure standing by the side of the bed. A tray rested in the other woman's hands. Recognizing the same kindly older servant who had helped her bathe and brought her food the night before, she sat up in a flurry of loose hair. Forgetting for a moment that she was naked, she quickly caught the sheet up and felt the tide of heat in her cheeks as she covered her bare breasts.

She must have fallen back to sleep after she had invited Ian McCray to bed her and he had accepted so . . . well, so *gloriously.*

Remembering their impetuous joining, she blushed deeper, guessing that what had happened was no secret once the woman saw the shambles of the bed and Leanna's completely undressed state.

The older woman—the one Laird McCray had called Rossie—sighed loudly, her pale blue eyes narrowing. "Poor bonny child, he couldn't leave you alone even at such an early hour, could he?"

"I . . . I . . ." Leanna stammered, reluctant to explain *she* had actually stripped naked and offered herself to the man in question.

"It's barely afternoon," Rossie snapped, looking indignant. "That beast."

"He wasn't a beast precisely—"

"No? Well, that still doesn't excuse him. Young, handsome scoundrel that he be, he had to have his way with you, didn't he? I saw it in his eyes when he carried you into the house last night. I am guessing he took your innocence."

"He didn't harm me." Leanna finally managed to get out the words.

Rossie still looked irate, the tray trembling in her hands. "I should hope not or I'd have his head. Tell me, child, are you tender? I have some salve I give to the village girls when they are married . . . something to ease the discomfort of the next day."

Utterly off balance, Leanna found that when she shifted, she *was* a bit sore between her legs. "I might be," she confessed, warmed by the older woman's frankness and the open concern and motherly protectiveness in her expression. Her own mother had died when she was only nine and she desperately missed her.

"I'll go get it." Rossie set the tray down. "You just rest and have a glass of wine. I'll pour it for you. There's also some lovely cold roasted chicken and a meat pie."

Soon, Leanna found herself propped against the pillows, sipping a glass of cool, sweet amber liquid, the tray balanced on her
lap, her mouth watering at the sight of the first real food that had
tempted her in weeks. She began to eat, drinking her wine at in-
tervals and marveling how life could change so quickly and completely. The food was delicious and the beverage lovely, and she
sighed in contentment just from knowing she was miles and miles
from the tower prison where she'd so recently awaited a hideous
fate. To her father, Frankton had presented a much different face
from the one she had discovered once he had arrived with his men
to escort her to his holding. The baron's gloating possessiveness
had first alarmed her, then disgusted her, and from that had grown
true fear. He was not a kind man, nor a good one.

"Here we are." The door swung back open as Rossie returned, a
small vial in her hand. The housekeeper beamed in approval when
she caught sight of the half-empty plate. "There's a good lass. Some
food will do you good, as you're too slender, my lady. Will you take
more wine?"

"No, thank you. It was all wonderful." Leanna let the woman
take the tray and sank back amid the pillows. Her room was well-
appointed and comfortable, bordering on luxurious, with silken
hangings on the bed and windows. The carpeting was thickly
woven, and the upper parts of the windows done in stained glass
that sent soothing colored shadows everywhere.

"Here." Rossie handed her the jar, telling her with brusque
practicality, "You have to rub it inside your female opening, using
your fingers and going as far up as possible. It may seem unladylike,
but you'll thank me when he visits you again this evening. The
good tidings are that after this, you'll be fine, and he can lie with

you as much as either of you desires it, and you won't have the same discomfort. Your innocence is lost, it cannot be regained, and your body will now accept a man and yield to him without causing you pain."

That actually *was* good news, because Leanna wanted Laird McCray to use her often.

Every time he took his pleasure inside her was another strike against Baron Frankton.

Accepting the offering, Leanna murmured, "Thank you. I'll use it right away."

Swords clashed, sending sparks flying. Stepping back, Ian parried a skilled thrust, anticipating his opponent's strategy and sending the other man's weapon skittering across the courtyard.

"Well-done." Angus panted in defeat, his black eyes narrowed, sweat pouring over his brow. Stripped to the waist, he resembled a bull: thickset and powerful, his shoulders huge, his chest massive and muscled.

Also shirtless, Ian was much taller but also leaner, and they usually made good adversaries, practicing with enough fervor that each of them frequently walked away with a cut or two, occasionally needing a stitch here and there to mend the damage. Ian grinned and shook the hair out of his eyes. "I am surprised I have enough strength left to beat you."

"Aye, I heard you were closeted with the fair Leanna most of the morning, and I can see for myself the love marks from her nails on your shoulders. You lose no time, do you, lad?" Angus sighed gloomily. "Damn you, boy, now I owe Malcolm good coin. I bet him you'd have enough self-control to last out the day, at least. His money was on the golden beauty of the English lass."

"I could hardly ignore her and prove a poor host, could I?" Ian laughed, then sobered. "I'm not jesting, and this is not for any ears but yours, Angus, but she hates Frankton, I'm guessing more than I do. You should have seen her face when she implored me to take her innocence, willing to bed a stranger rather than give it to the man she is pledged to marry."

"That's his loss—and your gain in more than just retaliation." Angus grunted as he bent to pick up his lost sword.

"It makes things a little . . . complicated."

Plucking at his beard, his friend straightened and said gruffly, "How so?"

"She knows she was taken to use for bargaining. I am sure she still thinks I wish to trade her back to him for my uncle's freedom, for I have not told her any different."

"Tell her you mean to kill him. Who knows, she might *reward* you." Bushy brows wiggled suggestively.

"And then what do I do with her?" Ian asked quietly, remembering soft, silken hair, long-lashed eyes, and the warm reception of her beautiful body. "When Frankton is stone dead and rotting in hell, what do I do with his intended bride?"

"Send her back to her family."

"You mean to the father who sold her to a toad like Frankton in the first place?"

"Perhaps the man didn't realize what he asked of her when he made the marriage arrangement."

"It was her father's responsibility to select a decent husband, not use her beauty to his own end. She told me she agreed to the marriage for the sake of her sisters, because the settlement offered was so large. You cannot tell me that if up north we know of Frankton's perfidy, her father was completely unaware of it."

Angus had a kind heart, though he tried to hide it behind his blustery facade. "I see your point, lad, I do, but other than keeping her, I don't see another solution."

Keeping her—that was an interesting notion. Ian elevated his brows, sweat dripping off his jaw.

Angus saw his expression and frowned ferociously. "She's . . . English and noble. It's out of the question, lad. Hell and blast, you're thinking with your cock."

"As long as that's not the only thing I do with it." Ian shrugged, grinning.

The room was warm, lit by only a single lamp against the subtle darkness outside, and Leanna straightened when she heard the lift of the latch. From her reclining pose on the seat by the window, she saw Laird McCray step into the room, filling it suddenly with his presence, his dark hair brushing his wide shoulders. "Were you waiting for me?" he asked softly.

"I hoped you would come," Leanna said with more than a little truth to her response.

"You told me to avail myself of your very lovely body whenever I wished," he said evenly, "and that offer was made so prettily that I cannot forget it."

"I am at your disposal, my lord." She meant it. Even though Rossie had brought her some clothing late that afternoon, she wore nothing under her dressing gown in anticipation of the laird's visit, her long hair brushed to a fine sheen and hanging loosely down her back.

Revenge. She planned to be as experienced as a whore by the time Frankton arrived to claim her.

"Come." Ian held out his hand.

She rose and approached him, her brows arching in question.

He swept her up into his arms, giving her that dark, mesmerizing smile she remembered from the morning. "My bed is bigger," he explained with a low, masculine laugh, his breath warm in her ear. "I anticipate we'll need the space, lass."

His room, she discovered, was just across the hallway. It was larger than the one she'd been given, and furnished plainly, but he was correct: The bed was massive, dominating the space. He laid her down there, untying her robe and swiftly stripping her bare, his gaze intent as he tossed the garment aside and stood staring at her with clear predatory lust. "You are incredibly beautiful, my lady."

"Which has brought me nothing but trouble," she responded bitterly, without thinking.

His brows shot together. "Did you not enjoy this morning?"

He knew she had. She blushed when she recalled how she had cried out loud during those peaks of intense pleasure. "I enjoyed it, my lord."

"Your beauty pleases me. It makes me very . . . hungry." His grin was wickedly charming, and he began to disrobe.

It unfortunately pleases Baron Frankton too. She watched Ian as he quickly and efficiently removed his clothing, his long fingers gracefully male as they moved. But if it had been the baron there undressing, she would be filled with disgust and repulsion instead of feeling the curls of unmistakable excitement in her stomach.

Reposed against the softness of the bedding, she realized that her breasts were changing too, feeling full suddenly, and heavy, and that a small ache had begun between her legs.

McCray was aroused as well. When he removed his breeches, she could see the stiffening of his erection, his large penis lengthening under her fascinated gaze, the tip distending and pulsing slightly, pushing against the flat plane of his stomach. Underneath, the sac of his testicles looked heavy and full in a nest of black curly hair.

He was a very handsome, very virile man—of that there was no doubt—and a skilled lover.

He was going to make love to her again.

Now.

She shivered.

The mattress dipped as he joined her on the bed, one of his hands immediately moving to cup her breast. His fingers glided over the weight of it, stroking lightly, toying with her nipple as he leaned forward to kiss her. One large male thigh slid possessively over her legs. She could feel the hard ridge of his erect shaft against her stomach, his mouth persuasive and seductive as he stroked her tongue with his in the same way his hand stroked her breast.

Allowing him whatever liberties he wished, she parted her lips to his intrusion, sliding her arms up around his neck, his skin hot under her fingers. She felt dwarfed by his size, his body so much larger, so different from her own. Corded muscle bunched under her clasping fingers, his heat palpable, as was the insistent throb of his desire next to the softness of her belly. His hair brushed her hands, dark and silky.

"You taste like heaven," he whispered against her mouth. "So sweet. Tell me, are you sore?"

"No," she denied, hoping Rossie was correct about the ointment. "You can take me if you wish it, my lord. I want you to do so."

For a moment, he lifted his head, his hand still holding her breast, his dark eyes direct and questioning. "I am your abductor and I want only the same thing from you that Frankton wants. Yet you give yourself so easily to me, just to spite him. I confess, I am not sure how to feel. I have never had a woman lie with me who didn't at least have some measure of wanting but instead only plotted retribution against another man."

"He isn't a man; he's a monster." Leanna looked up at the handsome Scot who covered her with his naked, powerful body. "And I feel the wanting," she murmured truthfully, half lowering her lashes, "if that means I like it when you touch me. I am just not used to it yet. Please do not turn away from me."

"That's hardly likely." His laugh was low and a little harsh. "I am glad you wish it too. It makes our mutual pleasure even more unholy since I planned on seducing you to make him squirm with the knowledge that I had you first."

"We are of like mind, then," she said faintly, very aware of how his fingers still touched her nipple, lightly stroking now, the sensation escalating beyond pleasant to arousing.

"Almost," he agreed enigmatically.

She would have questioned that equivocation, except he moved his hand from her breast to her stomach, sliding it lower to slip between her thighs. His long fingers sought, found, and then penetrated her female entrance.

"You are damp," he said, smiling, his mouth lifting, "but are you certain you are not too tender from our earlier encounter?"

The feel of him probing inside her was distracting, and she found his invasion wasn't in the least uncomfortable. She also liked the fact that he actually cared whether he hurt her. "I will welcome you, my lord," she declared in husky assurance.

"If you are sure . . ."

In a flash of time, he shifted, covering her and suddenly ready, his body poised to possess her. She closed her eyes as he began to enter her, opening her thighs wide in invitation, letting his intimate foray consume her senses. His erection felt large, incredibly hard and slick.

And wonderful—it was pure carnal sensation to lie there beneath the laird and spread her legs for him, allowing him the most intimate knowledge possible of her body.

It was easier this time, she realized with surprise when he sank deep, her vaginal passage expanding to accept the penetration, a sigh of pleasure leaving her lips despite her inner vow to not be so vocal in her enjoyment this time. She had been raised a lady, and it was a little embarrassing to recall the sounds she had made earlier.

But she found she couldn't help it. A small whimper escaped her throat as he withdrew and pushed back in, his heavy-lidded gaze holding hers, a sensual smile on those well-shaped lips. Leaning forward, he whispered in her ear, "You feel every inch of me, don't you, my sweet hostage? And I feel all of you, those soft walls milking my cock as you try to keep me inside you, your womb trembling as I push in deep. You learn quickly, beautiful Leanna."

She liked hearing her name spoken in his soft brogue almost as much as the glorious feeling of his thrusts, the sensation of his lips touching her ear, his hard chest above her. She rubbed her hands over the powerful muscles of his back and closed her eyes. Like the first time, she could feel his escalating need in the change of his rhythm, his hips flexing faster, the increased speed bringing her a building sensation of tension mixed with pleasure. As from a distance, she could hear her own small gasps, her hips lifting to accept each surge until she was clutching at his shoulders, mindless with desperate desire.

When the sublime pinnacle came and she fell, her body rippling with tiny convulsions of pleasure, she gave a small scream, uncaring any longer about anything as mundane as her dignity. With a low curse, he joined her, impaling her as far as possible, going rigid as he ejaculated, coating her passage with the warm liquid spurt of his seed. The pulsing of his shaft matched the beating of her heart, primal and wild, and she marveled at it as he filled her, lying there in limp, blissful afterglow.

To her surprise, he didn't pull out, but once his breathing slowed, he propped himself on his elbows and smiled lazily into her face. With his long, disheveled hair, he resembled a legendary pirate, all sleek, dark, and dangerous. No, more like a striking Scottish chieftain, she corrected with an inward smile, who had just thoroughly ravished some young maid.

Still half-rigid inside her, as if it weren't an odd position for a conversation, he said with his usual tone of unconscious command, "Tell me, how did you come to be engaged to Frankton? Surely your father understands what kind of man he is and, with your stunning beauty, could do better for you than a grasping, deceitful villain you obviously despise."

Leanna swallowed, averting her gaze. "My father is an earl, but inherited no fortune with the title. He has five daughters, my lord, and wished for good marriages for us all, despite the fact he could not afford to properly present us to society. On a trip to London, I had the misfortune to be at a small function given by one of my father's friends. The baron was there as well, and I caught his eye. At heart, my father is a decent man, but he has his weaknesses, and gambling is one. Frankton lost no time in completely destroying whatever small assets my father had. In order to save the family estate, the bargain was made. I could hardly force my family to starve by a refusal. This way my sisters will at least have a chance to marry well."

Despite her refusal to shed one more tear over her plight, a small sob caught in her throat, and to her dismay, her eyes filled with tears.

Ian's mouth tightened slightly. "I guessed something like that had transpired. Another black deed Frankton will answer for in hell."

Leanna shivered. "He is evil. I—"

"Yes, he is, and evil men do evil things," the laird interrupted with a grim smile. "I suppose that was why he locked you in the tower room and posted guards: to keep you from running off during his absence while he accuses my uncle of a crime he never committed."

She might be naive, but she understood McCray's need for a bargaining tool.

"And," she said with a small, triumphant smile, since his cock, formidably large even half-erect, was so potently inside her, stretching her, "to make sure I stayed pure until the wedding."

"That's certainly no longer an issue," he murmured teasingly, and shifted, leaning forward to nibble gently on the curve of her neck.

"No," she agreed, giving a muffled laugh mixed with a sigh of enjoyment as his tongue traced the line of her jaw and licked her lower lip. He kissed her as if he tasted her, savoring her mouth, and she responded, pulling him closer, parting her lips. To her amazement, though they had just had intercourse, she found that longing welling inside her as he began to touch and caress her body, saying outrageously erotic things in her ear, taking her mouth time and again until she could feel he was also growing once more, hardening, and stretching her vaginal walls with his swelling erection.

When he began to move, she felt the blissful abandon of pure sexual license, her body open for his use and pleasure, her own senses tantalized and heightened by the skill of her Scottish captor. She climaxed twice before he came again with a hot rush inside her, the dizzying, sensual joy unbelievable. Afterward, nestled against him, her body pleasantly exhausted, she saw the moon had come up, high and full. Ian's breathing evened into the cadence of slumber, but he still kept her close in his embrace.

She felt safe, Leanna realized, with those strong arms around her.

But also knew it couldn't last long.

Chapter 4

The horse clattered into the courtyard and Ian waved a hand in greeting. His cousin Robbie, he saw, eyeing the mud-spattered cloak and tousled hair of the young man reining in his heaving mount, had ridden hard and fast.

"Ian." Robbie swung out of the saddle and grinned. A graze of black whiskers graced his lean jaw and he looked weary, but his handclasp was strong. "I rode almost all night. I need a drink, maybe even a good bucketful, for my throat is dry as dust."

"It's bloody good to see you," Ian responded with a smile, "and we've whiskey and ale aplenty. Rossie knew you were coming, because I have sentries posted everywhere and one of them reported it. She's got food at the ready, anticipating your hunger."

"Bless her," Robbie McCray said with a low laugh. "I might marry her yet, you know. I cannot figure out another way to steal her away from this old castle."

"She can't be more than two score years older than you," Ian observed dryly. "And as she has always had a weakness for hand-some, worthless rogues, she might just oblige you."

"Is that why she has an uncommon fondness for you?"

"It might be."

"If she agrees to run my household with the efficiency she runs yours, I'll propose."

"Come inside." Ian led the way to the table, where Angus was already seated with a tankard before him. Robbie wasn't lying about his thirst, for he drained his first glass in barely more than a gulp, and immediately poured a second. And when a serving girl brought a steaming platter of meat, he devoured his food in record time. Ian and Angus ate a little more leisurely, and he waited for them to finish. When the plates were cleared away, Robbie sighed, rubbing his jaw. "That was damned good. Hell, I'm tired."

"What brought you here so neck-or-nothing, lad?" Angus asked bluntly, impatience one of his trademark qualities. "What news do you have?"

Robbie, the son of Ian's uncle who now languished in the New-castle jail, sobered at once, losing his easy smile. "I petitioned of-ficially to have my father released, as you wanted me to, Ian," he said abruptly, "using the proper channels, jumping through their infernal English hoops. I proved that two of the accusations were false, but the magistrate has been purely bought, beyond question. A dismissal of the formal charges was denied and my father is still being held. Damn all, I *told* him to not bloody do business with the vermin English."

"Held for murder," Angus spat out, lifting his ale and drinking heartily. "It's as ridiculous as asking Queen Anne to kiss my arse."

"A man who uses a cane and can barely walk across the floor,"

Robbie agreed, his fury evident in the set of his mouth. "The charges argue that he supposedly cut down a young, healthy buck with a sword thrust in the back. If the judge even bothered to see my father, he would realize it was a ludicrous accusation."

"I am guessing Frankton didn't do the evil deed himself, but hired some vicious killer." Angus ventured, "Perhaps if we could put out the word that we would pay a tidy sum to the person who could give us information on this carefully planned scheme, we could gain the truth. The baron clearly wanted Thomas's estate, as he is the one who approached with the offer to do trade and lured Thomas into his clutches. Never trust an English bastard, I say."

"With Frankton as the only supposed eyewitness to the heinous crime, the charges cannot possibly be pressed forward once he is dead." Ian's voice was calm, his hand steady as he reached for his glass. But inside, his fury raged at the injustice, and he could feel his cousin's fear for his frail father. As laird, it was Ian's responsibility to care for his people, and this unjust imprisonment of a man he revered grated on his pride and nerves. The only thing Thomas had been guilty of was a failure to realize Frankton's reputation was well deserved.

Robbie toyed with the handle on his cup for a moment; then he said heavily, "Any word that bastard has figured out you have the girl yet, cousin? He is keeping her abduction quiet, but he was in London when it happened, so it could be the news was delayed getting to him."

"We were over a hundred strong. The baron probably knows already that a large party rode north, and to where. He will also realize it is a McCray he is trying to rob and ruin, and put the pieces together. Frankton is amoral and ruthless, and it will be no loss to this earth when I kill him, but he isn't stupid."

"In the meantime, my father sits in jail."

Ian's mouth thinned at the hotheaded open criticism, and he regarded his young cousin from across the table. "I cannot rush out and handle this in a fit of anger. Neither can I allow you to approach the baron. He's too clever, and well guarded by his heavy purse, traveling with a hired force everywhere he goes. No, let him come here for his future bride and demand her release."

"What if he doesn't?" Robbie argued, the lines around his mouth showing his fatigue and resentment of his helplessness. "The world is full of comely lasses. He'll simply find someone else to ease his lust. I know you are laird and I rarely doubt you, but I am not sure of your plan, Ian."

As if on cue, Ian heard a soft, intimately familiar voice, followed by a melodic laugh. With a look toward the stairs that curved into the main hall where they sat, he saw that Leanna descended the steps, about halfway down. Rossie, at her side, was talking quickly, and both women, who seemed to have formed a swift friendship, were smiling.

"That's her," Angus stated in his forthright, gruff way. "Tell me, Robbie, lad, do you still think he won't come to retrieve this particular prize?"

Robbie glanced at the stairwell, his cup suddenly arrested in the very act of being lifted to his mouth.

Ian couldn't blame him. He caught his breath every time he saw her.

This evening Leanna wore soft blue, a dress that had once belonged to his younger sister—now married and living in

Stirling—altered by the village seamstress to fit Leanna's graceful, slender figure. Her shining golden hair, so lovely and unusual, was gathered softly away from her face, exposing her elegant bone structure and haunting dark blue eyes. It was more than her compelling beauty that attracted men, he'd decided in the past days—and nights—trying to analyze his own potent attraction to his English captive. It was her quiet femininity, the hidden passion under her demure, ladylike exterior, the refined way she moved and smiled.

"Jesus," Robbie muttered. "Is she an angel?"

"Or a beautiful witch?" Angus replied dryly, with a sidelong look. "She apparently casts a powerful spell. Ask your laird, lad."

It was true; Ian couldn't deny it. He was in her arms every night, taking her over and over so that she slept half the day away from the exertions of their lovemaking, her pale thighs sticky with his semen, her body sated from his passion.

Robbie tore his gaze away from the young woman coming toward them. "Are you bedding her, Ian?"

Since it was common enough knowledge around the castle and probably the entire countryside, Ian merely lifted a brow.

Robbie's gaze flew back. "Well, well," he said softly, "if you tire of fucking her, let me know."

"I won't," Ian replied, his curt lack of hesitation startling even him.

Angus shook his head in obvious resignation, dashing more ale into his cup. "Oh, my lad. I tried to warn you, Ian. I did. That busy cock of yours is currently head of this clan."

* * *

Leanna sipped her wine and smiled, though she was more than a little uncomfortable. Having a tray delivered to her room was lonely, but dining at a table full of men was sometimes too much the opposite. Since Ian, as chief of the clan, was unmarried, she sat just to the left of the head of the table. Besides the barrel-chested Angus's wife, she was the only female, and though she knew the men tried to do their best to remain polite, the conversation often became boisterous.

Ian's cousin, the good-looking young man introduced as Robbie McCray, watched her with steady dark eyes, looking so much like a younger version of Ian that it was unsettling. It was Robbie's father, Rossie had told her, whom Baron Frankton had accused unjustly of a crime, in an attempt to steal the man's property. The older woman was a font of information, and her hand firmly ruled all the domestic aspects of the castle's operation.

Robbie inquired pleasantly enough, "Lady Leanna, how do you like the Scottish countryside? Very often the English find it a bit . . . untamed."

Worried that this man in particular would hate her, since her fiancé was responsible for his father's plight, and because being put on the spot involved a dozen pairs of unrelenting male eyes upon her, Leanna took a compulsive gulp of wine before she replied. "I haven't actually seen much besides what lies outside my window. I would agree it is very untamed . . . but also very lovely."

"So are you," Robbie countered, and slightly lifted his glass in a salute that seemed to mock and compliment at once.

Untamed, she wondered, or lovely? She murmured politely, "Thank you."

"Ian needs to show you around more," Robbie continued. He

was tall and athletically built, his raven hair and face remarkably like his older cousin's, the handsome stamp of the McCray features unmistakable. "But then again, he's very busy. I am here for a few days. Perhaps I could oblige and introduce you to the beauty of the Highlands."

Relieved that the young man didn't seem to hold her accountable for the actions of her unwanted fiancé, she said sincerely, "That would be nice. Thank you."

"Tomorrow?" he suggested, his ebony brows elevating. "What do you think, Ian, shall I show her Loch Cray?"

For the first time, Leanna glanced over and saw the laird's expression, surprised to find it a mixture of annoyance and amusement. "I suppose," he drawled. "Loch Cray is worth seeing, and Lady Leanna has been cooped up in this castle for over a week."

"I'll be happy," Robbie answered in the same smooth, lazy tone, "to liberate her."

"Not *too* happy, I hope," Ian said curtly.

"I am simply being friendly."

"I see." Ian settled back in his chair, his fingers carelessly toying with his wineglass, his long legs extended. It took a moment, but he nodded. "Go well armed," he said brusquely. "I trust your sword arm almost as much as I trust my own, Robbie."

"In the morning, then, my lady?" the younger McCray asked her, his smile boyish and captivating with its charm.

Robbie McCray, Leanna decided then and there, was a rather dangerous young man.

She nodded and stood, and though they might be her Scottish captors, to their credit the men at the table all rose politely to their feet. "In the morning," she murmured. "I look forward to it.

If you'll excuse me, it is getting late and I am not used to so much wine. Good night." She smiled vaguely at the assembly and left the table, heading for the stairs. To her surprise, she had taken no more than a few steps when she found herself suddenly lifted up off her feet by large, masculine hands, and a small, startled gasp escaped her throat.

Ian held her firmly against his chest. "I wouldn't want you to fatigue yourself by having to climb the stairs, my lady. Allow me to escort you to your—well, *my*—bedroom."

Her arms circled reflexively around his strong neck. She was well aware that everyone in the dining hall had seen him sweep her up, and his destination was no doubt obvious. She flushed, saying in low protest, "My lord, must you be so . . . so open with your intentions?"

"They all know I want you; 'tis no secret." He took the stairs quickly, two at a time.

She agreed; they most probably *did* know it, Leanna acknowledged to herself wryly. His smoldering regard had been unhidden throughout dinner, as his dark eyes watched her eat her meal and sip her wine, and took in every single movement. While it was pleasing to so interest her handsome captor, she was also not comfortable with the notion that the people around them were well aware how they spent their nights. Ian was different—she understood that. He cared very little if everyone knew he bedded her time and again; after all, he was laird, and a law unto himself. Even Rossie scolded and reprimanded him with familiarity, but still undeniably deferred to her former charge in any matters of importance.

Pushing open the door to his bedroom, Ian carried her inside and impatiently shoved it closed with a booted foot. He set her down, and his hands went swiftly to fastenings on her gown, slipping them loose and disrobing her in no time, leaving her naked for his overt perusal. Sitting down on the bed, still fully clothed, he pulled her onto his lap, kissing her mouth with fervor, and bent her back over his arm so he could taste her upraised bare breasts.

Not used to such impetuosity from him, Leanna gasped as he sucked on her exposed nipples, laving them with his tongue until they hardened and peaked in his mouth. One of his hands went to her hair, pulling loose the few pins she used in her chignon, letting the mass tumble free down her back. "I need you," he said with command, his breathing slightly ragged as he looked down into her face. With little ceremony, he stood and almost tossed her on the bed, his hands going to his breeches, letting his erection free. He pushed her legs apart and settled between them, still fully clothed and booted, grasping her hips and entering her with such speed, she took in her breath sharply, her eyes shutting at his rash desire and invasion.

He hadn't lied; their joining was tempestuous, and he possessed her as never before, not roughly but with such vigor that she gasped with every thrust. And in a purely physical response, her body answered the force of his passion, her sex softening and growing wet and welcoming, her thighs opening, her passage accommodating even such insistent ownership. She was so close to climax when he suddenly pushed all the way in, holding her hips ruthlessly still as he erupted in a scalding rush of release, that it sent her over the edge, her body gripping his pulsing cock, rippling around it long after he had gone still.

The fabric of his breeches felt strange against her sensitive inner thighs. She was a little dazed by his urgency. Even the usually self-possessed laird looked ruefully amused when he finally met her eyes. "That was not," he admitted, "very gentlemanly."

"No," she agreed, sprawled backward on the bed, completely naked while he was still clothed, his manhood filling her, his powerful body wedged between her legs.

"Should I apologize?" he asked softly. "You seemed to enjoy it anyway."

She *had* enjoyed it, even though it hadn't been a gentle wooing but more of an exhibition of fierce desire. Did that make her a strumpet?

Leanna smiled up at him. "If you'll go a little slower next time, I'll forgive you."

Swiftly leaning down to kiss her, he said promptly, "It's a bargain, my lovely captive. Let me undress and prove to you that a McCray clansman always keeps his word."

Chapter 5

"McCray!" Frankton exploded, whirling around. "That highland barbarian all the women whisper over. They went north, more than a hundred of those heathen Scots galloping as if the devil were at their heels. *He* has Leanna, damn him."

Very calmly, Lord Falmouth, reigning magistrate of the northern courts, said, "Robert McCray was just denied his petition to have the charge you support dropped against his father. It was clever for you to lure the old man down to York to discuss the details of the livestock purchase. The deed to his border property will be in our hands soon enough when Thomas McCray is convicted and hanged." Falmouth's reptilian smile was thin and his eyes hooded as he sat in a red velvet chair, his skinny legs elegantly crossed at the ankle. "It does not surprise me that a lawless infidel like Ian McCray would take your woman and use her as a bargaining tool. And," he added with a chuckle, "use her in other ways, at a guess."

"That whoreson bastard." His vision obscured by his violent

anger, Frankton could hardly see through the red haze that seemed to envelop the room. "We met in Edinburgh when one of my cousins had the poor taste to marry a Scottish earl. I sensed then his distaste for me. It is completely mutual."

"You do have a certain reputation, my dear Frankton, that's . . . er . . . how shall I put it? For the sake of diplomacy, perhaps I'll just say rumor has it you usually get what you want, one way or the other."

"You are no better," Frankton answered.

"Indeed." Falmouth lifted a brow—an irritating, supercilious mannerism. "That aside, my advice is to forget the winsome Miss Arlington. Given McCray's status as an indiscriminate womanizer *and* the fact that she has been in his company—and undoubtedly his bed—for over a week now, she is no longer the tender, terrified virgin you wanted, not to mention she might have a McCray brat growing right now in her belly."

Baron Frankton halted, arrested by the knowledge that his friend—if you considered an amoral man who could be bought for a bag of coins a friend—knew of his secret pleasures. Gruffly, he said, "Every man wants a pure bride."

"But most do not anticipate with quite so much relish the notion of her terror and pain during her deflowering. Make no mistake, Frankton, I know exactly who and what you are." Leaning back, looking like Lucifer himself in black robes superimposed against the bloodred fabric of the regal chair, Falmouth smiled in a parody of the real thing.

"I know you as well," Frankton warned. "You speak of my *secrets*," he sneered. "At least I do not lust after comely young men, keeping them in my home disguised as footmen and scribes."

His lordship looked unperturbed. "Robbie McCray was particularly tempting," he drawled with introspection, one hand reaching for his glass of wine. "So young and intense, his good looks striking, his sexual prowess already the fodder for whispers among the ladies. Perhaps when you retrieve the girl, you can bring him along as well. For me."

"I thought you advised me to forget her."

"And leave her to McCray?" Lord Falmouth laughed out loud, the sound grating in the depths of the shrouded room. "You have no intention of listening to me. I knew it before I said the words. This young *woman*"—he said the word with obvious distaste—"has aroused your lust to a level I have never seen before in all the years of our acquaintance, and besides, I believe you paid a small fortune for her, and your parsimonious soul would never give that up without a fight. Take a large force; that is all I advise, and stay out of the reach of McCray's sword arm. He isn't to be faced in hand-to-hand combat."

"Oh," Dartmus assured him, his mind still working out the details of his counteroffensive, "do not worry. Now that I know where Leanna is being held, I have a plan."

Falmouth lifted a brow. "You always do, Frankton. It is one of the things I like about you."

The water rippled and moved, the air hanging heavy with shadows, the wind very light and teasing. The day was lovely and warm, the breeze redolent with the earthy scent of heather and pungent earth. As she strolled along the edge of the long loch, Leanna sighed, lifting her face to the slight wind and inhaling deeply. After spending weeks in her tower and the past few days inside the castle, she found the fresh air intoxicating and the feel of the sun on her face a lovely luxury.

"Loch Cray is over ten miles long," Robbie, walking next to her, informed her. "It has some of the best salmon fishing in Scotland, not that our clan lets anyone else test these waters with their lines. Of course, at least right now, it would be so difficult to cross our land a rabbit would be spotted trying to set foot on McCray soil. Ian has men posted everywhere, waiting for Frankton to come for you."

Suddenly, the sunshine seemed to fade a little, her joy in the beautiful day lessening. Unable to prevent it, Leanna felt a shiver ripple through her body, and she crossed her arms over her breasts in a gesture of self-protection. "I dread the moment," she confessed, "that I am returned to him."

"I beg your pardon?"

The long grass brushed her skirts as birds sang fitfully, filling the morning with sound. Glancing over at Robbie—at least a decade younger than the laird, at a guess, closer to her nineteen years—she saw him frown. "I am a hostage," she elaborated, stating the obvious. "When the baron comes, he will exchange me for your father's freedom. It is why I was taken from Frankton."

To her chagrin, Robbie McCray burst out laughing.

Obviously, he had never been ogled by the repulsive Frankton, or locked away in a tower for weeks without human contact except frightened maidservants and impassive guards. She said sharply, "I am glad you are amused, but perhaps if you found yourself in such a position of helplessness, you would feel differently."

Robbie's mirth faded, and he looked at her with those intense dark eyes. "Do you really believe Ian will hand you over?"

"I . . . I was captured to free his uncle."

"You were captured," Robbie said evenly, "to bring Frankton here so Ian could kill him. I doubt he counted on becoming so enamored of your person, my lady, but I would wager my soul to the devil that he wouldn't hand you over to anyone, much less a greedy, cruel pig like Frankton. Even if you were homely and covered in pox, he isn't the kind of man who would let a woman be abused or degraded."

Startled, suddenly vibrantly hopeful against her will, Leanna digested his words. It was true: Ian seemed to enjoy their nights together very much, but that was lust—lust he could vent on some other woman if he wished. She didn't dare to dream he would feel more, though . . . if she admitted it, she had begun to hope so. Stopping abruptly on the grassy path, she demanded, "Why didn't he tell me?"

Robbie shook his head, his smile sinfully attractive. The breeze ruffled the full sleeves of his white shirt, the garment open at the throat to show a hint of a bronzed chest. "He answers to no one. He's the laird. I can tell you from personal experience that Ian is not used to explaining his actions. You have his attention in many ways from what I can see, but this particular conflict only indirectly has to do with you. It is between him and the baron."

"What will he do with me?" she asked without thinking.

Next to her in the mellow sunlight, with his dark hair glistening blue-black and that slight, very charming smile on his face, Robbie McCray said softly, "I cannot say, my lady, as I do not speak for Ian. However, know this: If he tires of you or if you need protection in any way, my sword is ready and my arms are open. You need do nothing except send me word and I will come for you."

A little off balance at that generous declaration and the open admiration in his eyes, Leanna murmured, "Thank you. . . . You are kind to someone you barely know."

"It isn't kindness," he responded wryly, arching a brow, the corner of his mouth lifting, "which, after a week in my cousin's bed, I think you probably realize. You are the most extraordinarily beautiful woman I have ever met. That aside, I have never seen Ian so openly infatuated. I admit it intrigues me. Why are you so different?"

The compliment flustered her, as did the way he looked at her, those dark eyes almost familiar, they were so similar to Ian's. The heat in his direct gaze was also disconcertingly something she had seen many times before. He was audacious, she decided, the laird's young cousin, and she couldn't help but wonder how Ian would feel if he heard such an outrageous and blatant offer.

Perhaps he would be jealous. Suddenly remembering Ian's almost frantic need for her the previous night as he carried her upstairs, she wondered if Robbie's unconcealed appreciation had not fueled her lover's sudden overwhelming lust. The rest of the night, too, he had been more insatiable than usual, his lovemaking both tender and intense.

"Perhaps," she said faintly, "we should go back."

"As you wish." Robbie seemed to understand he had confused her, and was amused by it.

This time, when he lifted her onto his horse and swung up behind her, settling his arms around her as he took the reins, she felt a little unease at being so close to him. Robbie had asked her upon their departure if she wanted her own mount, but she was not a rider; her father had only the horse he rode himself in their stables since their poverty was such that he could not afford ladies' mounts for his daughters. When they rode together through the village on their way back to the castle, the people on the street waved in enthusiastic greeting, and Robbie answered in kind, but their stares were avidly curious as they gazed at her.

She was a hostage, she sharply reminded herself. Surely everyone knew she could not help being there.

And they probably also all knew she graced the laird's bed, she thought in embarrassed resignation.

But it was better than marrying the odious Frankton.

In the empty room, the large bed was turned back but unoccupied. As Ian stood in the doorway of his bedroom, he felt restless unease. Leanna had been very quiet at dinner, and he had the uncomfortable sensation that something was wrong and he was at fault for her preoccupation. He'd told himself to just leave her alone, but her withdrawn mood bothered him.

He was worried over a woman's mood. Hell and blast, *that* had never happened in his life.

It was ridiculous for him to concern himself, of course. She was little more than a pawn, a hostage, a plaything to be used to confound and humiliate the hated Baron Frankton, he reminded himself quickly.

And, looking at his empty bed, he told himself with painful honesty a second later that in such a short time, she had become much more than that. It was true, she warmed his nights, responding to his persuasive lovemaking with honest passion, but she was also sweet and innocently kind, gracious to the servants, and uncomplaining about her circumstances. Young as she was, he admired her courage and the loyalty to her family that had compelled her to accept the untenable proposal of the despised baron in the first place.

In short, he was . . . smitten.

Crossing the hall with long strides, he rapped lightly on Leanna's door and then pushed it open. To his relief, she was inside, clad in her dressing gown, her loose golden hair a mass of tumbled silken curls down her back. Her expression was unreadable, her long-lashed eyes veiled as she looked at him from across the room.

Ian said evenly, "I thought perhaps you would be waiting for me in my room, lass. I know I was late talking with Angus, but—"

"If I do not have to go back to the baron, I cannot see the point in continuing our . . . intimate activities," she interrupted in a cool tone, which was unlike her.

For a moment, her statement confounded Ian. Then the picture suddenly came sharply into focus. "Damn Robbie and his loose tongue," he muttered.

"If you had told me yourself, it would have been better." Leanna looked at him, composed, but her lovely blue eyes held a shade of accusation.

"But then," he pointed out in perfect honesty, "you might have no longer come to my bed."

"So you deceived me?"

He shrugged with a nonchalance he didn't feel. She was vexed with him and he found he didn't like it, but then again, he was laird, dammit, and since when was he accountable for not explaining his intentions anyway—much less to an English prisoner, and a woman at that?

"It wasn't calculated deceit; it was simply omission," he said, and was stunned to hear the defensive edge creep into his voice.

"Had you already decided you were not going to return me when I offered myself to you like a common harlot?" She put her hands on her slim hips and there was a flush on her smooth cheeks.

He never lied. It didn't occur to him to do so usually, but it did now. Yet honesty won the day, and he admitted, "Yes, and there is nothing common about you, Leanna; nor are you a harlot."

The compliment did not win him her favor. "I have seen the way women look at you, my lord, even the serving girls. You can vent your lust on someone else easily enough."

"I have seen the way other men look at *you*, especially my young cousin," he countered irritably, "and I want you only."

A startling sentiment, especially when uttered aloud.

But all too true. He wasn't sure which one of them was more surprised. A telling pause ensued in which they just looked at each other.

"What will happen to me if you do indeed kill Frankton?" she asked quietly, finally breaking the silence.

"Whatever you wish," Ian told her, torn between the urge to tell her he would never let her go, and the wisdom of vowing such a thing to a woman he'd known less than two weeks. He was deeply sexually infatuated with this beautiful girl, to an extent that had never happened to him in his thirty years—but how could he know it would last? Besides, she was English, and he was laird. Wedding a Scottish lass was something he always assumed he would do eventually.

"I don't know if I wish to go back to my father," she said, her slender throat rippling as she swallowed, the glow of the lamp turning her hair the color of molten gold. "He sacrificed me once already, and though I will always love him, my trust in him has been shattered. While I was willing to do my duty to help my family, he must have known more about Frankton than he revealed to me. I feel I was betrayed. I have an aunt who lives in Wales. Perhaps I could go there."

"It's too far away," Ian objected without thinking.

"All you have to do, Ian, is take me back to England. You owe me that much. But don't worry; I do not expect you to escort me farther. I will work out the rest myself."

Despite the scandal of her abduction and her lost virginity, Leanna would have no trouble finding a husband; of that he had little doubt. Her beauty was incomparable, and she was a lady in every sense of the word. Couple that with her innate sensuality, and a man would be a fool not to want her.

If she carried his child, which was a definite possibility after the past days and nights of sexual excess in his bed, he would not let her go; that he knew. Whether he could let her go *at all* was the question.

"I take it," he asked quietly, "you wish to sleep alone? I will accept it, since I have never forced myself on you or any other woman, but what of our bargain? I upheld my part, my lady. You asked me to take you and I did so, trying to give as much pleasure as I received. You captivate me, lass, and I want you and will continue to want you as long as you are here."

"I want you too," she confessed with her typical honesty, "but it was so easy to excuse my wanton behavior when I felt I was spitefully foiling the baron."

I want you too. . . .

A tightness inside him eased.

"You are not wanton, but passionate, and I personally prefer the idea that you lie with me because you wish it, not because of Frankton," Ian said persuasively. "Come to me, Leanna, and keep him out of our bed."

Encouraged when she did not refuse, Ian crossed the room and lifted her gently into his arms. He kissed her soft mouth, then looked into her eyes and said with perfect truth, "I am as confused as you are over what lies ahead. Perhaps it would be best if we simply enjoyed what time we have together before he comes. When this matter is settled and my uncle freed, we will decide the future."

Her slim arms went around his neck, and the smile she gave was both wistful and alluring. "Has any woman ever denied you, Ian?"

He grinned. "Not in my memory."

"Then perhaps that's what I'll tell myself." She touched his cheek and offered her mouth for another kiss. He obliged, pleasure and arousal flooding his body.

This need, he thought, tasting and stroking her even as he carried her across the hall to his bed, *is almost frightening.*

It was just before dawn, that dead hour between night and day. Leanna stirred and rolled over, seeking the solid warmth of Ian's body. To her surprise, his arm came around her like a band of iron, and his hand covered her mouth. In her ear, he breathed, "Don't move or make a sound, love."

Startled, she came fully awake, obeying his terse order and blinking in the darkness. He let her go but was tense; she could feel the rock-hard bulge of his impressive muscles and hear the steady, increased thud of his heart. In a moment, she understood why. The door gave a small, almost inaudible creak as it inched open.

Lying on her side facing Ian with her eyes half-closed, she couldn't quite see what was happening, but feigned sleep as he obviously wanted her to, trying to stay relaxed even though her pulse raced and throbbed in her throat. Sprawled next to her, Ian also gave the appearance of deep slumber, his dark hair disheveled on the pillows.

There was more than one man; she could tell that from the sound of their breathing. How many she wasn't sure, but a scream built in her throat as Ian still didn't move. When she saw the silhouette loom over the bed, she wasn't sure she could keep still a moment longer.

Suddenly, the scene erupted as Ian flung himself upward, his fist connecting solidly with flesh, and a yelp of pain echoed out. Shrinking back against the bed, Leanna saw in terror there were at least three men in the bedroom, all dressed in black clothing, undoubtedly armed, for she caught a gleam of metal in the darkness. Ian too, she saw in the dim light coming through the window, held a wicked-looking knife, and as she watched, he swung it in a precise movement toward the closest of their assailants, cutting the man across the neck, the spurt of blood horrifying. The invader fell, clutching the gash, and hit the floor with a solid thud. Losing no time, fast as a dancer and as graceful, Ian slashed again and she heard the ripping of cloth and a bellow as another man stumbled backward to hit the wall. It happened so incredibly fast that the injured man looked astounded even as his knees buckled.

The one man left standing seemed undeterred, but was smart enough to not let Ian close, and they faced off warily. Magnificently nude, his dark hair sleek around his shoulders, Ian was not only unafraid, but obviously furious. His eyes were narrowed and he resembled a menacing mythical warrior, perfectly proportioned and muscular, his dripping knife attesting to his deft skill. He kept between the attacker and the bed, protecting *her*, Leanna realized.

"I'll spare you," he said through his teeth, "despite the cowardly approach and the fact that you are a paid killer, if you put down your weapon."

"Save your breath, Scotsman," the man spat. He was huge, every bit as tall as Ian, and even heavier, with hulking shoulders.

"Very well. It was your choice. When you wake up in hell, remember it."

Feinting a slash to the stomach, Ian charged and then dodged left, his movements a blur. All Leanna knew was that suddenly the large man went rigid, his face convulsing, his knife falling from lax fingers, never even having the opportunity to attack. He crumpled and Ian let him fall, his long knife buried to the hilt in the man's back. Barely breathing hard, Ian stood there and surveyed the chaos with a cool gaze.

Huddled in the bed, shocked and suddenly shivering, Leanna could not believe she had just seen three men killed before her eyes, and that the tender lover who had brought her to the peak of ecstasy time and again had cut them down with such ruthless skill—it all seemed a dream. The sickening stench of coppery blood made her stomach lurch, and she fought the urge to scream hysterically at the sight of the sprawled bodies. It was a nightmare, she promised herself, and closed her eyes.

The commotion had roused others too. She could hear doors opening, and seconds later, a low whistle rang out. Reluctantly, her body trembling, she lifted her lashes. Robbie stood in the doorway as he took in the carnage. His sword hung in his hand and he was bare chested, clad in only a pair of doeskin breeches. "What do we have here, cousin? By God, Ian, couldn't you have saved one for me?"

Ian shrugged, still naked and blood spattered. "I tried. He wouldn't listen."

"Oh, dear Lord in heaven," Rossie cried, peeking out from behind Robbie's tall form, her horrified gaze fastened on the fallen men. "What kind of madness is this?"

"Frankton's work, no doubt," Ian explained with a grim smile. "He has discovered where Leanna is and, in his usual way, tried the underhanded approach first. If I weren't a light sleeper, I suspect I'd be dead and she would be on her way back to England as we speak."

Frankton. England. Ian . . . dead?

Belatedly, Leanna remembered she was nude and snatched the sheet up to cover herself, but not before Robbie noticed her state of undress, his smile holding a wicked glint. Shifting his gaze back to his cousin, Robbie said, "He'll know now you are on your guard. That helps, because he won't have a choice but to come himself."

"And believe me"—Ian's voice was chillingly cold—"I can't wait."

Chapter 6

"I ordered Harry to follow them and take two more well-armed men." Ian stood high up on the castle walk and watched as, far below, Robbie led Leanna from the courtyard, the gleam of her bright hair unmistakable in the sunlight. "I am reasonably sure that no one else could slip through the guards I have posted, but then again, I certainly did not think three men could penetrate our defenses so easily and gain entrance to my own bedroom."

"They murdered the sentries in cold blood," Angus said bitterly. "Typical brutality for such a conscienceless Sassenach, damn his black soul straight to hell."

"I should have doubled the watch. It is all my fault."

"Don't flay yourself any more over it, lad. You killed the English hireling bastards. That's some justice for our fallen men."

It was easier said than done to salve his conscience; Ian knew that. The men the baron had hired to murder him had been thorough and well trained, and they had killed four of his clansmen, loyal McCrays with families. He would provide for their wives and children, but that didn't make up for the loss of a husband or a father. "Dammit," Ian muttered, "I just want him to come and face me."

"All of this over one woman." Angus shook his head.

"It isn't about Leanna. It's about Frankton's greed." Ian was quick to defend her, surprised that Angus would dare voice such a thought out loud.

"Aye, yes, but there's more trouble ahead, the dastardly baron aside."

Ian glanced over with a low sigh. From their high perch, Angus watched the young couple as they left the protective courtyard walls, Robbie courteously taking Leanna's arm to aid her over the rough patches in the path. "You mean Robbie, of course."

"That I do, lad. He fancies himself in love with your woman, Ian; make no mistake about it. You are not there to see his face when you follow her so eagerly upstairs. His tortured expression tells me he goes to sleep imagining you between those pale legs, taking your pleasure."

"He has more lasses than he knows what to do with," Ian protested in open disgust.

"Yet he yearns for yours." Angus chuckled suddenly, stroking his beard. "It's retribution, I am guessing, for all those years you so easily bedded any woman who caught your eye. Here you are now, having to defend your claim to none other than your own cousin."

"I am defending nothing," Ian snapped. "She's mine. Robbie knows that. He won't challenge me. If I thought he would, I would hardly let them go off and picnic or fish or God knows what particular ridiculous outing he has planned today, the besotted fool. Leanna enjoys being out of the castle, so I allow it. Nothing will happen."

Mildly, his friend remarked, "You seem testy for someone so sure of young Robbie."

"He would give his life for her," Ian said with conviction. Then he added on a breath, "But I don't want to have to ask that of him. Therefore the extra guard. And you are right as usual, Angus; I am growing peeved with him. He does nothing to conceal the way he looks at her, as if he is imagining her naked and willing in his arms. By the fires of hell, what does he expect I will do in the end?"

"His eager cock is thinking, not his mind. Last eve, I thought you were going to tear his young head off."

Remembering the way his cousin had stared at Leanna's admittedly lovely full breasts, the creamy upper curves bared by a low-cut gown that flattered her entrancing figure, still made Ian's mouth tighten in irritation. "He annoyed the devil out of me," he admitted, thrusting his fingers through his hair. "Will I have to endure this for a lifetime, every man who sees her wanting her?"

"A lifetime? Ah, I see, you've decided then to wed her? I guess I am not surprised."

Had he? The question set him off balance. To avoid answering it, he said quickly, "I want no part of a quarrel with Robbie, quite the contrary. He is like a brother to me, closer than anyone else in my family. I am fond of him, and I also see how he is with *me* now these past days: jealous and angry as well. Tension like this between us is the last thing we need, especially considering the threat from Frankton. However, I cannot see how to fix it. I suppose I could forbid Leanna to be near him, but I haven't seen that she encourages him in any way, so it would seem as if I were punishing her and regarded him with mistrust. It might make things worse."

Putting his hands on the wall in front of him, Angus looked thoughtful. "Perhaps the best thing to do would be to let him consummate his passion for her. Give him permission to bed her for one night."

For a split second, Ian could not even speak. Then he exploded in uncharacteristic fury. "Are you insane? One second, you tell me you aren't surprised I want to marry her; the next, you tell me to let her fuck someone else."

"Just to get a reaction from you, lad." Angus chuckled, but then his smile faded and he said gruffly, "I saw how it was from the beginning between you and Lady Leanna. So did Rossie. Not much slips past her keen eye, and she is fond of the girl. For an Englishwoman, the lass is acceptable for the wife of our laird. When a woman is truly in love with a man, it is hard to miss."

Pushing aside the unpalatable vision of his cousin and Leanna in bed together, Ian asked tersely, "You think she is in love with me?"

"By the gods, it's obvious, boy, to someone not so involved. And since she told Rossie plainly so, I am guessing it is true."

Leanna in love with me—the idea was not new, if he admitted it. He *wanted* her to be in love with him.

As he was with her. And apparently his cousin was as well.

Damn, this was a complication he didn't need.

"What should I do about Robbie?" he asked. Though he was used to making decisions affecting the lives of his clan with calm, cool logic, clearheaded thinking escaped him when it came to Leanna.

"Perhaps you should let her handle it."

He was not used to letting others handle anything in his life. He'd been laird since he was twenty. Ian said curtly, "I'll talk to him."

Angus's bushy brows lifted and he snorted. "You can try, lad. Let me know when you plan to reason with him so I can be there to help mop up the blood."

"These are for you."

The flowers looked strangely delicate next to Robbie's sinewy, masculine fingers. Leanna took them, unable to suppress a smile, though she shook her head. "You are very sweet."

"I am *not* sweet," Robbie told her with a cheeky grin. "Though I imagine you are." His gaze drifted suggestively over her body, boldly lingering on her bosom. "I own I wouldn't mind a taste."

Leanna did her best to give him a quelling look. "Rossie tells me your reputation is already more notorious than Ian's was at the same age, and I think I see why. Flowers and compliments aside, you must know Ian is becoming annoyed by your attention to me."

"And I am so damned envious of him, I can barely exchange a civil word," Robbie admitted sharply, glancing away. "I see his disapproval; don't worry. We are at odds for the first time in our lives. He wants to throttle me. I want to castrate him and take you for myself."

Put that bluntly, the sentiment was a little shocking. "Robbie," she said reproachfully, feeling uncomfortable. "You've been here a week. We barely know each other."

"You were at the castle half a day before Ian bedded you."

She could feel her cheeks heat. "How do you know that?"

"Everyone knows it," he said restively. "And I wish we *knew* each other," he countered, giving her a meaningful look from dark, direct eyes. "The amount of time elapsed since I met you is but a detail. But don't worry. I wouldn't betray Ian, however much I might want to do so."

They sat on a small hill, a blanket underneath them, with the remnants of their lunch packed back into the basket Rossie had provided. Twirling the lovely blooms in her fingers, Leanna pondered how odd it was to be so far from home, with the threat of Frankton still looming, and feel so . . . settled and happy. "Ian is a wonderful man," she admitted softly. "I know you admire him and that he cares for you. Don't let this infatuation spoil anything between you, please. It would make me feel terrible."

"I am not happy with it either." His tall body propped on one elbow, looking every inch the frustrated young lover, Robbie gazed at her. "I want you. He wants you. The trouble being, of course, he *has* you. Every night."

Over and over. Leanna blushed again, recalling how ardent and skillful Ian was as a lover, taking her again and again, eliciting delicious sensations and incredible arousal as he enjoyed her body.

"It's that good, is it?" Robbie muttered, his mouth twisting as he watched her expression. "Damn him," he added blackly.

Not having dared to say this to anyone but Rossie, whom she now considered a friend, Leanna acknowledged quietly, "I love him."

"I know."

Her brows went up. "You . . . do?"

"Oh, hell, yes." Violently he ripped up a long blade of grass, crushing it in his fingers. "Who better to see it? I love you; you love him, and Ian . . . who knows if he will recognize what he feels? He's older, guarded, used to women besieging him because of his looks and title. He takes them to bed, but as far as higher emotion, I doubt he even allows it."

"I hoped . . ." Leanna swallowed and looked away. The fields were very verdant, the sun high again, the scent heavy with summer. "I . . . well . . . hoped he might come to care for me."

"If he doesn't, I'll rip his heart out."

She couldn't help it; she laughed out loud, a choked sound. "Nothing so drastic, if you please, Robbie. Chivalry has its place."

He laughed too, looking boyish again and not so seriously intent. "It might not be so easy. The other night when the baron's assassins attempted their attack, he was so murderously angry, I was almost afraid to come into the room. I think he was so ferocious because you might have come to harm. Had he left one of them alive, we might have gotten information about Frankton's plans."

"I was very frightened, but it was over so fast."

Robbie's eyes darkened and grew heavy. "You looked delicious there, amid those tumbled sheets. I saw you naked."

He had, and she was still mortified, because though everyone might know she and Ian slept together, it was quite something else to have half the household come rushing up to witness her occupying his bed. "Three men were dead. I wasn't paying attention to my state of undress."

"I guess if I can't have more, I will always remember how you looked, so soft and enticing and smooth. Even now I can picture you spreading your legs for me, inviting me inside." Robbie looked at her meaningfully.

"Don't," she said softly, biting her lower lip, her face heating.

"I've had women . . . they have been throwing themselves at me since I was fifteen." His voice was restive and the errant breeze stirred his dark hair. "Satisfying myself has never been an issue."

She didn't imagine it was. He was so young and vibrantly handsome.

"Why," he asked, exhaling a ragged breath, "do I want *you* so badly? It is against my principles to feel this way about Ian's woman, and I *hate* the English. Blondes are not even my preference!"

A laugh over his irritation rose in her throat and burst out. Leanna put her hand over her mouth, stifling her mirth. "I apologize for disrupting your world."

"So you should, my lady."

She grew serious. "Please don't contest Ian over me."

"I cannot promise anything. I would not seduce you dishonorably, but a challenge is different."

The sentence was said with such conviction that all her concerns resurfaced. "If either of you came to any harm on my behalf, I am not sure what I would do. Please, if you truly do care for me, do not cause me such grief."

His expression tortured, mouth tight, Robbie looked away. "Perhaps," he said remotely, "we should be heading back."

Cameron McCray was covered in dust, sweating, and trying to catch his breath. Handing him a glass of whiskey, Ian said abruptly, "For God's sake, out with it."

"They're coming, my lord. They will be here tomorrow afternoon. Three or four hundred strong each, maybe more, three different parties, all moving toward us." With impressive speed, Cameron drained his glass, his throat working. "They ride up the west road, bordering our land but staying out of it. Trying, I would guess, to remain undetected for as long as possible."

Ian glanced over at Angus. "How many men can stand ready, knowing we might have to fight?"

Angus said immediately, "Close to a thousand, all eager to drink the blood of the brutish baron, lad."

"I'll do that." Ian crossed the room, thoughtfully pausing at the window. It was a hazy night, much like the one on which he had abducted Leanna. "He wants a fight," he murmured. "He means to win by numbers, since treachery failed."

"He wants Leanna." It was Robbie who spoke, quiet and yet restless, sprawled in a chair in Ian's study, a glass dangling from his long fingers.

Very dryly, Ian said, "I'm sure you can understand that." Then, turning, he nodded. "Thanks for the good work. Cameron, go home to your wife. Angus, you need to alert everyone of what might happen tomorrow. I want all children and women safely inside their homes, with a perimeter of men around the village. I trust Frankton not at all."

"Yes, my lord." Cameron bowed and then left the room, but for a second Angus lingered, glancing back and forth. He said, "You won't kill each other now, will you? This isn't the time for a jealous brawl. That English toad is almost here. It's what we've all been waiting for. Lady Leanna will have no protector if you are both weak and wounded from your rancor over her."

Ian spoke firmly. "We're fine, Angus. Go."

Suddenly uncertain that he had spoken the truth now that they were alone, Ian eyed Robbie's long body lounging in the chair, the tension in his cousin's face belying the casual pose. Robbie's lashes were half lowered, his gaze glittering with enmity.

"Thunder take it, Robbie," Ian said tersely. "You test me; you truly do. Hell, we've always been friends, close as brothers."

"If you think I like this situation, you're wrong." Aggravation was clear in every word. "But if you think I can help it, you're wrong there too."

"What will it take to make you lose this obsession?"

"Jesus, that seems obvious enough, Ian." Robbie laughed without mirth. "Care to relinquish your spot in her bed? If the answer is no, there isn't any easy solution to this problem."

"That isn't about to happen. You must agree to stop your determined pursuit. Leanna is worried I will hurt you. . . . Hell, I'm worried I will hurt you, if you want the truth." Ian ground out the words, as alarmed as Angus over the growing enmity between them. Dashing more whiskey into his glass, he took a solid drink.

"You could," Robbie said insolently, "try, of course. You seem confident of the outcome. I am not so sure you would win. As you said a few days ago, my sword arm is as skilled as your own."

"I said almost," Ian pointed out, "and we shouldn't quarrel over this."

"Have you asked her?"

"Have I asked her what?" Ian fairly snarled, staring at his cousin, his cup arrested near his lips.

"Where she wishes to go. She has no idea what you intend to do with her. I extended my protection. Mayhap she would like to accept it. At least I openly offered. Would you stop her?"

"What the hell did you offer?" It was tempting to test their battle skills right then and there. Except, Ian reminded himself with a steely hold on his control, that he was older, supposedly wiser, and he knew Robbie was pushing him on purpose.

"A future. One that you won't. And she was tempted."

Ian felt a pang of searing jealousy, like a knife to the heart. If Robbie offered her marriage, maybe Leanna would consider it. He knew full well that she was not the kind of woman to live her life as a man's mistress. Only her circumstances had driven her to lie with him in the first place, and Ian knew well enough she would not consent for the arrangement between them to stay as it was once the matter with Frankton was settled. "Are you so sure she was tempted?"

Robbie sprang to his feet, pacing across to grasp the whiskey decanter. "She loves you . . . but she also likes me, and the way I feel toward her . . . She cannot be indifferent toward it."

It was true. Ian wondered what young woman wouldn't want to hear how a handsome young man ardently adored her. "That is not enough for a future."

Robbie poured whiskey into a glass and turned around, an infernally smug smile on his face. "All I know is, she didn't refuse me."

Chapter 7

The soft glow of the lamp was aided by the brilliant starlit night outside, and Leanna sat near the window, her book half-closed in her lap, sometimes opening it and reading a few words, but mostly gazing out into the night. She enjoyed the waiting, she found, because the anticipation of Ian's arrival heightened her senses. As the latch lifted, a small, telltale shiver of excitement edged up her spine.

To be replaced by dismay a moment later as a tall, dark-haired man stepped into the room. Her book dropped to the floor as she stood in alarm. "Robbie, what are you doing?" she asked quickly, feeling a sudden fear for this impetuous young Scot who was so openly infatuated with her. "This is Ian's bedroom. If he should find you here—"

"If he should find me here now, he'd probably skewer me posthaste, but he's still in the main hall with the men. Frankton's forces have been spotted. They'll be here tomorrow."

Leanna felt the blood drain from her face.

"Don't look that way, lass," Robbie said, and before she could protest, he caught her in his arms, holding her gently against his lean, strong body. "You're trembling over nothing. The bastard won't get near you. Ian would never allow it, and I would die to protect you."

She took a deep, quivering breath to compose herself, and pulled away. To her relief he let her go without protest, and truthfully, there had been nothing but comfort in the brief embrace, though as usual, he was unable to conceal the hot-blooded desire in his eyes, his gaze flickering over her thin nightdress.

"That is just it. I don't want anyone dying over me."

He shrugged in careless dismissal of her concern. "I hope you don't include Frankton, because his chances of returning to England are about the same as Lucifer being invited back into heaven, but that English vermin is not what I wanted to discuss with you."

"What's wrong?" she asked, wondering what would make him dare Ian's wrath.

"Nothing is wrong," Robbie said softly. "Quite the contrary." He smiled—a wickedly boyish grin that made him even more breathtakingly handsome. "Ian wants to flay me alive because I desire you."

"If you think that is something I don't already know, you might remember I told *you* just that the other day at the loch."

"Aye, you did. I might have mentioned to him the rest of that conversation. His expression was a sight to behold when I told him I offered you my protection. It shook him, and Ian doesn't shake easily. Maybe it will help make the stubborn fool declare himself."

Astonishment momentarily replaced her worry over the coming confrontation looming on the horizon like a dark cloud. Leanna stared at Robbie. "Are you telling me you, of all people, played Cupid between Ian and me?"

Something flickered in his dark eyes. "If I can't have you, then I would see you happy with Ian. He needs to honor you with his name."

During those horrible weeks of being held captive by Frankton, she had experienced such despairing loneliness and dread. It was hard to imagine that being kidnapped and held hostage by another could improve her lot in life so dramatically, but it had. Here she was with two handsome men vying for her favor, ready to protect her with their lives. Leanna smiled. "Thank you."

Robbie hesitated as if he had more to say, but instead inclined his head briefly and swung on his heel, leaving the room. His exit was fortuitous, because only minutes later Ian entered, a faint scowl on his face. He snapped out, "I just passed my irritating young cousin on the stairs. Was he—"

"He told me about Frankton's approach," she interrupted, her happiness fading. "Oh, Ian, I dread what might happen."

"I'm surprised the blackguard's death would bother you," Ian said casually, sitting down on the bed to remove his boots. "I hope he's enjoying his last night on this earth."

Leanna looked so ashen, pale, her arms wrapped around her chest as if she was chilled, her eyes like dark pools. Rossie had told him once that women had the worst of it during any battle, for they were the ones who had to wait and worry over those they loved. At the time he'd been bleeding from a painful wound to the shoulder and wasn't in the mood to believe her, but maybe it was true.

Leanna wasn't riding out to confront the English on the morrow, but while Ian looked forward to the confrontation as a means to defeat Frankton, she looked anguished over the matter.

Did Leanna love him? Apparently everyone thought so, including Robbie, damn the audacious lad, but *she* had never said the words.

For the first time, Ian wanted to hear them from a woman. In the past, he'd always severed any liaison when he sensed the direction was headed toward heartfelt declarations of that sort. He'd dallied with all sorts of females, from serving girls to fine ladies, and never once had he wanted one of them to say those discomforting three words.

Until now.

I love you.

"You know I mean I fear for you," she told him, her slender form bathed in the candlelight. She'd been reading, for an open book lay on the floor as if she'd risen hastily from her chair.

Ian rose and extended his hand. "Come here and demonstrate your concern."

"You need to rest. Frankton will be here tomorrow, and I know he will bring a large force, because he would seek the advantage."

"I need *you*," he countered, his smile slow and deliberate. "Any warrior needs his woman before a battle. It reminds him he has something to fight for, lass. Come to bed."

"You are trying to distract me." She narrowed her eyes and didn't move.

He chuckled. "What is amiss with that? I hope to distract us both. I want you to think of nothing but how I feel inside you when we lie together."

For a moment he thought she would refuse him, but then she came forward, her slender fingers resting in his grasp as he took her hand. They kissed, softly at first, then with more urgency, and she fumbled with the buttons on his shirt until it was open enough she could touch his bare chest, one fingertip grazing his flat nipple until it puckered and his breath caught deep in his throat. Ian molded her soft form to his larger body and reveled in the change in her breathing as he nuzzled her neck and inhaled her sweet fragrance.

For all his confidence that Frankton would prove a cowardly foe, there was always a risk when a man drew his sword. Tonight he would love her differently, Ian vowed, not with hotspur sexual need, but with gentle giving, though it was not his nature to go slowly.

Perhaps he could say with his body what he wasn't ready yet to put into words.

Then his English lass surprised him. "Lie down," she ordered in a demanding tone even Angus would obey. Ian lifted his brows, but one look at the expression on her face convinced him, as did the way she slid the robe off her slender shoulders, and he complied, lying down on the bed.

Immediately she went to work on his breeches, unfastening them to free his already stiff cock, pulling his shirt out so she could push it off his shoulders. Very lightly, she scored her nails down his bare chest and looked into his eyes. The muscles in his stomach tightened as she brushed the tip of his throbbing cock. "Perhaps I will distract you instead, my lord."

If she even so much as walked into a room he could notice nothing else, but he didn't say so. "Do your best, lass," he murmured. "I am at your mercy."

Her hand dropped lower, to touch his rampant erection between the parted material of his opened breeches. Usually Leanna was not so bold, and he sucked in a startled breath. Her cool fingers wrapped around his heated flesh. "Yes, I believe in this position you are. Shall we negotiate? If you want me, I have a few conditions."

"Hostages do not give terms," he managed to say, though his voice sounded thick even to his own ears. Her touch drove him to near madness.

"This one does," she murmured, an angel clad in only a thin nightdress, her loose pale hair begging for his touch, her lashes lowered in a demure contrast to her possessive hold. "My first demand is that you be careful and anticipate treachery tomorrow."

"Done." He was a seasoned warrior, and a part of him was amused at her concern, and another part intrigued by her unexpected approach. "With the English," he said in a silky tone, "I am always prepared."

"Like now?" She stroked him, her hand gliding down his erection. "I've noticed. Care to hear my second condition?"

"Of course, lass."

"You cannot get hurt."

That he couldn't promise, but he shamelessly did so anyway, because her caressing hand held him in thrall. "I'll not get even a scratch."

"And don't let Robbie do something foolish."

Ian gave a grunt of dissention. "Like any man could stop him from acting like a belligerent idiot."

"I'm fond of him," Leanna admitted. She added softly, "Not nearly as fond as I am of you, but he is a charming scapegrace and

I know you love him. Keep him from harm for my sake, Ian, and also for yours."

Damn her, she literally had him by the bollocks, her hand sliding downward to cup that sensitive sac. "I'll do my best," he promised sincerely, knowing he'd protect Robbie regardless of his current state of annoyance with the young rogue.

"Since you agree"—she let him go, much to his disappointment—"I think we have come to an understanding." She pulled the ribbon on her bodice free and let the nightdress pool around her feet.

The perfection of her body never failed to give him pause, and he didn't reach for her at once, but just admired every lush curve, every tempting hollow. When she joined him on the bed, he shed his breeches so quickly he heard the material rip, and rolled her over to her stomach so he could stroke her graceful back, trace the line of her spine and the curve of her buttocks as he kissed the nape of her neck. "I'll take you like this first," he said in a low, heated voice, "and make you scream your pleasure. Then you can ride me perhaps . . . and for the third time, I'll come up with something even more inventive. Are you intrigued, Lady Leanna?"

She was, he discovered as he touched, caressed, and took her, enjoying each singular gasp, every muted moan, and, finally, her cry of surrender when she climaxed.

He was both victor and vanquished.

Which was, he decided when hours later he drifted to sleep with her damp, sated body in his arms, exactly as it should be.

Chapter 8

The company glistened in the sunlight, hundreds of bayonets and swords winking as they approached.

From one of the windows in the main hall, Leanna watched them advance, her gaze focused on the man who rode just behind the front line of riders. He was graceless in the saddle, his hair pale blond, his face lean and hungry like a starving wolf's. Almost forty, going to fat in the middle, Frankton looked as she remembered him, and it was with utter and complete relief that she knew she would never have to endure his touching her.

Ever.

Angus, stocky and impassive, stood next to her, sword in hand. He murmured with precise intent, "If that bastard even looks at you, my lady, I will cut him down like a rabid dog. Aye, you have my word on it."

Glancing over, she knew she should feel shocked at that sentiment and his language, but instead, considering Ian was out there, ready to face the encroaching horde, she was glad he was by her side. If Angus was anything, he was stalwart, and he would protect her, and she knew that was why Ian had left him behind.

Both the laird and Robbie sat almost motionless, waiting, a sea of McCray clansmen behind them. They looked impressive on their restive horses, dark, handsome, and dangerously formidable. Robbie had his hand on his sword already, his dark hair gleaming in the sun, his young face openly hostile, one expert hand controlling his mount.

Ian was different. He exerted no visible effort to keep his huge stallion quiet, sitting on the beast like a part of it, his gaze unwavering on the baron, his sword still sheathed at his side.

"Bring her out," she heard Frankton call, his voice sending a shiver of revulsion up her spine. "If I don't see Lady Leanna, McCray, your uncle will rot in his cell."

The front line of English riders halted only about a hundred feet from the waiting Scottish lords, their clan filling the entire courtyard.

Robbie said something low, and Leanna saw his horse dance sideways, his sword coming out, his lethal stance unmistakably threatening and volatile.

"Don't," she said in a half sob to herself.

Ian, remember your promise.

"That's one plucky lad," Angus murmured, grinning openly, "but not to worry. Ian will keep him in check."

"I hope so," she managed to whisper, so afraid for them both she could hardly breathe. "The baron isn't known for his charitable actions and honor."

"Nor is our Robbie for his discretion. Given how he feels about you, if he doesn't run the baron through at once, I will be surprised."

"Oh, God."

"I agree," Angus said conversationally. "It would be better if he waited and let Ian do the deed."

Ian lifted his hand just a fraction.

"Come on, lass. We're to just step outside the doorway, no farther. Let that English pig see what he will never touch." Angus took her arm and escorted her to the massive front door. Two Mc-Cray clansmen, draped in their plaid and well armed, opened it. Stepping outside, Leanna stood there in the golden afternoon sunshine. Angus, with his sword drawn, was at her side.

Lifting her chin, she stared at her fiancé. He stared back, a slow, evil smile spreading across his face. Since Ian's force was twice the number of the men he'd brought, she wondered uneasily what that smile might mean.

Though it was a beautiful day, not a cloud in the sea of blue above them, thunder rumbled suddenly. Troubled, she glanced up. Neither Ian nor Robbie moved, and she realized to her dismay that it was the sound of horses and a small army spilling down the hill to the right of the castle, an impressive cloud of dust rising behind them. To her horror, she saw that to the left, as well, more cavalry came, their swords drawn.

Considering that made the baron's opposing numbers now greater, her heart sank. She felt like the mythical Helen, launching battleships to war. Her voice was agonized. "Angus, I don't want a bloody fight. Men will be hurt, killed. I . . . I would rather go with him and endure whatever he wishes than allow a single blow to fall."

"Don't worry, my lady; Ian knew perfectly well that the baron had three separate forces. And he doesn't mean for this to come to anything other than a contest between him and Frankton. Besides"—he grinned, his small black eyes twinkling—"do you think he would let you go? And Robbie, do you picture that hot-blooded rascal allowing you to leave? I am sure he feels that if any-one besides Ian could bed you, he would be the one."

Leanna's cheeks flamed, though she was certain everyone knew of Robbie's interest. "I don't want either of them hurt."

"They won't be. Now watch. Look." Angus was openly gleeful. "Ian is riding forward. Though we cannot hear what he is saying from this distance, I know he is inviting the stupid, greedy Sas-senach gutter rat to settle the matter between them, just the two of them. See there: Frankton is refusing, shaking his head, skulking behind his men."

It was true; Ian had advanced alone and sat his horse directly in the front of the advance line. He spoke again, and though she couldn't discern the discussion, his face was impassive, his hands still on the pommel of his saddle.

Whatever Ian said must have concerned her, for the baron glanced back toward where she stood on the high steps, and the glower and fury in his expression were unmistakable. Chortling, Angus said cheerfully, "I believe our laird just informed him of his fondness for your . . . er . . . charms, my lady. See how red the beast's face is getting. I wish I could hear him. Ian will continue to humili-ate and goad him until he accepts the challenge."

"I rather wish an entire army couldn't hear him," Leanna mut-tered. "It's mortifying to have hundreds of men know you share the bed of a man who is not your husband."

"He'll marry you, lass; never fear. And how many of us with true hot passion wait until our wedding day? I know I took my Rowena before our vows were said. I couldn't help but press her, and she understood my need."

Ian truly wants to marry me? Robbie had mentioned it, but she hadn't dared hope.

Despite the fact that two armies stood poised, and it seemed probable blood would be spilled, Leanna felt a surge of joy through her fear.

"I think perhaps Ian just informed his noble toadship that he couldn't possibly let him take you, as you are probably breeding his child." Angus was so obviously delighted and so openly loathed the baron that even Leanna allowed herself a small, nervous laugh. He pointed. "My lady, look—see how Frankton's hand strays toward his sword, even though he knows better. Perhaps Ian detailed just how *many* chances there have been for his seed to take inside you." Glancing over and seeing her pink cheeks, Angus said contritely, "Forgive me, lass, but Ian has a lusty appetite and his hunger for you is obvious to us all. You also sleep late most mornings and the two of you retire fairly early, so the assumption that he is at you all night is easy to come by."

It was close enough to the truth that Leanna said nothing despite her embarrassment as she watched the two men. It looked as if the line in front of the baron had split a little, Frankton's men perhaps realizing that even their cowardly commander might take up the challenge. With Frankton's foul temper, she began to pray he would snap and lunge at Ian, who was surely ready for such action.

Taking advantage of the fact that his opponent was no longer shielded by a wall of men, Ian urged his horse through the gap, his hand now resting on the hilt of his sword, his dark hair gleaming in the sun. Robbie still sat in front of the McCray clansmen, watching, his weapon drawn. Face-to-face with Frankton, within reach, Ian leaned forward. His lips moved, his voice saying something obviously meant for the baron's ears only.

Whatever it was, it was amazingly effective. As Leanna watched, Frankton jerked furiously at his sword and attacked with rabid fury, his face contorted with hatred, his first swing narrowly missing Ian's right shoulder. Stock-still and riveted, she saw the tall laird parry two more murderous blows before he neatly and gracefully turned his horse at the same time he plunged his sword into the baron's throat. For a second, Frankton seemed more surprised than anything, and then a river of red poured down his shirt and he dropped his weapon, slumping forward.

Ian pulled his sword free and swung his mount around to face where she stood on the steps. He lifted the bloody weapon in a salute, smiling.

Next to her, Angus murmured, "That was well-done, wasn't it? I wonder what the lad said to make the grasping rodent finally go over the edge."

Leanna gave a choked laugh. "I have a feeling I don't want to know."

Considering the events of the day, he should have been weary, but Ian found his step was light as he climbed the stairs. Robbie was on his way to Newcastle with witnesses willing to testify to both Frankton's death and his gloating admission that he'd lied about Thomas's guilt. His uncle should be free in a few days. The English forces too were off McCray land without so much as a scratch to either side, which pleased him. Not terribly loyal to their now dead leader, they had quietly retreated without protest.

Leanna, if he could persuade her to stay, was his. Never having proposed marriage before, he was actually nervous about asking the question, and perhaps even more so over admitting he'd fallen in love with her. Not the kind of torrid, urgent, passionate love that Robbie claimed to feel for her, but something deeper. A need to have her by his side, not only in bed but all the time, a desire to see her smile, to picture her round and heavy with his child . . .

Love. Not just passion, but . . . love.

With a pause at the door of his bedroom, he took a deep breath and pushed the door open.

Arrested in the doorway, he stopped, able only to stare.

She obviously had wished to please him, but she had also had a long, distressing day, and it had taken its toll. She was asleep, breathing easily, her hair a golden, glorious mass against the linens. He took in the wine by the bed, two glasses ready, the soft light of a dozen lamps, the scent of perfume in the air. His gaze strayed back to the woman in his bed, and he drank in the sheer beauty of the sight.

Leanna was completely naked, her thighs parted, and he could see the soft, tempting darkness of her female cleft between her long, slender legs. Her breasts lifted slightly with every inhale, the pale mounds firm and high, and her face was serene, long lashes pillowed on her perfect cheekbones. Though he should probably let her sleep, he acknowledged wryly to himself that it wasn't going to happen. He was already hard and heavy from standing there for just those few moments, the throb in his hungry cock matching the beat of his heart.

Undressing quickly and quietly, he joined her on the bed, his fingers finding that sweet softness between her parted legs, beginning to stroke her awake. He marveled at the beauty of her body, at the mystery of her feminine allure as his fingers explored her most private place, threading through her soft thatch, circling gently the small, enticing opening that would stretch to accommodate his need, finding the nub that was even now beginning to swell in sexual arousal.

Ian grinned as she moaned in her sleep and spread her legs further. Her eyelids fluttered as he slid a finger into her passage, and she breathed, "Ian."

"No one else, my love." He continued to arouse her, using his thumb and fingers, until he could feel she was wet and wide-awake. She watched him with half-closed eyes, her enjoyment of his touch unhidden. And when he moved over her, she opened for him, welcoming him as he pushed inside. Usually voracious, especially the first time, he exerted enormous control and loved her gently, with consummate skill, concentrating solely on her pleasure. When she wildly clutched his shoulders and he knew she was ready to peak, he whispered in her ear, "Will you marry me, Leanna?"

Her eyes flew open and she gasped. "That's not fair. Oh, God, Ian, don't stop, please."

"Answer me first," he demanded, holding back the thrust he knew would send her over the edge.

"Yes. Just . . . please . . ."

He obliged, smiling, sliding forward deeply so that he could feel the tremors in her womb and the undulation of her inner muscles as she climaxed. Luring her to that sensational crest twice more, he finally let himself find his own release: a burning, fiery burst of joy that shook his entire body and left him gasping.

"You beast" was the first thing she said indignantly, and she slapped him on the shoulder with surprising force for one so slender.

Laughing and opening his eyes, he feigned an innocent expression, looking into her lovely flushed face. "How am I a beast, may I ask?"

"Marriage proposals are not supposed to be made when . . . when . . ."

"The lass is about to experience a very loud, very intense climax?" he supplied, lifting a brow in arrogant amusement.

"Ian." Her protest was muffled, her expression charmingly chagrined.

"It seemed like a good time," he told her, lightly kissing her mouth. "I didn't want to risk your refusing me."

"Why would I? I love you."

At last. She said it at last.

The moment seared his soul.

When he could speak, he said hoarsely, "I kidnapped you and seduced you. That isn't exactly a romantic courtship. I am . . . unaccustomed to what women want when it comes to marriage. I know you enjoy this"—he gestured at their intertwined bodies—"but are you sure you want to stay here, in Scotland, with me for the rest of your life?"

Leanna smiled, a curve of those soft, tempting lips. "Oh, yes."

Ian smiled back, elation making his voice thick. "Thank heavens, or else I am afraid I might have to abduct you again, my sweet hostage."

Book Two

Seducing Robbie

Chapter 1

*M*oonlight slid along the walls and cobbled streets, giving the city a ghostly glow. A waist-high mist made the buildings appear like something out of a macabre fairy tale, as if Edinburgh floated on a supernatural cloud like a lost mythical kingdom. In the shadows, Julia Cameron shivered as she heard a creature scurry by, feeling something actually brush her skirts.

"A cat," she told herself firmly, murmuring under her breath, stifling a surge of despair. She'd been waiting now for hours, and not only was it ill-advised for a woman to be out alone in the middle of the night even in a fashionable neighborhood such as this, but she was chilled and exhausted. Perhaps this had been a fool's errand. . . . God knew the infamous McCray spent the night often enough in someone else's bed, if all reports were accurate. He might not come home at all.

Was she really going to follow through with this rash, reckless plan?

Yes, you are. She squared her shoulders resolutely.

Then, as if on cue, the sound of a horse approached, just as she was actually contemplating giving up. Within moments, a silhouette loomed above her, the tall rider and sleek black stallion emerging from the mist. The stables were behind the house, and he headed that way, coming within a few feet of where she stood in the shrouded alcove of an angled wall. Julia waited, knowing the man had spotted her when he started in surprise and gave a sudden low curse, his skittish horse dancing sideways in reaction, rearing up like an ancient statue.

As she stepped out into the moonlight, she cleared her throat, staring upward. "Robert McCray?"

"Whoa, Solomon." Hooves clattered to the cobbles. Patting the neck of his animal to soothe it, the man astride said harshly, "Blood and thunder, what the devil are you trying to do, lass? Scare me out of my wits?"

It is him, Julia thought, standing so close she could reach out and touch the muscled shoulders of the restive stallion. Even in the uncertain light, she could see the man's legendary masculine good looks, the stories not exaggerated. Tousled dark hair brushed his wide shoulders, and his long, lean body looked powerful and athletic. Eyes as dark as midnight stared down at her with a startling vitality. Even though it had been years and she was little more than a young girl the last time she saw him, he was not a man one could forget.

She said with remarkable composure, considering her nervousness, "It was not my intention to startle you, but I need to speak with you. It's . . . urgent."

"So urgent you lurk in the dark like some brigand?" McCray

retorted, holding the reins in one long-fingered hand, staring down at her. "Have we met?"

He was at a disadvantage, since from his height on the huge horse, he couldn't see her clearly. Julia nodded. "We've met. It has been quite a while, but we have met. I am Julia Cameron. My father counted your father as one of his closest friends."

How much the weight of that friendship would hold would be tested this evening if the infamous McCray would just hear her out.

His attention sharpened. She could see it in the thin moonlight. "Laird Cameron's daughter?"

"The same," she acquiesced.

"But she is a child."

Apparently he could see a little of her, enough to notice she was *not* a child. She smiled in a tremulous effort. "I am almost twenty. The years pass quickly." After a deep breath, she added, "And I need your help. I've traveled from Hawick by public coach to see you, arriving after dusk, but was told you were not home. I decided to wait."

"You traveled by yourself and waited here in the dark, alone? Are you daft, lass?" He sounded both astounded and disapproving.

She lifted her chin, the sting of tears pricking her eyes from both fatigue and the awful stress of the past year. Her hands were shaking and she clenched them into fists. "Perhaps. But when one is desperate, there are often few choices. I just need a moment of your time, McCray."

"Why?"

Julia hesitated. "It is . . . complicated."

"Wonderful," he muttered. "I've just spent the evening drinking and gaming. I am not certain I am up for complicated conversations with desperate young ladies. Can't this wait until tomorrow?"

She couldn't help the edge of bitter urgency that crept into her voice. "No. Please, McCray—"

"Call me Robbie," he muttered abruptly, before she could finish her plea. "And I suppose for the daughter of an old friend of my father's, I can spare a few moments, even at this unorthodox hour. Let's go inside."

The fire in his study took the chill from the autumn air. Robbie McCray poured himself a brandy; then, taking a look at the pale features of the girl who claimed to be Julia Cameron, he poured a small second glass and handed it to her. "Drink this. You look like you might need it."

She accepted it with hands that trembled visibly and sank down in one of the chairs by the fire. Old Rufus's daughter, he saw now that she wasn't just some dim form lurking in the shadows, was indeed a grown woman, and a beautiful one at that. The thin, quiet child he remembered vaguely had blossomed into a stunning young woman with hair so dark it gleamed like ebony in the firelight, a striking contrast to her creamy, flawless ivory skin. Her features were delicately fair in her oval face: a straight, small nose, soft coral lips, high cheekbones, and long-lashed eyes an unusual greenish color, almost the same shade as the depths of Loch Cray. In fact, he considered himself—and was considered by most of Scotland, if his reputation was any indication—a connoisseur of lovely women, and he was not certain whether he had ever seen such perfect female beauty. Her body too, when she slipped out of her damp cloak, was revealed to be both lush and slender, though her gown was modestly cut and the drab color indicated her mourning. That she would travel anywhere alone was unthinkable.

"I am sorry about your father's death," he said truthfully. She was correct: There was a time when his father and Rufus Cameron had fought side by side against the English and stood firm together against the inner dissention that seemed to constantly plague Scotland and weaken its defenses. Standing by the hearth, he propped his shoulder against the mantel and watched his unexpected guest, openly curious about her presence.

The young woman's eyes glittered with tears suddenly. "He was murdered."

"I heard there was an accident and he drowned." Robbie frowned and took a sip of his brandy.

"When a man is found floating in shallow water with ligature marks around his neck, it is murder," Miss Cameron declared in a flat, unemotional tone, though her eyes still looked suspiciously luminous in the firelight. "And the detail that my older brother disappeared three months later is even more damning."

That got his attention. Vaguely Robbie remembered hearing of the missing young man, but he hadn't been entirely sober for about twelve hours now, and the facts were a little fuzzy in his memory. "He still hasn't been found?"

"No." Her soft mouth trembled slightly, and the liquid in her glass sloshed toward the rim. "It's been nearly a year. There is little doubt in my mind that he's dead as well."

"Who profits from their deaths?" It seemed a logical question.

"My cousin Adain." The conviction in her voice was soft but lethal. She took a quick sip from her glass and swallowed with a choked cough. "He denies any part in either crime, but I know he must be the one. He controls everything with Randal gone. At one time"—her slim throat worked—"I actually was fond of him, but I cannot ignore the stark truth. Adain is a criminal, slaughtering innocent men for gain. I mean to thwart him, and—for a few weeks, at least—it is still in my power to do so. I foolishly kept hoping Randal would return, but time is running out. That is why I am here."

Considering it was the wee hours of the morning, and the amount of hock and claret he had ingested, not to mention his pleasant but strenuous interlude with a certain young courtesan famous for her inventive sex play, Robbie was damned tired. He said with ungentlemanly bluntness, "How the devil can I help you, Miss Cameron? It seems to me this matter is something you should take up with the proper authorities. Besides, other than the fact that our fathers knew each other, pardon my honesty when I say your problems are none of my business."

"What about ships? They are necessary to your business, correct?"

She spoke so quietly, it took him a moment to register the words. Ships? Blast it, yes, they were necessary to his business, and two of his precious three ships had been recently seized by the English navy while on their way back from Rotterdam full of wine and silks. His attempts to haggle for their return had been useless so far, and since the alternative to too much protest was to be charged formally as a privateer, he'd had to grit his teeth and let the confounded Sassenach have their booty. All his efforts, all the frugality of the past years, for naught . . .

His unexpected guest went on. "I'm rich. The two ships could be replaced, free and clear, as payment for your aid. All outfitted with crew and captains, ready to take your wool anywhere in the world, and bring back wine, ivory, silk, whatever you wish to trade."

Since he had been working diligently to rebuild his family's fortunes, partially lost when an English blackguard named Baron Frankton had falsely accused his father of murder and had him arrested, Robbie froze in the act of taking a drink. Frankton was dead now, but the money and land confiscated by the English courts were lost forever. He asked in an even voice, "How do you know I need ships?"

The young woman gazed up at him, her dark skirts damp and pooled around her feet, those glimmering emerald eyes direct. "People talk about you. In the Borders, you are somewhat famous . . . or perhaps I should say infamous, both for your skillful sword arm and your . . . amorous exploits. Word is that you were expanding your shipping business until the English interfered."

"Don't remind me," he muttered. *Bloody bastards.* To his credit, he didn't say it out loud.

"I wouldn't, but it is pertinent to this conversation, McCray."

"Call me Robbie," he bade her again, slightly amused at her girlish blush when referring to his reputation with the fairer sex, but still infinitely puzzled. "And I admit the bribe intrigues me, but what is it for? I am not a magistrate who can convict your cousin of his crimes."

"No, but you are a . . . dangerous man. Legendary, almost, when it comes to duels and raids on the English. Your skill with a sword is supposedly unsurpassed."

His eyes narrowed. "I am not an assassin."

"Nor do I wish you to be. As much as I have grown to distrust and despise Adain, I don't seek his death. What I need is protection for the fortune my father left me, and perhaps the same for even my life."

"Hire a guard." His glass was empty and Robbie moved restively to refill it, a vague headache throbbing behind his temples.

She shook her head. "Once Randal has been gone a year, he will be declared dead by the courts and my cousin will be laird; there is nothing I can do about that. However, my father left it in his will that I would become heir to half his wealth and some land, but only if wedded." Miss Cameron paused and her voice quavered. "He was pleased over my engagement to Adain and fond of him. I think it was his way of leaving some of his fortune to my cousin, who, even though I detest him now, I admit would manage it better than Randal. As it stands, if I married him, Adain would inherit it all now. If I *don't* marry at all, he still inherits everything."

"I can see how the situation would be a dilemma." Still a little mystified, Robbie added, "Someone who looks like you is probably vulnerable with or without a fortune if she is unwed, Miss Cameron."

"With *you* as my husband, no one would think to threaten me. Adain couldn't force me into marrying him, and he would think twice about attempting murder a third time if you were the potential victim."

Perhaps his confusion was due to the late hour and his slight inebriation, but Robbie wasn't sure he quite understood. "You wish *me* to marry you?" he asked incredulously.

She nodded, her green eyes as mesmerizing and as lovely as wind on rippling grass. "Think of the ships, Mr. McCray, and land, and flocks of sheep to subsidize your wool trading. All I ask in return is your sword arm." Julia Cameron lowered her long lashes slightly, veiling those verdant depths. "I think you would be very hard to . . . kill. Stay alive long enough for me to inherit, and you can see your shipping business prosper. It would be pointless to murder me if all I have is yours."

The fire snapped and gnawed at the logs, the clock on the mantel ticked, and the brandy in his hand emitted a heady fragrance. All those things he registered only absently, staring at the gorgeous young woman sitting so upright in the chair only a few paces away.

Marriage?

She was undeniably very beautiful, but . . . marriage?

"You don't know me," he finally managed to say.

"My father liked you. He would laugh over the tales of your exploits, and said more than once in my hearing that when you settled down, you would make some woman a fine husband. I think he would approve."

"I would think it more important if *you* liked me."

"Most women seem to, don't they?" She gazed at him from under the veil of her dark lashes.

God spare him from illogical, innocent young ladies. Robbie rubbed his jaw, not sure if he'd ever been so confounded in his life.

He struggled to add some sanity to the conversation. "Be that as it may, Miss Cameron, are you truly willing to turn over every coin and your personal well-being to my care on the unproven assumption that your cousin is a villain? It isn't prudent. Isn't there someone else, a friend, a lover, who can fulfill the role of husband?"

"It isn't unproven, I'm afraid. I tried to deny Adain was the culprit but I can no longer. And if there were another man I felt strongly enough about to wed, would I willingly put him in danger?" She spoke with an almost chilling practicality. "Rest assured, this offer is not made lightly. I have pondered long and hard over who might be a suitable husband. Adain has still tried to pressure me for marriage, which would nicely wrap up his ill-gotten fortune, but I have resisted and will continue to resist. For months, I have prayed Randal is alive and will return, but I need to face the awful fact that he is gone. I will not allow my cousin to control my life, and I most certainly refuse to become his wife. Marrying someone else not only gives me my father's wealth, but it protects me from being forced to share the bed of a murderer. Yours is infinitely preferable."

Yours is infinitely preferable. . . .

His bed. Julia Cameron in it, her glossy ebony hair spread over the linens, her luscious lips damp from his kisses, her breasts in his hands . . .

No, this is not the time to think with your cock, Robbie, my lad. . . . She is a delicious piece, but there are plenty of those to be had without the permanence of a wedding.

Except for two ships. The loss had set him back years. Besides, a part of him knew his father, who had never fully recovered from his unfair imprisonment and died a few years ago, would want him to help his old friend's daughter.

Damnation.

Still off balance, Robbie muttered, "I have been propositioned before, but this is unique. I congratulate you on the distinctive approach."

Julia Cameron twirled her half-empty glass. "I will do whatever you wish if you will help me."

"Don't say that," he protested darkly, unwillingly picturing again her lovely, slim body beneath him, her legs spread open to accommodate his need as he pushed inside her delectable warmth. . . . Would she be restrained and ladylike in bed, or sensual and responsive?

"Why not?" She frowned, too innocent, obviously, to understand the lascivious direction of his thoughts.

"Take my word."

"Do you not find me attractive?"

That delicately asked question exacted an unwanted laugh. Hell, yes, he did, unfortunately, and it was currently clouding his thinking. "That isn't the issue."

"The issue being, I suppose, that you have a celebrated aversion to marriage."

"I am only seven and twenty. Just because I am not wed does not mean I have an aversion to marriage, Miss Cameron. It's just that I haven't met the right . . ." He trailed off abruptly, having already said more than he intended, feeling a slight chagrin that was no doubt due to too much drink and too little sleep.

Her ebony brows rose above her lovely eyes. "Don't tell me you are a romantic, Mr. McCray. Were you just about to tell me you haven't met the right woman?"

"Hell," he muttered, sipping his brandy, giving her a dark look. "Forget I said anything, will you?"

Julia Cameron laughed, but there was no mirth in the sound. "This is just my luck. I offer myself, body and soul, to the most notorious rogue in Scotland and he refuses because he is secretly a sensitive, idealistic man who yearns for true love."

She was being sarcastic, but it was close enough to the truth that Robbie growled defensively, "What of it? Marriage is supposed to be a holy union, and I, for one, have seen firsthand how happy it can make two people who are truly in love, not just lovers. My cousin Ian and his wife, Leanna, are a perfect example of actual wedded bliss. If I can find that for myself, I will grab it with both hands. Forgive me for not living up to your expectations of jaded indifference."

The firelight shaded the hollows of her lovely face. With bitter humor, she responded, "This heretofore unknown facet of your personality is inconvenient to my purposes. Rumor has you seducing women, fighting duels, and drinking till dawn, all with legendary prowess."

Considering his activities on this particular evening, that assessment was close enough to the truth. Robbie said neutrally, "Sometimes things are exaggerated."

Her soft mouth thinned stubbornly. "What can I do to make you consider my bargain? Can you not imagine trading your illusion of a love match for financial stability and the opportunity to expand your family fortunes, not to mention acquiring more grazing land?"

"I would also acquire a wife," he said pointedly, gazing at her with deliberate scrutiny. "And while your physical appearance is appealing, Miss Cameron, I know little else about you."

"What do you need to know?" she countered coolly. "It is not as if I am asking you to live with me for any longer than it takes to settle things. A month or two and we can go our separate ways. You can have your ships and land, and I will be rid of Adain. I intend to build a house somewhere quiet, and as long as I have enough to live on comfortably, I don't care if you take the rest."

A month or two. Ships, and a month or two in her bed . . .

"But we will be wed forever," Robbie objected as he fought for a rational argument, his shoulder hard against the mantel. "It is not a matter to dismiss lightly. I am very fond of Ian and Leanna's babes and want children of my own. What do you say to that?"

For the first time, her pale cheeks took on color. "I am surprised you don't already have children."

"The rumors aside, I am a careful man. I do not run around siring bastards."

Obviously, she didn't quite understand how one avoided such a thing, and her flush intensified with charming innocence. "You want . . . babies?"

"Absolutely." If this was leverage to dissuade the very tempting but unrealistic Miss Cameron and deflect his own carnal urges, he'd press the point. Besides, it wasn't a lie. He *did* want children someday. "I want a nursery full. Perhaps I stand as accused and am truly romantic down deep, but I do wish to have a large family."

Her green eyes were luminous as she stared up at him. She stammered, "I—I suppose we could. . . . That is . . . I anticipated you would expect—"

"Often," Robbie said flatly, taking silent pleasure in so flustering the determined young woman who had the audacity to come to him with such an unusual offer. He added softly, "Some things are *not* exaggerated. I have a very healthy sexual appetite. As my wife, I would expect you to accommodate me frequently."

That should take care of the laird's winsome daughter.

He was wrong.

Lifting her chin, she swallowed visibly, but said with unerringly firm conviction, "Fine, McCray. Do we have a deal?"

Hell and blast. The truth was, he was tempted. Even without the ships . . . *she* was temptation incarnate. He'd always been partial to dark-haired lasses. His gaze traveled over her slender, shapely body once more, inspecting the tempting curve of her full bosom, the narrowness of her waist, the glorious contrast of her pale, perfect complexion to the raven silk of her hair. Taking his time, he studied her mouth, so soft and rosy, and pictured himself plundering inside, twining his tongue with hers, looking into those green eyes as he moved inside her wet heat when he took her.

He was never wrong about women, and Miss Cameron, he sensed, would make a passionate partner. In fact, despite his fatigue, he felt himself harden at the thought of bedding her.

Her glorious body at his disposal *and* new ships, a reckless voice in his head reminded him. *One hell of a bargain, laddie.*

Well, he was a gambler at heart, and he almost always won.

"I believe we might," he answered with a wicked smile.

Chapter 2

*E*dward Gibbons paced across the room, for once unmindful of the shabby rug and worn furniture. His face was pale and puffy from a night of excess, and his hands shook slightly as he reached for the half-empty bottle of claret that sat on the sideboard. "I cannot believe I allowed you to talk me into this . . . this madness," he muttered.

"How is it madness?" Therese, his sister, asked in her usual deceptively placid voice. "Julia is gone and everything is falling into place."

He turned, lifting the glass in his hand to his mouth with a shaky, convulsive movement. Taking a drink, he coughed slightly and narrowed his eyes. "Where is she?"

At the table, her plate nearly empty, Therese calmly helped herself to another slice of jellied veal. "I have no idea. The pretty little bitch has decamped and that is all that concerns me. Poor Adain must be beside himself."

Edward asked haltingly, "You are certain you've done nothing to her? We've taken enough risks as it is, and another body wash-ing up—"

"You worry like an old woman," Therese interrupted shortly, taking a generous bite of her food. She chewed and swallowed, making him wait for her reply. "I haven't touched the silly chit." With a ladylike touch of her napkin to her lips, she added sweetly, "More's the pity. Her slender neck would snap like a twig. I've pic-tured it more than once."

Inelegantly, Edward dashed away the sweat from his upper lip with the back of his hand. "I am still not completely convinced Adain will marry you."

"When we stand by him in the face of the accusations, giv-ing our stalwart support, he'll be most grateful." A feral gleam in her eyes, she continued. "Of course, it would have been easier to convince Randal, but he isn't ever predictable; he never has been. That branch of the family has always been volatile, hasn't it, Edward?"

Not bothering to answer, he drained his wineglass.

"Don't lose your nerve now."

When he didn't comment on her admonishment, she took an-other generous bite.

Outside, in the crisp autumn air, the sky was so deep a blue it seemed surreal. The countryside was beginning to deepen in color, growing rich and mellow, but the city looked the same in all seasons: sprawl-ing, busy, and crowded. Usually Julia despised the bustle and inces-sant noise, but as the carriage rattled along, she found she barely noticed anything except the tall man sitting across from her.

The man she had just married minutes before. The ring was there on her finger; she could feel the hard, round, unfamiliar shape of it.

Her *husband* . . . The undeniably handsome, wickedly wild Robbie McCray was her husband. Julia had the uneasy feeling she might have sold herself to the devil, but Adain was checked, and that was all that truly mattered.

She certainly hoped her father's liking for the rogue sitting across from her reflected his usual keen judgment.

"We'll stop by and pick up those papers before we head out," Robbie remarked, stretching out his long legs, one dark brow arching upward.

She said nothing but just nodded, sitting still and covertly studying him from under her lashes. It had taken three days to iron out the details of their arrangement, days in which he had visited her father's solicitors, consulted with builders on the costs of construction of his precious ships, and even dragged her to a meeting with the minister who would marry them. The clergyman—she suspected he was an old friend of the McCray family—had lectured her at length on wifely duty. During that particular stern sermon, her intended had lounged lazily next to her, an arrogant smirk on his well-shaped mouth, his dark eyes openly mocking.

She hadn't found it nearly as amusing. In fact, she was quite horribly nervous now that all was said and done and their vows exchanged. It was one thing to bribe a known profligate rake into marriage, and quite another to imagine lying with him. He was used to the experienced women usually associated with the whispers about his exploits. She was neither experienced nor a flirt, and his easy assurance shook her.

But she *had* prevailed. And while she was apprehensive about the upcoming wedding night, she was certain of one thing: If a woman had to sell herself into marriage for protection and the preservation of her family fortunes, surely it was prudent to choose a man celebrated throughout Scotland as a talented lover. Mc-Cray's physical appearance too was a boon. He was well above medium height, wide shouldered, and athletically graceful when he moved, his chiseled features the epitome of male beauty, with a lean, straight jaw, firm mouth, and those infamous dark, seductive, long-lashed eyes. Julia had lived a sheltered life in some ways, but her father had been laird, and there had been a constant flow of visitors and members of her clan through Castle Cameron, so she had seen her fair share of men. There was no doubt of McCray's potent attraction, and she felt the powerful magnetic pull just as had the legions of women who had come before her.

"You are remarkably quiet, Mrs. McCray." His deep voice softly interrupted her reverie. "Having regrets already?"

Sitting up a little, Julia looked him in the eye and said in firm—but not honest—denial, "No."

Her new husband looked amused, his arms crossed over his wide chest, his booted feet carelessly brushing her skirts. The corner of his mouth lifted in a cynical smile. "I know you are anxious to reveal your devious plan to all and sundry upon our arrival at Castle Cameron, so I arranged for us to leave Edinburgh at once. After our stop at the solicitor's office, we will collect our baggage and be on our way. There is a small inn that I know of a few hours from here. We can spend the night there."

Unable to keep from blushing, Julia did manage to hold his gaze, though it took all of her bravado. "That sounds fine."

What a lie. A host of butterflies danced in her stomach.

"You must tell me," he asked reflectively, "during the past several days in the proper company of my aunt, who I must say was stalwart at suddenly finding herself chaperone to my unknown intended, did the two of you discuss the actual wedding night?"

It was true; to her surprise the notorious McCray had insisted that she be protected from scandal by staying with his elderly aunt, and had dumped her off on that poor but resilient woman with little more than an introduction and an announcement of their impetuous engagement. More surprising was the fact that such a respectable matron was related to a roguish scoundrel and also fond enough of him to accept the arrival of his heretofore unknown fiancée with admirable aplomb.

Julia said truthfully, "She was very kind, but obviously off balance at the notion of her rakehell nephew wanting to marry anyone. I assume she thought that we had already . . . that is"—good heavens, she was blushing again—"that you had seduced me. The speed at which you arranged the wedding didn't help."

His brows shot up, but if he took exception to the term *rakehell*, he didn't say so. "You *wanted* speed."

"Yes, indeed. The sooner Adain learns of our union, the better. I am not particularly concerned over what people think."

"I am going to venture a guess that when word of our marriage leaks out, society in general will expect us to have a seventh-month child," Robbie said, rubbing his jaw, his dark eyes narrowed.

"When we don't, that will take care of that rumor."

"Yes, I suppose so. Are you always this practical, lass? It seems to me, upon our short acquaintance, that you approach matters in a very straightforward fashion for a woman."

Not bothering to hide her flash of irritation, Julia responded, "Since when is directly dealing with a problem a trait regulated only to men? I am intelligent, educated, and—"

"Very beautiful," he interrupted smoothly, "and I usually find the more beautiful the woman, the more spoiled, clinging, and demanding. I was giving you a compliment, not deriding your sex. Since you have apparently listened to reports of my scandalous conduct in the past, I am sure you know I am a great admirer of women in general."

With a falsely sweet smile, Julia retorted, "When one's name becomes synonymous with skilled seduction and the hot-blooded pursuit of passion, there has to be a germ of truth somewhere in all the whispers."

His laughter rang out, and suddenly he looked more than starkly handsome; he looked dangerously attractive and all large, potent male, filling the small space inside the carriage. Still smiling, a wicked, sensual curve to his mouth, he said, "I can't wait to fuck *you*; that's for certain, Mrs. McCray. I, for one, am looking very much forward to tonight."

Blinking at his deliberate use of a word she had never heard before, Julia could easily guess what it meant, *and* that it wasn't something a gentleman would ever say in front of a lady.

But then again, she hadn't married a fine gentleman. She had married an infamous Border rogue.

Lapsing into shocked silence, she looked pointedly out the window, trying to ignore his amused stare.

Good God, he was right. It would be nightfall soon.

* * *

Robbie watched his beautiful bride take her last sip of wine and set aside the glass next to her empty plate.

And then he moved. In a flash, he was on his feet and around the table, pulling her out of her chair.

Sweeping her into his arms in a flurry of pale skirts, he ignored her outraged gasp and grinned at the other startled occupants of the inn's small dining room. "It's our wedding night," he announced loudly as he carried Julia toward the stairs.

"McCray," she hissed, clutching at his jacket as people chuckled over their abrupt exodus and his declaration.

"I hope, in bed," he said, ducking through the low doorway and starting to climb, "when I am between your undoubtedly very lovely legs, you will call me Robbie. I guess we'll find out in a few moments, won't we?"

"And you have made sure everyone staying here knows what we will be doing," she said furiously. Julia's cheeks were pink as she stared at him with those tantalizing green eyes. "Are you just living up to your reputation, or are you truly so impatient you had to drag me publicly upstairs?"

Their room was one of the first doors in the upstairs hallway, and he shouldered his way through it, kicking it shut with deft skill behind them. "Both," he said succinctly, and deposited her on the large four-poster bed. Stepping back, he surveyed her sprawled figure with pure male appreciation.

She had chosen a soft pink gown for the wedding, the color a perfect complement to her creamy skin and dark, shining hair. The neckline was modest, but the fullness of her breasts still mounded over the top, revealing the enticing upper swells. She wasn't technically what he considered to be voluptuous, but because she was so slender, the very narrowness of her waist and slim hips made her appear to be opulent and lushly female. Even if she weren't beautiful in every other way, her body alone would make men want her, he decided, not bothering to hide his deliberate perusal.

Nor could he hide his burgeoning erection. He'd been told he was well-endowed more than a few times—it wasn't just his reckless charm that made women appreciate him in bed—and when he slipped out of his jacket, the bulge in his tight breeches was already very visible. Even his untutored bride noticed, her soft mouth parting as her long-lashed eyes widened in alarm.

"See?" he said, elevating one brow and sitting down to tug off a boot. "My reputation aside, I am *definitely* impatient."

"It's rather hard to miss confirmation of that fact," Julia retorted, still staring at his crotch, but to his surprise, she didn't try to sit up and edge away or do anything except lie there and watch him begin to undress. Other than the arousing quiver of her breasts as her breathing quickened, she didn't move. At all.

Like a damned virgin sacrifice. From the look in her eyes, she was more intimidated than she was willing to admit.

In his heedless youth, he'd bedded a virgin or two, but it had been a while. A wedding-night deflowering certainly posed a unique challenge, for beyond all else, he wanted his bride to enjoy it.

Truth was, he intended to have her begging beneath him, so hot for his hard cock inside her she would be wild in his arms.

Since he'd tied himself to one woman for the rest of his life, he certainly didn't intend for her to be anything except willing and even eager in bed. He was just the man to educate the delectable new Mrs. McCray in the art of love, beginning with this evening.

Taking off his other boot but still wearing his shirt and breeches, he settled on the bed next to her. Propped on one elbow, he traced the delicate curve of her lower lip with a forefinger. "How much do you know, beautiful Julia?"

Her emerald gaze was wary, but she lay there on her back, compliant and quiet. "Know about what?"

Fucking, he wanted to say, since they certainly didn't love each other, but it was her wedding night, so he substituted, "Sexual congress between a man and a woman."

She flushed, the color rising from her slender neck and suffusing her cheeks. "Certainly not as much as you," she said tartly.

"Hell, I hope not," he said bluntly, the scores of sexual encounters in his past coming instantly to mind. He'd had his first experience at fifteen.

"That's hypocritical," she pointed out, watching him from under the fringe of her dark lashes. She trembled a little as his fingers glided over her smooth cheek and slid down the graceful arch of her throat. Her pulse beat fast and light, and he didn't miss the telltale sign of agitation.

"Hypocritical? Perhaps," Robbie admitted with a small smile, "but every man would prefer his wife came to his bed chaste and inexperienced. If you aren't a virgin, I have no choice but to accept it at this late hour, but tell me now, for it changes what comes next."

"How?" Her perfectly shaped ebony brows lifted a fraction.

The question alone was his answer, for no one but an innocent would be that naive. Robbie gave her a dark, glimmering smile and ran his hand lightly down the length of her arm. "You'll see. Tell me, have you ever been kissed?"

Her expression changed then, growing a little bleak. "Yes," she admitted. "At one time I was certain I would marry Adain. I let him kiss me . . . and a little more. That's all. Once I realized he was a monster, I was disgusted."

A *little more*. It was ridiculous, but Robbie didn't like the idea that another man had ever even touched her. "How much more?" he asked, his hand slipping to her waist, tugging her closer. Lowering his head, he brushed her mouth softly, just a feather touch of their lips. "Tell me."

She whispered, "He unbuttoned my gown . . . and touched me. I was a little shocked, but I thought I loved him."

The murderous bastard had fondled her breasts. Perhaps it would be a pleasure to challenge Adain Cameron after all. Robbie pulled Julia closer, kissing the soft spot below her ear, breathing in the fragrance of flowers that drifted from her hair. "I see. Well, tonight you will experience a great deal more than a few kisses and some fumbling through your clothing, lass."

"That I gathered." Her voice was dry, but she shivered in his arms.

He kissed her then, a soft, slow melding of their lips, discovering that she had indeed been kissed before, for she opened willingly to the pressure of his tongue, allowing him access to the intoxicating warmth of her mouth. Leisurely, he alternately stroked and delved inside, taking his time. Her body felt light and deliciously curvaceous in all the right places, her breasts resilient and firm against his chest. Through his shirt, he could feel the increasing push of her nipples, indicating at least some measure of arousal. Deepening the kiss so he could taste every bit of her, he seduced her mouth with practiced ease, leaving Julia breathless when he lifted his head. Wickedly, he licked her lower lip, enjoying her art-less response. "You taste like fine wine."

Her eyes were wide, the depths darkened to a verdant color like a pine forest. "I don't think Adain ever quite kissed me that way," she confessed.

"Good." Robbie settled on top of her, keeping his weight bal-anced on one arm. "Let's get rid of these." He pulled the pins from her hair, letting the silken raven mass cascade over the blankets, sifting his fingers through it gently. "God in heaven, it is like mid-night satin, so soft and fine. I cannot wait any longer to see the rest of you."

With deft fingers, he unfastened her gown, easing it from her shoulders and down the length of her body. He did the same with her chemise, pulling the ribbon loose at the bodice and taking in a sharp breath as he revealed the ripe, sumptuous, pink-tipped mounds that had drawn his attention all evening. With her tum-bled, luxuriant dark hair and ivory skin, his new wife was more than simply beautiful; she was magnificent, and as he stripped off her stockings and shoes so she was completely nude, Robbie felt the throbbing need between his legs with uncharacteristic urgency.

He stood, unlacing his shirt and jerking it off, and then re-moved his breeches just as quickly. As he settled back over her, he could feel her uneasy reaction as the erect length of his rigid cock heatedly pressed against her outer thigh. "See how much I want you, Julia?" he murmured, deliberately holding her gaze as he cupped the pliant weight of one gorgeous breast. His thumb grazed the rosy crest, and he savored the soft texture and form of her nipple. Continuing to stroke, he murmured, "Look how lovely you are, womanly and full, your flesh filling my hand to overflowing, your nipple utterly round and such a delicate color. You will suckle my children here"—he caressed her again, hearing her small intake of breath with satisfaction—"but I must be first."

She gasped when his mouth closed over the peak, and for the first time, she touched him voluntarily, her hands clasping his head, sliding into his hair. Teasing her with his tongue, swirling it over the succulent flesh until the nipple became firm and tight, he sucked on one breast and then the other, his hand smoothing the curve of her hip. When he heard the unsteady rhythm of her breathing increase, Robbie smiled to himself and licked a hot, wet trail down her stomach.

His own heart beat fast as he examined the dainty patch of soft black hair at the apex of her thighs with salacious interest, his face inches away, inhaling her womanly scent. Julia had her legs tightly together despite the fact that she was becoming aroused, the instinct to protect herself from a marauding male not yet overcome by desire. When she experienced what he was about to do to her, she would open for him willingly anytime—he knew that with confident assurance, and he gently placed his hands on her upper thighs. "Open for me, lass."

Gloriously beautiful, her breasts flushed from his attentions, Julia looked slightly panicked. "What are you going to do?"

"Nothing but kiss you," he promised, his gaze roaming with pleasure over the sight of her naked, alluring form, marveling at the vision of perfect female beauty and the promise of unadulterated sexual fulfillment.

"It seems to me you are in the wrong position to kiss me," she argued in the forthright manner he was learning was one of her traits. Her thighs stayed tightly clamped together.

With consideration for his own pressing need, Robbie fought amused impatience and explained, "There are many forms of sex play, my sweet virgin, not just the actual penetration of a female by a male. Now trust me as you promised, and remind yourself that I should know what I'm doing."

"That's the truth, McCray," she muttered acerbically.

He couldn't help it; he laughed. With an impudent grin, he coaxed, "Spread your legs and find out if the rumors are all true, my lady. I challenge you. I vow to warn you before I actually am going to mount you."

It was certainly the right tactic to dare her, for under the pressure of his palms, she reluctantly allowed her thighs to fall apart, exposing her sweet cleft. Once again the splendid perfection of her body took his breath away, and he lowered his head between her legs, holding her open for what he knew would be a shocked reaction to his intentions.

Her labia was soft, utterly sweet as he began to press his mouth to the apex of her sex, ignoring Julia's incoherent protest. He gently licked those luscious lips at first, letting her become accustomed to the notion of oral contact in such a private place, and when he felt her relax a fraction, Robbie slipped his tongue between the intriguing and increasingly damp folds, seeking the tiny nub he knew would illicit intense sensation.

At the very first contact, she moaned. "Stop."

Since he had never encountered a woman who didn't like what he was doing, he simply chuckled and swirled his tongue around with persuasive purpose. In moments, his innocent wife arched in supplication, that telltale bud swelling under the attention of his mouth, her orgasmic peak building predictably. Using his experience to gauge exactly when her climax was going to peak, he waited and at the last second pressed his mouth and suckled with scintillating pressure, rewarded when she shattered with a wild cry, her hips surging high, her head falling back as she twisted in utter abandoned carnal release.

Waiting until her breathy sobs no longer filled the room, he finally shifted, moving over her damp body and staring into her dazed eyes. "Now," he said simply, easing between her open legs and positioning himself.

McCray must be some sort of warlock, a sinful, darkly seductive creature made to lure women into unspeakable acts that gave incredible and unearthly pleasure. Beneath the man who had so shockingly tantalized and beguiled her body into a place she hadn't ever imagined existed, Julia felt the hard and inescapable push of his rigid sex into her body begin, his entrance burning and stretching her female passage.

But after that glorious burst of rapturous sensation, she found her trepidation had abated, replaced by a languorous anticipation. Robbie McCray's devilish reputation might just be well earned. The subtle excitement and enjoyment she'd experienced when Adain had touched her was dwarfed by what had just happened to her body. She'd never dreamed such pleasure was possible.

Her new husband knew it also, for she could sense it from the seductive half-smile curving his mouth, and his heavy-lidded eyes. "Are you ready for me, lass?"

"Yes." If she knew anything, it was that it was too late to turn back now. She'd married him, and this was part of the bargain.

Robbie's advance didn't precisely hurt, but it felt very odd, as if she were too full and her passage distended impossibly wide to take his erection. Her hands came instinctively to grasp his shoulders, and she marveled at the hardness of his body compared to hers. His scent was also so different, utterly male—like whiskey with a faint hint of clean sweat. Dark eyes glittered with undisguised need as he penetrated her body, and he wasn't unaffected either, for as he possessed her, she caught the increased cadence of his breathing and the tension of his bunched muscles under her hands. Even in her inexperience, she realized he was exerting a great deal of self-control.

"God, you are so tight," he muttered, half lowering his lashes. "It feels damned good, lass. Too damned good."

"How can"—she gasped as he advanced another inch— "something feel too good?"

"For a male it can. . . . If I come too soon, you won't enjoy this fully." His hips moved forward and he slid in farther. "Tell me when it hurts."

She felt it seconds later, a sharp pricking sensation. "Stop." She clutched his shoulders, knowing he was tearing her in two pieces. "Robbie . . . stop. It hurts."

His gaze softened a moment and he did halt, leaning down to kiss her mouth, just once, very lightly. "It has to hurt a little but will be over quickly. Now hold on."

Julia bit her lip when he thrust suddenly forward, more surprised than anything to find him completely impaling her with his erect staff, the pain a sharp flash, and abating almost as quickly as it happened. His hips forced her legs very wide apart, his stiff cock entirely inside her vaginal passage. "Oh."

"Tell me it isn't that bad." His voice sounded strained, as if he had just run a great distance, and a light sheen of sweat graced his skin. "Sweet Jesus, have mercy and assure me I can move."

Since she wasn't in actual pain, Julia acquiesced. "You just seem . . . overly large."

His laugh brushed her cheek. "Most women prefer a larger size. Just wait," he muttered, and to her amazement, he began to withdraw, the backward slide of his sex within hers actually pleasurable.

And then, when almost completely out of her, he surged back inside.

He was right, she found. The deep, hard penetration felt . . . wonderful, and a peculiar excitement began to coil in the depths of her stomach. When he withdrew again, she sighed in anticipation of the next slick thrust, lifting her hips to take him as deeply as possible.

In seconds, she found she naturally undulated her body to the tempo of that erotic rhythm of withdrawal and thrust, almost as if she already knew this ancient dance of mating, her body gaining a will of its own under the possession of the man above and inside her. Julia felt herself helplessly float again into that magical place her skillful husband had taken her, her need building. She fought for it, but it wasn't until he slid his hand between them and touched her where they joined that it happened, a flash of white-hot sensation, and she might have even screamed; she wasn't sure. She trembled in sheer blissful gratification, only barely aware that Robbie stopped moving at the same time. Buried deep, he groaned and his shoulders flexed powerfully as she felt a forceful, hot rush of liquid inside her. Time and again, he seemed to quiver, until he lowered himself and rested his face in the mass of her outspread hair, whispering in her ear, "By the gods, maybe marriage will agree with me."

Chapter 3

Cameron Castle had been modified over the years, so it wasn't actually a castle at all, but a vast manor house sporting in portions the turrets and thick walls of the medieval structures often found across Scotland. More modern additions gave it a huge, sprawling appearance. It stood on a small rise in Roxburghshire, surrounded by a park of beech and pine. Rolling green hills stretched as far as the eye could see in the distance. Since he had been there before and his family home was not a great distance away, Robbie felt quite at ease in the familiar countryside, though the cold gray walls before him did not resemble in the least the warm and inviting facade of Cray House.

"Perhaps you had better enlighten me as to your anticipation of the impact of our arrival," he drawled, watching warily as two men, both wearing the Cameron plaid and mounted on fine horses, rode out to intercept the carriage. "I am armed, but don't care to start trouble by appearing to be looking for a fight. After all, you are a Cameron, and you did marry without the permission of your laird. Resentment of your new husband is both likely and expected."

"Adain won't be happy," Julia said with an edge of steel in her voice, "but then again, if he hadn't murdered my father and brother, he could have had me himself, so his feelings are not an issue."

As Robbie inherently disliked that notion, he disregarded it. "He has guards posted. Is that usual?"

"I suppose he thinks that I have *disappeared*. Much like what he wants us to believe about Randal."

"You didn't tell anyone you were leaving?" Robbie settled back in his seat, gazing at his wife in amazement. "By the devil, lass, Cameron is probably tearing the countryside apart."

"That's his problem. I owe him nothing." Julia's soft mouth had a stubborn set.

"Will he openly challenge me?" Older and more experienced, Robbie wasn't as certain of dismissing the unknown Cameron male's sense of outrage. As acting laird, Adain wielded a good deal of power.

Julia shrugged her slender shoulders. "I doubt it. Adain isn't so much hotheaded as he is . . . proprietary."

That wasn't very reassuring. "You belong to me," he commented without equivocation, loosening his dirk in his boot as a shout slowed the carriage.

Across on the opposite seat, Julia sat sedately, but her green eyes sparked. "Watch yourself, McCray," she said tartly. "This is a marriage of convenience, but that means for both of us."

Cocking a brow, he readied himself to get out and face the Cameron clan troopers. "Odd, last night you called me 'Robbie, my dear. . . .' It must have been when I was about to rupture the barrier of your maidenhead. . . . Oh, yes, I recall, just after you were wild with release with my mouth on your very tasty—"

"Stop it." Her cheeks stained with color, Julia sat bolt upright on the seat and glared at him, her incomparable beauty only accentuated by her obvious chagrin.

Though he admired her physical appearance, he definitely also liked her spirit. Attraction was based on many things. He'd met beautiful women who didn't interest him at all because of their personalities, and others who might be considered plain, but their inner sparkle drew admirers like moths to a flickering flame. His new wife had both beauty and a lively intelligence. It was a bewitching combination.

With a deliberately cheeky grin, he remarked, "Let's greet your kinsmen in perfect accord, my lovely Julia. It wouldn't do to start off on the wrong foot. I'm a damned good swordsman, but there *is* only one of me."

Even though there was a fire leaping in the huge hearth that was the focus of the main hall, it felt cold under the vaulted ceiling, as if frigid air seeped from the stone floor beneath her feet. Next to her, Robert McCray, a man whose famed dangerous pursuits were not limited to bedding lovely ladies, fairly radiated male possession, the tensile strength of his hand at the small of her back. Their reception had not gone well so far, and Adain had ordered the room cleared so they were alone, just the three of them. Servants had scattered gladly, and even the housekeeper, Mrs. Dunbar—the only motherly figure Julia had ever known, as her own mother had died giving birth to her—had left quietly in shocked silence over the news of her unexpected marriage.

The two men facing each other so grimly were two of a kind; Julia wasn't sure she quite realized that until now. Both were dark, tall, good-looking, and muscular; both were self-assured and confident. They were even dressed similarly, in white shirts, fitted doeskin breeches, and knee-high boots. Adain didn't have her new husband's dashing aura of careless charm, but was instead more serious, with an air of grave responsibility.

Only that impression was false. Adain Cameron was treacherous and evil, while Robbie McCray might be many things—arrogant, too handsome for his own good, undoubtedly reckless—but she still didn't think he would ever murder someone for personal gain.

Of course, she hadn't thought it possible of Adain either until offered proof so convincing it forever shattered her faith in the man she'd thought she'd marry.

The main hall of the castle was huge, but still did not seem big enough for the two men looking at each other with such open enmity. Adain fairly snarled, "You are . . . *what?*"

"As I said, Julia's husband," Robbie answered smoothly, but there was a warning implicit in his dark eyes that no one could miss, and his stance was tense. "We're here so she can collect her belongings and settle things before we travel to Cray House. Don't worry, Cameron; we'll be gone in a day or two."

Her cousin's eyes were a light gray, almost silver, and when his glance flicked to her, Julia saw the fury there mingled with an unmistakable pain. "You *married* him? Tell me, Jules, I want to hear *you* say it out loud."

The raw sound of his voice and the use of the nickname he alone used nearly made her flinch, but she stiffened her shoulders, reminding herself she didn't truly know this man. She'd thought she did, but the Adain she had once admired and even loved didn't exist. "We were married in Edinburgh," she said evenly, tilting her chin and looking her cousin in the eye. "I am Mrs. Robert McCray."

"Why?" Adain shoved his hand through his hair, rumpling the dark strands. "By the gods, I wasn't aware the two of you even knew each other. When you turned up missing, I feared the worst. Men have been out looking for you for four days. I've barely slept or eaten."

"Just like you looked for Randal?"

Adain stiffened at the scathing tone of her voice. "*You* were here when Randal disappeared. I came at once, abandoning my own affairs to help organize a search for him. Yes, exactly like we looked for Randal. I did everything I could."

It was true. He did look tired, she registered involuntarily. There was the slight shadow of dark stubble on his lean jaw, and lines she had never noticed before around his mouth. "How odd he has never been found when you so competently directed the hunt," she murmured ungraciously. "Or perhaps it isn't odd at all."

"Jules, we have had this discussion before." His voice held weary reproach, and his eyes were shadowed. "How can you believe I would ever harm Randal? He is like my brother."

"And what am I? The sister you never had?" she asked sweetly, her gaze burning with contempt.

"Not even close, though I don't deny I love you."

At one time, she'd thrilled to hear those words. Now they rang with the hollow sound of deceit.

Adain switched his focus once again to the man by her side.

"I'd like to see the marriage lines, McCray. For some unfathomable reason, Julia thinks I am a villain, but the truth is, her welfare is my responsibility, and despite her hatred, I would not see her shamed by a false ceremony."

To her surprise, Robbie didn't seem to take offense, but instead inclined his head. "Aye, Cameron. I would do the same in your position. You will find it was all legal and . . . now, irrevocable."

His meaning was absolutely clear. Their marriage had been consummated. Recalling the erotic details of that union brought heat into her cheeks, but Julia didn't flinch from staring her cousin in the eye, letting him see the truth.

"Damn all," Adain muttered, his mouth tightening, those telltale lines deepening. "I suppose I am not surprised on that score, given your reputation, McCray."

"I am not one to disappoint a lady." Robbie lifted one dark brow suggestively.

"Especially when she is not only arrestingly beautiful, but also an heiress like Julia?" Irony weighed heavy on the words, as if Adain felt every bit of his defeat. "I assume you know she will inherit half her father's wealth, and that is the purpose of this hasty union. Word has it the English commandeered two of your ships recently. What an inventive method of recouping your loss."

"Let us not forget also a pleasurable one," Robbie drawled in a casual voice, but his gaze was watchful.

Adain didn't flinch outwardly, but his eyes glittered. That silver gaze came over to rest on her one last time, as hard as diamonds and as bleak as winter. "I hope," her cousin said quietly, "that in your zealous pursuit to damn me to hell, you haven't also sent yourself there, Jules."

Then he turned on his heel and stalked away, through the large main entrance into the courtyard.

A little shaken, Julia took in a breath and said caustically into the resulting silence, "That went well, didn't it?"

The huge room was now deserted except for the two of them. Robbie turned to look at her, his regard penetrating. "You might have mentioned, when you said Cameron was pressuring you for marriage, that he is deeply in love with you. I was under the impression he wanted your inheritance."

His dark gaze was speculative and, unfortunately, discerning. Julia steadied herself and replied curtly, "A man who kills members of his own family for coin does not know the meaning of love, Mc-Cray; keep that in mind."

Her husband's brows lifted a fraction, a rueful smile on his mouth. "I haven't yet heard of any proof of this venal, murderous action on the part of your cousin, sweet Julia. You seemed so certain he was the one that I didn't question your convictions, but truth to tell, upon meeting him, aside from his understandable current desire to run me through with the nearest weapon he could find because I have bedded you, I don't sense that side to the man. Are you certain he is the one who killed your father and brother?"

With complete assurance, Julia said bleakly, "Absolutely."

"Care to tell me why?"

"No." She turned to where a long stairway curved up the left wall. "My room is upstairs. . . . I suppose we will be sharing it." She could not help it; she blushed, recalling the night before and his scandalous use of her body. "Right now I wish to bathe and change after our journey."

From the expression on Robbie's face, she had the distinct feeling he was not satisfied with her refusal to explain, but he merely inclined his head. "I need to see to Solomon, for he won't let anyone touch him but myself. Stabled in an unfamiliar place, he can cause quite a stir unless handled properly."

With a nod, she turned away, grateful he didn't press her further about Adain's perfidy.

"Sweet Julia?"

Glancing back, she saw him standing with a cocky grin on his beautiful mouth, his dark eyes gleaming. "What is it?" she asked warily.

"Don't hurry," her husband said softly, "for I will be up to help you with your bath in just a few moments."

Traitorous excitement shot through her veins at the open sensual promise in his eyes. "I am perfectly capable of bathing alone, McCray."

His grin widened. "Yes, but my way is infinitely more enjoyable, lass."

"So *you* are Julia's husband."

Glancing up as he measured out oats from a wooden bin, Robbie saw a young man in the doorway of the stable watching him with a slight frown. He was slim to the point of being almost girlish in appearance, dark haired with a pale complexion, and unmistakably a Cameron. Straightening, Robbie said neutrally, "I am. Robert McCray."

"My brother didn't murder anyone." The young man leaned heavily on a crutch fitted with a small leather saddle under his arm, his expression not precisely hostile but definitely not friendly.

"It certainly sounds like someone did," Robbie commented, dumping the grain into a trough and reaching up to rub Solomon's sleek neck. "Your uncle is dead and your cousin missing. Understandable conclusions can be drawn, since your brother profits from their deaths."

"It isn't profit to lose the man you loved like a father, a good friend, and the woman you desire, now, is it?" Not more than sixteen or seventeen, Adain's younger sibling certainly sounded bitter.

"Nay, not if it isn't at your hand."

"Julia didn't think it was him at first."

Thoughtfully Robbie regarded Cameron's younger brother. "That has occurred to me. She waited almost a year to do anything about trying to preserve her inheritance. She claims she hoped her brother would return."

"We all hoped so . . . but it has been so long." The boy paused and added in a rush, "There's more than one who has claimed to see his ghost. It haunts the cliff path after dark. People avoid that way now."

Robbie wasn't much interested in superstitious rumors. If one were inclined to believe every report of a restless spirit, Scotland would be fairly overrun with apparitions. He was more interested in the living, and his wife in particular. "Tell me when Julia changed toward your brother."

"Had it not been for her mourning, she and Adain would have wedded months ago. Then suddenly, rumors spread he was implicated in the murder of her father, but no one really seems to know how it all started. Randal's disappearance made it worse. At first she stood by Adain, but then . . ." The boy trailed off and made a helpless gesture with his hand. "He doesn't know why she turned against him, but it happened all at once."

"That's my impression." Something Julia was reluctant to talk about, if her reticence just a few moments ago was any indication. And while she hadn't directly misled him, Robbie had the sense this was all a great deal more complicated than he first assumed.

"I'm not denying there's a shadow over this family, for I may be crippled, but I've got eyes and ears. Still, Adain is suffering more than anyone."

"And my marriage to Julia is a twist of the knife already slipped between his ribs, is that it?" Robbie could feel the enmity radiating from the doorway halfway across the stable.

Staring at him, the boy said bluntly, "Yes."

"You resent the devil out of me, I take it."

Blinking at that forthright statement, the young man reddened slightly. "I do, and so I should, sir."

"Perhaps. But would it surprise you to know I'm damned curious about all of this now that I've met your brother? I've saved my neck more than once by being able to measure a man's nature in just seconds, and I find I agree with you. Adain Cameron strikes me as an honorable man, and that puts an interesting twist on things." Distractedly, Robbie gave the stallion a final pat. "Tell me, lad—"

"Arthur."

"Tell me, Arthur, what have those eyes and ears of yours picked up that Julia does not know?"

"She's a woman, if you'll pardon my saying so—"

"I've noticed." Robbie smiled wryly. "But explain to me how that affects her powers of observation."

The hand that wasn't wrapped around his crutch made a gesture of poignant frustration, and young Cameron said, "Dash it, would *you* strangle an old man with a bit of rope and toss him in a stream? No, I would guess not. You have a skilled sword arm and would cut him down face-to-face. Adain may not have your reputation, sir, but he is damned good with a blade; ask anyone. If he had wanted to kill our uncle, he would not have done it in the fashion it was done. He isn't a coward, and that was the work of a slinking serpent afraid to show his face."

Robbie elevated a brow, crossed his arms over his chest, and leaned against a post near Solomon's stall. "I agree . . . but logically, there are those who would say the deed was done in a fashion to deflect suspicion on purpose. Julia seems utterly convinced your brother is behind the loss of her immediate family, and her happiness and safety are now my responsibility."

"I would venture to guess believing such a thing does not make her happy," Arthur Cameron said with conviction. "Before all this they were not just engaged, but . . . well . . ."

"I'm aware it wasn't just an arranged match, but there was a romantic attachment on both their parts," Robbie said shortly, sparing the young man from having to go on. He didn't want to hear it, which was a little unsettling. He'd known she was engaged before, but having come face-to-face with Cameron, he wasn't quite so blasé about their former relationship. It was unsettling enough to have a wife, much less to know another man was in love with her.

"Well"—though his cheeks had suffused with color, Arthur went doggedly on—"if you are responsible, as you say, for her happiness, shouldn't you find out the truth? She will be miserable always to think Adain killed her father and Randal."

"We won't be here long enough for me to really look into this,"

Robbie stated pragmatically. "Besides which, this is your brother's problem. He will be laird soon enough, and I'm sure if you look on my presence here with less than enthusiasm, he feels even more antipathy. I know I would. The woman he desires shares my bed."

"To clear his name, he would tolerate a few more days of your company." Looking pathetically sincere, Arthur said quickly, "Aside from your marriage, the two of you have nothing against each other, do you? You are both strong, capable warriors and would make a formidable force if you joined together to seek out those who committed these crimes. Up until now, Adain has been crippled by the fact that he is the main object of suspicion. Your faith in his innocence would go far in helping him in his quest for the truth."

Amused and a little touched by such stalwart brotherly devotion, Robbie said, "I am not at all as certain as you are, young Arthur, that your brother would welcome my help in any capacity. In fact," he added under his breath, "if he could cut off my balls, he would, and gladly."

That made the boy laugh, a hiccup of sound, his thin face lighting. "I have a feeling that wouldn't be an easy undertaking."

"I am rather attached to them," Robbie said with a grin.

"Julia is very pretty." It was a careful observation. "Do you not feel sorry for Adain if she unfairly despises him and chooses to lie with you instead?"

"I doubt he is interested in my pity."

"No, but if he were accepting of your help, would you give it? We are now family. You are beholden, to a certain extent, to aid us."

Moving to close the stall door and leave Solomon to his oats,

Robbie said firmly, "You have loyalty to your brother, and I admire that in a man. However, I can't think of a thing I could do to help."

With surprising grace for one so handicapped, Arthur Cameron scooted back on his crutch and said doggedly, "If there was a way, would you do it?"

Gazing at the boy's pale, set face, Robbie muttered, "You are as tenacious as a terrier after a rat, lad. I suppose that if there were a way I could help any good man clear his name, I would."

Julia looked up quickly at the sound of the door opening, her heart increasing its pace. *It took the dratted man long enough*, she thought, sinking a fraction lower in the water and feeling it lap over the tips of her breasts as Robbie walked into the room. The water was cooling and she was beginning to shiver.

Though she would never admit she had lingered longer than necessary at her ablutions because she was waiting for the gloriously attractive Robbie McCray, she was undoubtedly curious as to just what he'd meant when he'd said a bath could be fun.

"Thanks be to heaven I am not too late." His warm, drawling brogue was full of amusement, and he shut the door carefully, dropping the latch into place. "I cannot think of how disappointed I would be to miss the sight of my enchanting wife all beautifully naked, wet, and . . . slippery."

Giving her roguish husband a cool look from under her lashes, Julia said, "Actually, I am quite finished, McCray. If you would hand me my towel, I would appreciate it."

"I can do better than that." As he crossed the room, he didn't seem to notice the wide window overlooking the rolling hills, the lush carpet underfoot, or even the bed hung with pale blue silk and covered with a delicately embroidered blanket. His dark gaze was fastened on her alone as he moved toward the tub and sank down suddenly to his haunches, picking up the drying cloth she had left on a small stool. "Please, my lady, allow me the honor."

She let out a small squeak of surprise as he plunged his arms into the tub, heedless of the water sloshing out or her dripping nakedness soaking his clothes. Julia clutched at his shoulders as he lifted her out, a warm anticipation spreading through her body like wildfire. The towel was tossed carelessly on the bed, and Robbie laid her on it, his avid gaze traveling over every damp, gleaming inch of exposed skin.

"I cannot wait to be inside you," he said, a half-smile touching his lips as he deliberately unfastened his now half-sodden breeches. "Can you tell?"

She could, of course, the instant the last button was undone and his magnificent erection was free. It looked large through the open material of his breeches, and seemed to lengthen further as she watched with fascinated attention. "I'm not blind," she muttered, feeling oddly flushed.

His wet shirt was plastered to his wide, powerful chest, and he pulled the lacings free, stripping it off and tossing it aside. "You make me hard as hell, wife," he said in a low, almost hoarse voice. "Especially as you are now. Like some dark-haired siren from the sea."

If his cock was any indication, he told the truth. It stood high and engorged against his stomach, pulsing slightly, the distended tip gleaming. "Tell me you're going to take off your boots," she protested as he began to climb on top of her. "By the gods, McCray—"

"Later," he growled, and captured her mouth in a hard kiss, his insistent tongue delving deep, the fine wool of his breeches an abrasion on her inner thighs as he settled between her legs, nudging them apart. Julia wanted to be outraged, for not only was she dripping wet, but he was still half-dressed. Yet the sensation of his skillful mouth plundering hers silenced her protests, as did the warm foray of his long-fingered hands across her bare skin. He kneaded her breast as he thrust his tongue deep between her lips, his long fingers massaging the taut flesh, the nipple tingling and hardening.

Hot, insistent lips roamed across her jaw, and he whispered in her ear, "Jesus, you feel damned good underneath me. You have beautiful tits, sweet Julia. Firm and full and begging for my mouth."

He was infernally right, she realized in dreamy rapture as he moved lower and sucked one puckered tip into the recess of his mouth, his tongue swirling around the crest in long, tantalizing strokes. She wanted him to suckle her, to make that singular sensation coil in her belly. Clasping his dark head, her fingers slid through his silky, thick hair, holding him close as she shamelessly pushed her aching breast deeper into the heated depths that so relentlessly teased and aroused. He chuckled a little as he lifted his head and she immediately tugged it to the aching, needy opposite nipple, but he obliged with enthusiasm, cupping the pliant weight in his hand, making the dusky tip stand high before he licked it gently, eliciting an involuntary moan.

"Please . . ." Julia could not believe she was actually begging, but for the moment did not care. "McCray."

His dark eyes were alight with both arousal and mischievous command. "If you want me to suck on it, sweet Julia, you must call me Robbie."

The long weight of his body pinning her to the bed had her nearly delirious with anticipation, and the feel of his hand molding her flesh was both unnerving and glorious. "Fine," she bit out, watching him from beneath half-lowered lashes. "Robbie, please."

He smiled in a dangerous curve of his beautiful mouth. "I might even be persuaded to . . . *taste* you again if you are very, very nice to me."

The idea of his mouth between her legs was enough to make her squirm slightly, her hungry breast forgotten for a new, more tantalizing need. "I'm lying naked underneath you, McC— er . . . Robbie. How much nicer can I be?"

He lapped lightly at her straining nipple. "I don't know. Let's see . . . how far can you spread your legs? I mean very wide, my lovely wife, so I know exactly what you want."

There was no question the man was utterly outrageous. But she could not forget the memory of his tongue between her thighs as it delicately brought her to the summit of pleasure. . . .

Julia eased her legs apart slowly, rewarded when he slid down her body and settled between them, his dark head nestled in that shocking position. One large palm rested on the inner softness of her open thighs. "Now, this is a beautiful sight, lass. Here, let me have a nibble."

Her eyes drifted shut at the first light pressure, long fingers pushing her folds open as he pressed his mouth to her sex and began to lick and probe, a low sound of pleasure locked in her throat. Held prisoner by both acute sensation and his light grip, she listened to the wet sounds of his mouth feasting at her cleft, feeling a rising tide of excitement clench in her stomach and take her body captive. Within moments, she moaned, arching her pelvis upward, his hands sliding to cup her buttocks, lift her higher, and hold her in place for his delicious sexual torture. Dark hair brushed her quivering inner thighs, and his lashes lowered to veil his eyes as he alternately penetrated her female opening with his tongue, then he licked upward to toy with the sensitive nub that seemed the center of her pleasure.

Panting, her hands tangled in the bed linens, Julia reached for that wondrous peak and found it, a small shriek of pure rapture echoing outward as she climaxed hard against his wicked mouth, her body shaking and trembling. Gently suckling, he held her there until she twisted away, unable to bear another moment of such intense, glorious release.

"My turn, sweet," her husband murmured as he shifted, and suddenly she felt the pressure of his demanding entrance between her open legs, the tip of his cock stretching her wide as he pushed slowly inside to fully rest inside her still pulsing vagina. He said thickly, "You are tight as a gloved fist, Mrs. McCray, and so wet and hot I think I've gone to heaven. Hold on, lass, for a hard, fast ride."

Still languorously drifting in the aftermath of her orgasm, she found he was true to his word, for he withdrew and then plunged back inside with rapid long strokes, his lean hips thrusting his hard shaft as deeply as possible before sliding back almost completely out. The fluids of her sexual release lubricated his insistent movements, and Julia could not help but give small, breathless sighs of pleasure at the slick possession of her body, enjoying the carnal rhythm with shameless abandon. Bending her knees, she spread her legs as far as she could to allow him full penetration, arching upward to accept every throbbing inch. "Oh . . . Robbie, yes."

"That's it," he said through his teeth. "You were born to give a man pleasure. Come again for me."

She obeyed when his hand slid between their mating bodies and touched her, his fingers gliding over that swollen nub with excruciating pressure that seemed to make her body explode. Clutching his shoulders wildly, she convulsed around his hard cock, her legs locked around his waist. In response, he gave a groan and ejaculated, the forceful spurt of his hot semen bathing the mouth of her womb. With his face resting against the side of her neck, Julia could feel the warm rush of her husband's breathing and the wild pounding of his heart against her breasts. Keeping his weight braced on his elbows, he finally lifted his head and gave her one of his signature lazy smiles. "Now, that is the way to take a bath, lass."

Chapter 4

*A*dain Cameron reached over and poured more wine into his glass, trying with every fiber of his being to tamp down the impulse to heave himself to his feet and shove his fist right down Robert McCray's throat. The problem was, of course, that violence at this point would be fruitless, for besides proving to Julia that he was the murderous fiend she believed him to be, it would not undo the fact that the infamous McCray had already fucked her.

It killed him, like a knife straight into the heart, to think of it.

The infernal McCray had done a decent job of it too, if the small blushes that graced his beautiful cousin's smooth cheeks whenever she glanced at her husband were any indication of what had transpired between them. Of course, Adain thought in grim resignation, sipping his claret and looking down the long length of the dinner table where the newlywed couple sat, the man had a reputation for seducing everything in skirts, from aristocratic, highborn tarts to scullery maids, so he *should* be good at it. Sleeping his way through the countryside might make the arrogant Robbie McCray's name synonymous with sexual conquest, but there was also the undeniable fact that he was a fighter as well as a lover.

At least Julia would be protected, along with well bedded. A man like Robbie McCray would take care of his own.

Damn him to a burning hell. . . .

The light touch of a hand on his arm broke his distraction and he glanced at the woman sitting next to him in question. Her wide brown eyes held a glimmer of sympathy. With a rueful smile, he said quietly, "I'm sorry I'm not much company this evening, am I, Therese? You should have sat next to someone else."

Lady Therese Gibbons, the sister of their closest neighbor and his old friend Edward Gibbons, the Earl of Larkin, simply shook her head and answered in the same subdued tone, to keep their conversation private from the ears of the people eating and drinking around them. "Nonsense. And no one can blame you for being affected by the callous way Julia is treating you, Adain. It cannot be easy to sit here as the host to her new husband, not to mention how you have endured her open suspicion and enmity."

"It is her house too," he automatically defended her.

"But need she rub your nose in it?"

Therese had a point there. His fingers restlessly smoothed the stem of his wineglass. "She believes so fervently that I am a criminal that perhaps she feels I deserve it. I admit it: It gives me pain. . . . And now this sudden marriage to a man she barely knows adds salt to the wound. I am a little off balance; it is true."

Though not stunningly beautiful like his wayward cousin, Therese was still pretty in a buxom fashion, with brunette curls and milky skin, her figure voluptuous to the point of being almost plump. Brow furrowed, she glanced down to where Robbie McCray sat in conversation with her brother, Lord Larkin. Julia sat at her new husband's side, studiously refusing to look Adain's way. "He is a handsome rogue and no doubt preyed upon her sorrow to get around her. It is too bad, but it is a bed she has made and must lie in. There is no reason for you to—"

"I wish I knew why exactly she is so convinced I'm a vile murderer, when a few months ago we were still betrothed." He was being rude—snarling out the words and interrupting her, but he couldn't help it. "Therese, you have been Julia's friend since childhood. Has she spoken of her sudden change of heart? I have asked, tossed aside my pride and even implored, but she refuses to say why she no longer believes in my innocence. When the rumors first surfaced, she was stalwart by my side."

"She can be very stubborn. 'Tis a Cameron trait, you must admit." Therese looked unhappy. "I wish I could tell you what you seek to know, Adain, for we are as much friends as Julia and I. Yet, I cannot, for she has not explained her thinking to me. You are not the only one she won't confide in any longer."

Julia grieved. He knew it. It was one matter for a parent to grow ill and die, and quite another for one to be found the victim of a senseless crime. Couple the first tragedy with her brother's disappearance and it was no wonder she was distraught. There were no witnesses to his uncle's murder, or at least none had come forward, and Randal's body had not even been found. Adain muttered, "I do not suppose it matters why she feels the way she does, for she is lost to me anyway."

Therese leaned forward a fraction. "There are other women in this world, Adain, women who see you for the fine man you are.

Julia is a good friend of mine, yes, but I say she was a fool when she ran off to marry McCray. Her impulsive behavior will make some other woman very lucky."

Though he had always looked upon Therese as simply a friend, Adain was a little startled at both the vehemence in her tone and the look in her toffee-colored eyes. He also couldn't help but notice that the low-cut bodice of her gown displayed a great deal of her bountiful breasts, and her body was certainly angled to afford him a generous view. In love with Julia most of his life, he hadn't ever even thought of any other woman in a serious context, and considering the flux of his current emotions, this was not an opportune time to encourage an interest he did not reciprocate. Clearing his throat, he replied neutrally, "Your faith helps ease the hurt, Therese, and I thank you and your family for not suffering the rumors over my culpability and standing by the Camerons in their need. Your brother has been my friend for a long time."

A swift flash of something that could have been disappointment moved across her face, and she leaned back, her lashes lowering demurely. "What are friends for, Adain?"

Robbie stood outside the door for a moment, wondering if he was so bedazzled by his new wife's passionate abandon and captivating beauty that he'd lost his good judgment. All through dinner—which had been a long affair of endless courses, and complicated by guests who apparently visited often—it was clear that Adain Cameron could barely bring himself to be even marginally polite. Robbie had been made welcome only because it was also Julia's home, and even the servants seemed to eye him as an interloper. Their courtesy was lukewarm, to say the least.

So why the devil was he going to talk to the man who obviously considered him an enemy? Because, Robbie acknowledged ruefully to himself as he lifted his hand and rapped sharply on the thick wooden panel, trouble drew him like a bee to a blooming flower. His cousin Ian was fond of pointing out that Robbie could no more keep out of whatever mischief might be at hand than he could keep from eyeing the pretty lasses.

When he opened the door to the growled response and stepped inside, he saw Adain Cameron look up and stiffen visibly. Whoever the man expected, it wasn't Robbie, which wasn't a surprise. Behind a large desk made out of a massive slab of hewn wood, papers scattered across the top and a ledger open in front of him, Cameron said coldly, "McCray, what the devil do you want? I would think you would be upstairs, enjoying your new bride."

"To be sure," Robbie answered evenly, "that is still part of my plans for the evening. However, I wanted to talk to you, if I may."

"If you are here to discuss the terms of Julia's inheritance, you would do better—"

Interrupting with curt emphasis, Robbie said, "I've most certainly discussed it already with your late uncle's solicitors, Cameron, and the money is not why I'm here."

Leaning back in his chair behind the desk, Adain narrowed his eyes. "But you admit that's why you married her."

"It's a little more complicated than that, but yes." Robbie gave the other man a small, sardonic smile. "Tell me, Cameron, what would you do if a beautiful woman waylaid you one evening outside your home, offering both wealth and the opportunity to bed her as often as you wished?"

Adain's answering smile was more a baring of teeth. "I suppose if I were a libertine who thought with his stiff cock, I would accept at once."

The insult was enough to make Robbie wonder once again just why the hell he was trying to talk to this man in the first place, but he tamped down the urge to spin on his heel and stalk out of the room, and simply lifted a brow. "I married her, offering my name and protection, and not all of it was avarice or lust. Our fathers were friends, and to a McCray that means something. I will see the lass safe, honor my vows of fidelity, and breed my children in her body. Could you ask more? My sword arm is hers, and I would gladly die to keep her from harm. Whatever you might have heard about me, Cameron, no man suggests I am dishonorable."

There was a short, tense silence. Then Adain Cameron nodded, a brusque movement of his head, his silver eyes bleak. "Aye," he said heavily, "no man suggests you are anything besides brave and honest, McCray. However, do not expect me to welcome you with open arms. Julia was supposed to be mine."

"Of that fact I am well aware." Robbie glanced pointedly at a half-filled glass next to a decanter sitting on the desk. "Is that whiskey?"

"You wish for me to share a drink with you?" Adain shook his head, an incredulous laugh escaping his lips. "I give you high points for audacity, McCray."

"I'm here because I think you are innocent of murdering your uncle and cousin," Robbie said mildly, "so I think the least you can do is offer me a little whiskey while we discuss it. What say you,

Cameron? I have no quarrel with you, and if I can make Julia happy by giving her the answers she needs to heal her losses, I wish to do so."

"You want to make her happy? That is an odd statement from a man who wedded her for her money and the use of her body."

"There's more to her than just her beauty, Cameron. She's a spirited lass with a quick mind and," Robbie admitted with a twinge of wry humor, "a sharp tongue."

"She has that," Adain muttered. For a moment he hesitated, and then he gave a reluctant nod. "Sit down. I'll get you a glass."

There was a leather chair across from the desk, and Robbie sank into it, accepting a glass of amber liquid, then leaning back and stretching out his legs. Taking a stiff swallow, he cocked a brow. "Let's get down to it. Tell me exactly what happened to your uncle."

"There isn't much of a story. I wish I knew more, but the facts are straightforward and infuriatingly simple." Cameron looked somber, his eyes the color of a winter sky. "It was more than a year ago . . . in late summer. Arthur and I came for a visit. All seemed well here—my uncle was in good spirits, Randal was his usual self, lost in some bit of poetry or in the midst of composing a ditty to please Julia and Therese—"

"Ah, Therese, the earl's sister. I noticed at dinner she seemed to be quite neighborly toward you. Is that usual?"

The other man shook his head, his mouth tightening. "There has never been anything between myself and Therese. We are friends, as Edward and I have known each other a long time. That is the extent of it."

That might be true, Robbie reflected over his whiskey glass, but the buxom Lady Therese would fall on her back and spread her legs for Adain Cameron in the wink of an eye, if he was a judge, and he was fairly practiced in gauging such things. "Go on, then. Julia tells me her father disappeared midafternoon and wasn't found until after nightfall."

"We naturally did not become alarmed until he missed dinner. His horse wandered into the courtyard a little while later without a rider, and I immediately organized a search party."

"*You* organized a search party? What of Randal? As first in line to be the next laird, I would think the responsibility to be his."

Cameron gave him a moody look. "My cousin wanted nothing to do with becoming the head of the clan, McCray. He is a gentle, romantic soul who occupies his time with literature and music. My uncle gave up years ago on trying to get his son to lift a sword or ride a horse at anything above a slow amble. It simply isn't in Randal's nature to command, and he was more than grateful to let the responsibility for finding his father fall to me. Unfortunately, we did just that, though I was thankful I was not the one to actually stumble across the body. Julia is correct about one thing: There is no question of murder, for the marks on my uncle's throat show clearly he was strangled to insensibility and then put in the water to drown."

"A gruesome and cowardly manner of killing, to be sure," Robbie commented, watching the man sitting across from him closely. He'd just used the present tense to describe his cousin, as if he believed Randal was still alive. It hardly exonerated Adain Cameron, but it was a positive sign. "Since I assume you exclude yourself, do you have any suspects?"

"The Cameron clan has enemies, naturally. This is Scotland.

If you breathe the air, you have foes." Adain's long fingers toyed with his glass, his face looking shuttered and bleak. "However, we have no open disputes that I am aware of, no quarrels over land or livestock, so the only conclusion is that the deed was personal in nature, for a purpose that is not obvious."

"Unless, of course, you were the one, for you stood to inherit his lands."

There was a flash in Cameron's silver eyes. "Damn you! Randal inherited, McCray, not myself. And yes, if you are thinking my cousin is no match for me in a physical confrontation and I could kill him easily and dispose of the body, that's true. But I am no more responsible for his disappearance than I am for my uncle's murder."

The corner of his mouth lifted in a sardonic smile, Robbie said, "I've known all along that you are the most likely candidate *physically* to be the villain, Cameron. I simply don't think you committed either crime. Tell me, once Randal became laird, how did your gentle cousin handle the responsibility before he disappeared?"

"He loathed it, naturally. Anyone will tell you that."

"Enough to leave on his own?"

"Perhaps." With a weary frown, Adain sighed. "Whether you believe me or not, I've sent word to friends in Edinburgh, Glasgow, Inverness . . . anywhere in Scotland he might go. His father's death shook him deeply. I returned to my own home once we had buried my uncle, so I cannot firsthand describe Randal's actions, because I wasn't here, but Mrs. Dunbar tells me he was more distracted than ever and very melancholy. I am still trying to straighten out the mess he made of the accounting and soothe the merchants who did not get paid or receive ordered goods. As far as I can tell, he was too steeped in his grief to effectually fulfill his new role."

"And then he mysteriously disappeared."

"Yes," Adain confirmed.

Tipping his glass to his mouth, Robbie drained the contents. Then he said grimly, "I think, dead or alive, we need to find Randal Cameron."

"He's quite . . . devastating, isn't he?" Therese rubbed her finger idly on the arm of her chair, but her gaze was bright with open speculation.

Julia stifled a laugh. "I suppose that's one of the many words one could use to describe Robbie McCray."

"I have more. How about wildly handsome, wickedly male, gloriously tall, and wide shouldered—"

"Let's not forget impossibly arrogant, notoriously fickle, outrageously hot tempered. His reputation is undisputed," Julia interrupted, lifting a brow. Her new husband had all of the aforementioned attributes Therese extolled, but Julia was still adjusting to the traits he had that didn't conform to the persona of the legendary Robbie McCray. The tenderness she hadn't quite expected, or the genuine sense of humor, and certainly not the potency of their mutual attraction. He'd been a means to an end, and she really hadn't anticipated that his roguish charm would be so appealing.

She *liked* him.

"Yet you married him." Therese gave her an understandably reproachful look. "I cannot believe you didn't tell me your plans, Julia. I thought we'd become close, like sisters."

It was true. Before her father's death, Julia hadn't thought of Therese as more than a neighbor she saw occasionally, pleasant enough but not someone she had a lot in common with beyond as a casual acquaintance. But both Edward and Therese had been supportive since the tragedy, especially after Randal's disappearance. They called often, and she and Therese had grown to be good friends.

"It made sense to choose McCray," Julia explained in a halting voice, remembering how much courage it had taken to follow through with her plan, actually leave the castle, and travel to Edinburgh to proposition a man she'd met only when she was a child. "All of Scotland has heard of his lost ships, so I knew I had something to tempt him to agree. I needed a husband, he needed to replace his confiscated property, and his ability to defend himself is undisputed. I doubt Adain would challenge him; nor can Adain treacherously catch Robbie McCray off guard."

"But you really did not know him."

"It is a common enough practice for young women to be betrothed to men they don't know," Julia pointed out, though that had bothered her as well. "I believe my father would have approved of the match, and that is important to me."

"And your new husband is extremely talented between the sheets," Therese commented with a hint of question in her voice. Leaning forward slightly, she murmured, "I mean, that's what they say, Julia, and having seen him, I somehow believe it."

Since it was absolutely true, Julia couldn't suppress a blush, but as good of friends as she and Therese might be, she wasn't willing to elaborate. She said primly, "His prowess in any capacity except wielding a sword is immaterial to me. At least tonight I know

I'll sleep safely, even if it takes sharing my bed with the infamous McCray."

As if it were a hardship.

They were in the guest bedroom Therese always used when visiting, since her brother's estate was far enough away that dinner invitations often included an overnight stay. Therese sat in a blue brocade chair by the fireplace, her expression softening from mischievous to sorrowful. "A part of me wishes Edward had never found that pin next to your father's body, Julia. I still wonder if I should not have told you or given it back. I agonized for months over what to do."

"Had you *not* given me the pin, I might have married Adain," Julia murmured, recalling that awful moment of disclosure—when Therese showed her absolute proof of her cousin's treachery.

"True, but—"

"Therese, you surely do not think for a moment that you could deny me the knowledge. I might have tied myself for life to a conscienceless monster."

Her friend's eyes held a troubled look. "I am sorry Edward refuses to testify to the authorities. He and Adain have known each other a long time. A stubborn part of him still thinks the pin got there by some accident."

Since Julia had commissioned the pin herself and had it fashioned as a gift—a pledge of both love and friendship—then given it to her cousin for his birthday just before the murder, the evidence was all too damning. It made her ill now to recall just how much she had looked forward to the expression on Adain's face when he opened the box and saw the Cameron crest with their initials entwined. He'd displayed it daily on his plaid, like a pledge of their love. That is, until her father's death. Adain never mentioned losing it, and now it was clear why. Julia got up from her perch on the bed and paced restlessly across the spacious room. "Edward harbors false hope. He found it on the shore of the loch right where he spotted my father's body in the water. What else am I supposed to think?"

"Neither my brother nor myself believe Adain is capable of such a crime. That is why Edward told no one but me about finding the pin. I kept the knowledge to myself for almost a year, but as your wedding approached, I . . . well, I finally opted to let you know about it and draw your own conclusions."

"Your loyalty is admirable." Julia stopped by the window and gazed out to see the moonlight gilding the countryside in a pale glow. "It is my father who is lost, my brother who is missing, and Adain gains land, title, and wealth from both circumstances."

"It does look bad," Therese admitted with reluctance in her tone. "However, if it weren't for Edward joining the search and finding the pin—"

Whirling around, Julia said bitterly, "He *did* join, he *did* find it . . . and not once has Adain even mentioned it missing. I despise myself for feeling enough for him that I have kept the discovery of the pin a secret, but I refuse to hide my loathing for the man he is. Do not try to argue that he is too honorable for murder, Therese, lest you forget the child even now growing in the belly of one of your female servants, conceived during one of Adain's visits to your home months ago *while* he was still betrothed to me. I had always thought him a good man, but Adain is in truth despicable and callous, apparently not past shoving up the skirts of a young scullery maid to take his pleasure even though he had pledged his heart to another woman."

Therese looked at her with sympathetic eyes, her brown curls glistening in the firelight. She said softly, "He is a man, and the girl did not say she was unwilling. And Adain denies it is his. Edward asked him."

"So he says." It was stated with grim disbelief. "But the girl swears to you otherwise."

"Don't worry. Edward has every intention of providing for her welfare and that of the babe."

Taking a deep breath to steady herself, Julia said, "Edward is a gentleman, something my cousin only pretends to be."

"And what, then, does that make your new husband?" Therese asked, tactfully changing the subject to something lighter. "I would think that Robbie McCray, with his famous sword arm and even more famous . . . um . . . Well, I suppose it *is* a sword of a different sort. . . . What would you call him?"

With a small, confident smile, Julia answered, "Dangerous."

Chapter 5

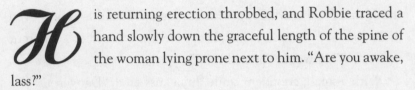is returning erection throbbed, and Robbie traced a hand slowly down the graceful length of the spine of the woman lying prone next to him. "Are you awake, lass?"

With a sleepy stretch, Julia rolled on her side and looked at him, her gaze immediately dropping to where his cock rose high and hard against his stomach. She gave a muffled laugh. "God in heaven, McCray, I just obliged you."

His grin was wolfish, and he caressed her bare hip, admiring her firm, pale breasts with an avid masculine examination. "I obliged *you*, and I have the marks of your nails on my back to prove it."

His delectable wife looked remarkably unrepentant, her lush body slightly flushed and damp from their recent intercourse. She shook back her ebony curls against the tumbled bedding. "Are all men so insatiable? I had no idea."

With swift, lazy grace, Robbie tumbled her to her back in response to that observation, settling on top of her. His mouth hovered teasingly over hers for a moment. "What other men are like is not your concern, Mrs. McCray. I am your only lover, and pleasing me often was part of our bargain, remember?"

Julia squirmed slightly, and he hardened further at the feel of her lissome form rubbing his shaft and testicles. Her green eyes flashed as she looked at him, but her arms came up to clasp around his neck with gratifying enthusiasm. "I remember, McCray."

Robbie wickedly licked her soft lower lip, a deliberately slow, languid contact. "Besides, you knew I liked to fuck before you married me, lass. You are constantly throwing my reputation in my face. What choice do I have but to live up to it?"

Before she could answer with one of her tart replies, he captured her mouth in a long, hot kiss, his tongue leisurely exploring, his hands roaming freely. He fondled the generous curve of one tight breast, weighing it deliciously in the palm of his hand, and then moved his attentions downward. Julia made a small sound in her throat as he slid a finger along the delicate folds of her wet, warm sex and found the entrance to paradise, then slipped it inside her. Her legs parted willingly as he explored her vaginal passage, his thumb slowly rotating around the small nub of her clitoris, and she shivered in his arms.

He lifted his head and smiled. "See, you like this, beautiful Julia, don't you?"

"It's . . . tolerable," she muttered, her eyes half closing as he applied just the right amount of pressure and her hips lifted in supplicant need.

What a stubbornly independent lass he had married. The journey as she discovered her sexuality was surprisingly entrancing. Usually he avoided inexperienced women, but she was . . . different.

She challenged him and he found it intriguing. His brows shot up and he laughed. "Just tolerable?"

"Don't . . . stop." She arched against his hand and panted.

He slid his finger out almost all the way. "You seem a little needy, lass. Shall I replace this"—his finger pushed back into her velvet-soft passage—"with something more substantial?"

In answer, she moaned, and her arms tightened.

His smile was dark with desire. "I'll take that as a yes."

With expert ease, he entered her a second later, his stiff cock urgently penetrating her slick heat as he began a rhythm of long, quick strokes between her legs. His hunger surprised him, for he had just climaxed inside her not long before, but he still had an almost adolescent sexual need to claim her again, to find exquisite and sensational pleasure in her arms.

Beneath him, Julia made breathy sounds telling him she was enjoying it every bit as much as he was, and she rubbed his shoulders with a restless motion, her head tilted back and her dark lashes fans on her pink-tinted cheeks. The bed they occupied was a little small, and not designed for someone as tall as he, but in truth, he didn't mind, for it meant they had to sleep in very close proximity.

He couldn't think of a more delightful way to spend the night.

With an inward glide, he closed his eyes at the onslaught of pure pleasure, his whole body on fire with carnal joy, and embedded himself to the hilt before he slid backward, her small inner muscles clenching in response to the luscious friction. His heart thundered along like a band of running horses as his sexual peak rose and built, and he controlled his intense need to ejaculate only by sheer will, waiting until Julia's unrestrained moans turned into a small, orgasmic scream that echoed in the darkened chamber.

The tightening of her contracting muscles around his surging cock sent him wildly over the edge. He erupted inside her, the rapturous release making him tremble, his arms shaking as he held himself still and poured his seed into his wife's lovely, warm, soft body.

When he was finally able to put together a coherent thought, it was that he was a damned lucky man.

Her husband's chest was hard, yet oddly enough a very comfortable place to rest. Julia lay sprawled on top of Robbie's lean body, relaxed and pleasantly exhausted. It was a little discomfiting to realize just how easily and eagerly she had fallen under the spell of the notorious Robert McCray, at least in a sexual sense. Of course, she thought in sated, sleepy reflection, there was some truth in every legend, and beyond a doubt, the man was a talented lover.

Snuggled in his strong arms, their damp bodies fitted together, his fingers lightly tangled in her hair . . . she felt safe and cherished.

"Tell me about your brother, Julia."

That quiet question made her lift her head. They occupied her bedchamber, and as always, when the moon was full, the long windows let the white light spill in, making it possible to see him clearly. The expression on his handsome face was neutral, and he lay back against the white bedding, watching her through half-closed dark eyes. Frowning, she said, "You wish to talk about Randal *now*?"

One ebony brow twitched upward. "I'll regain my strength in a bit, and we can eschew conversation for a more pleasurable activity, but, yes, I wish to talk about him now."

"Why?"

"Because I wish to find him for you." His hand lifted and his fingers grazed her cheek in a light caress, his gaze holding hers. "Tell me what he is like. Who are his friends? What does he like to do besides write poetry and compose music? Did he have a favorite spot to go to? Did he—"

"I get the idea, McCray." She said the words more sharply than intended, but in truth, she was very touched. Her cheek on Robbie's bare shoulder, Julia murmured, "He has always been a dreamer. That I admit. Not practical at all. I suppose he spent a great deal of his time out-of-doors because he wished to avoid being drawn into the affairs of my father's many holdings. He liked the cliff, where he would sit and sketch or compose music. There is also a man who lives on the other side of the village, near the woods. He was a famous bard at one time, or so they say, and even served at court. Randal often visited him. They shared a love of poetry."

"Has he been questioned?"

"I would guess Adain has done so, if just for appearances' sake." She couldn't keep the bitterness out of her voice.

"Tomorrow we'll pay this rhymester a visit. All right, go on. Your brother is my age and therefore he must certainly have at least considered the idea of taking a wife. Did he have a sweetheart? A mistress? Was he courting anyone?"

"Not all men spend most of their time chasing after women," Julia muttered dryly, "but I somehow doubt you could understand that." After a moment, she added, "I always thought that maybe he would marry Therese, but I never saw him display anything more than courtesy toward her, I suppose. My father would have been in favor of the match, for the Gibbonses have been our friends and neighbors for years."

"Would she have been in favor of it?"

"I think she expected it would happen." Julia yawned deeply, unable to help it. There was something soothing about being so intimately nestled against her attractive husband, and indeed, sexual intercourse was a tiring exercise in a physical sense.

It was odd, but she felt comfortable with him. Maybe it was because they had become lovers so quickly and the intimacy fostered an immediate bond.

Maybe she had fallen all too quickly under his legendary spell. Whatever caused it, she found lying in his arms to be seductively enjoyable.

"But now the resilient Lady Therese has fastened her sights on your cousin," Robbie said neutrally.

"Adain?" The idea of that interrupted Julia's slide into slumber, making her blink. "Whatever makes you think so?"

"My dear, sweet wife, with all due modesty, I think I can recognize the signs of flirtation and invitation." Robbie's tone was full of amused mockery.

"But he is supposed to be engaged to me."

"But you went and married someone else, remember?" There was a light tone of masculine warning.

Her cheeks flushed as she realized how absurd her statement had been. "Of course I remember. It seems to me I'm here naked in bed with you, McCray. I just meant that Adain and I have had an understanding a long time. Therese knows that he claims to have a passion for me, and she also knows better than anyone that he's a murderer."

Robbie's long fingers, which had been idly stroking her bare shoulder, went still. "Why better than anyone?"

Though it was one thing to realize her cousin's heinous deed and despise him for killing her beloved father, it was quite another to send Adain to the gallows. Once, Julia had dreamed of being his wife. When Therese had given her the damning pin that had been found near her father's corpse, Julia had hidden it. Besides, Edward had loyally refused, according to Therese, to ever testify against his lifelong friend. The one thing that cast doubt on Adain's guilt was the lack of physical evidence linking him directly with the crime. If Julia had made the discovery of the pin public, Adain might well have been charged openly with her father's murder but not necessarily convicted. Arthur would suffer through the trial—they all would—for the boy adored his older brother, and with the outcome not certain, she declined to come forward.

Maybe she was as foolish as Edward—but she did not want to see Adain hang. Her own loyalty was shaken, maybe even broken, but it wasn't gone completely. Once, she'd loved him. The conflicted state of her emotions had sent her to Edinburgh and into Robbie's arms and bed.

Julia stayed silent, inwardly cursing her loose tongue. Robert McCray was many things—rogue, warrior, rakehell—but he was not a fool.

"What does she know—and obviously you as well—that the rest of us don't, lass?" Her husband's question was gentle but relentlessly firm.

Against his chest, she muttered, "This isn't your affair."

"The devil it isn't," he said firmly, his hold tightening slightly. One long-fingered hand stroked her hair. "Everything about you is my affair, wife."

"I'm tired," Julia said stubbornly. "And I don't wish to continue this discussion."

"I'm not tired in the least. And make no mistake, we *will* discuss this tomorrow."

A moment later, she realized he spoke the perfect truth about not being too tired. An iron-hard ridge of erect male flesh rose along her thigh, and her husband's moonlit grin was both lazily attractive and tantalizingly male.

"Already?"

"Already," he confirmed.

His kiss was so ardently persuasive that she sighed in wayward anticipation when he pulled her closer, forgetting everything else in the world except the hard feel of her husband's arms around her and the heavy promise of sensual pleasure in his dark eyes.

They were only three doors away.

Hell!

Adain Cameron punched his pillow with force, his fist going deep into the soft down, his body too tense for slumber. He'd downed half a bottle of the best whiskey a man could buy, and it seemed impossible he could still be wide-awake. He was drunk; he'd known he was drunk about an hour ago, and . . . he was miserable anyway.

And so damnably aware of the bedroom three doors away from his.

Oh, it wasn't that he'd never lain in his bed before in the darkness and thought about Julia sleeping just a short distance down the hallway. He'd imagined her as tempting as one of the legendary sirens, her glossy dark hair strewn over the embroidered softness of sheet and coverlet, her slender body relaxed and pale in the moonlight, those soft lips he'd tasted, parted and inviting. . . . It was just that in his fantasies Robbie McCray's rangy body wasn't in the bed with her.

Thunder and blast, there was no doubt of what they did in that bed, either. Heaven help him, he'd even heard them as he'd staggered down the hall past their door earlier this evening, Julia's voice raised slightly, McCray's deep tones in a chuckle, and then a telling sigh, light as the crystal moonlight, obviously female.

You would think—Adain rolled over again and grumbled darkly to himself—that in a house as old as Castle Cameron, the doors would be built thick enough for privacy. This past year had been a nightmare, and it seemed he was not going to find any relief from it now. Not only had he lost his uncle and his cousin, but Julia as well. His head spun a little and he shut his eyes, fiercely willing the sweet oblivion of sleep to come.

Instead, he heard a small knock, and a second later the creak of the hinges on the door of his bedroom. One eye cracked open and he saw someone slip inside, the door clicking shut with a quiet sound. There was enough light that he could see the tumble of long hair and he sat up, one hand going to his aching head. "Who's there?"

"It's me." The voice was feminine and light, the tone hushed. "Shhh, Adain. I shouldn't be here."

"Therese?"

"Of course." The fragrance of lilies came to him as she approached the bed. "I couldn't sleep and was worried about you."

"You are correct. You shouldn't be here," he said forcefully, and then winced at the echo of his own voice. "Edward would have your head . . . and mine too, come to think of it. It isn't proper." He snatched up the sheet, which had fallen to his waist. "I'm naked, for God's sake. Please go back to bed."

"Are you thinking about them together? Surely your heart is breaking."

The soft question made his temples throb harder, the whiskey in retrospect not at all a good idea. Wearily, he muttered, "Therese, there are some things a man does not discuss, friends or not."

Now by the side of the bed, Therese smiled, the gleam of her teeth showing in her pale face. She wore only a dressing gown tied at the waist, and her hands went to the sash, deftly tugging it open. "I can help you forget, Adain, if you will let me."

Damn his traitorous male reaction; he couldn't help but stare at the parted cloth, catching a glimpse of her generous pale breasts and the dark brown thatch between her legs. Where Julia was slim and shapely, Therese was full and rounded in every way a woman could be, and she shook back her hair, widening her robe to obviously tempt him.

However trying the day had been already, he hadn't anticipated *this*.

"You're an untouched maid," Adain said thickly, "and the sister of an earl. Not to mention that your brother and I have been friends for years. I will not dishonor him by taking you to bed, Therese."

"Edward doesn't have to know." She stepped forward and her

hand came out to touch his shoulder persuasively. Her fingers felt cool and firm, and her brown eyes were wide and sincere. "Take me, Adain. I am willing."

Whether Edward knew or not, Adain was sober enough to realize that a tumble with Therese Gibbons meant a trip to the altar and a wedding band on her finger. Besides, she was not the one he desired. Julia was lost, but not yet gone from his heart.

This was the very *last* complication he needed. "I won't do it," he growled ungallantly, trying hard to ignore the thrust of her prominent nipples so near his face.

In answer, she shimmied closer and reached for the sheet covering the lower half of his body, quickly pulling it back. "You deny me but your body doesn't, Adain. Look at you, at half-mast already."

She was right. He was getting hard, but it wasn't because he was truly tempted, just that her nudity and nearness triggered an almost automatic response. "Dammit, Therese," he said in impatient argument, "I am flesh and blood, and you are a pretty woman and all but naked. Please leave and speak to no one about this. I cannot use you and then hold my head up in the morning."

Her gaze glimmered and she frowned, her brows shooting together. "That is all it would be to you?" There was a steely undertone to her voice.

"My love for Julia is strong," he answered with painful honesty, not looking away but holding her gaze so she could see he was sincere. "I know she is married. I know I will never have her, but I will not get over it lightly, I fear. Until then, another woman is not an option. Not if I want to offer her an honorable courtship."

"I see." Her response was short, her hurt feelings evident in her voice. "I suppose I have made a fool of myself, then."

Why the hell he felt guilty when he hadn't even invited her was a mystery. Adain said thickly, "Not at all. And who knows, I may feel differently very soon." He doubted it, but summoned enough politesse even in his inebriated state to say so. "Julia's betrayal is recent, and I am still in shock because of it."

"I assume that is true, since even now she sleeps in the arms of the infamous McCray."

The jibe was more than a little cruel, coming from a woman who supposedly wanted to offer him the solace of her body, but then again, he'd rejected her. Adain said quietly, "I am aware of where she is and whom she sleeps with, Therese."

She jerked her robe back together and averted her face. After a moment, she said in a more conciliatory tone, "I apologize. I came here to offer my comfort and instead upset you."

"I doubt I will even remember it tomorrow," he lied, "considering the amount of whiskey I consumed this evening. And as for McCray, he swears he believes in my innocence and wishes to help me clear my name. I may begrudge him every moment he spends with my cousin, but if he is sincere, I am glad he's here."

"I told you not to try tonight."

Therese Gibbons stopped pacing and whirled around, so furious her teeth ground together. She snapped, "I miscalculated, Edward. Fine, I should have waited until our next visit to try to seduce Adain. But at least I am attempting to do *something*, while you sit around like the feeble-brained, liquor-soaked fool you are."

In the dimly lit room her brother's eyes glittered suddenly like those of some feral creature, his lazy pose—sprawled in a chair by the fireplace—at odds with the nasty twist to his mouth. "Be careful, dear sister, in case you forget I wrung the life out of Rufus with my bare hands. Your neck is much more slender."

If there was one thing in this world Therese was not afraid of, it was her sniveling brother. "You used a chain to strangle an old man, you buffoon. And perhaps you should recall that I am the one who lured Randal to the cliff and rid the world of his useless existence."

"Ah, yes," her brother taunted, "yet another Cameron male who did not desire you."

The sting of Adain Cameron's recent rejection was still fresh, but Randal's refusal to touch her, once she discovered his secret shame, did not rankle. "He didn't fancy any woman, you sotted idiot. You would have a better chance than I at bedding the late weakling Cameron laird."

"That's disgusting," Edward muttered, sinking lower in the chair, a glass of wine dangling from his fingers. "I am not a sodomite."

"No, indeed. Instead you are a whoremonger who has brought our family to ruin with your gambling excesses and perverted appetites. At least passing off to Julia as Adain's the brat that you sired that swells even now the belly of one of our maids served a purpose. She brought it up again earlier. Stealing the pin was a good idea, but that story was a flash of brilliance. Jealousy is a powerful emotion, and a moral lapse like that one is not easily forgiven. Since you are so pathetic you will tumble anything you encounter that is breathing, we might as well use it to our advantage."

"Much better than being a washed-up spinster unable to snare the title and wealth she covets except by deceit and murder," her brother countered with a nasty snarl.

Considering the volume of his voice, Therese was indeed glad that Robbie McCray was undoubtedly keeping himself occupied between Julia's open legs and that Adain had drunk so much whiskey. She hissed, "Shut your mouth, you ineffectual excuse for a man. Arguing and insults are pointless; don't you see that? Our plan is working so far. Everything is falling into place. Though I worked on Julia's doubts over Adain's innocence, I never dreamed she would aid us so well by marrying someone else. The only trouble we have right now is that McCray apparently has promised to help Adain clear his name."

"The man is too occupied with his pretty wife," Edward scoffed. "He isn't a threat. Give him a willing wench and he's happy enough."

"Don't be so sure." Therese remembered the speculative glance Robbie McCray had given her across the dinner table when she sat next to the soon-to-be Cameron laird. It had not been typical male appraisal—no, not at all. It had been more an awareness of her flirtatious behavior toward his wife's cousin.

The man had looked at her if he *knew*.

Edward drained his glass, a dribble of scarlet liquid running down his weak chin. "So what the devil do you want to do about him?"

"Julia's new husband? I am not sure yet." At the window, Therese pulled back the faded silken drape, staring outside. Almost absently, she said, "Adain is openly jealous. If something happens to the bonny McCray, no one will doubt who had the most cause, now, will they?"

With obvious unease, Edward objected, "Julia might well produce the pin if something happens to her husband and her cousin looks to be the guilty party again. That is not to our purposes at all. So far you've convinced her not to go the magistrate, and she seems to have enough uncertainty to go along with us."

"The little bitch is as unsuspecting as a newborn babe, and besides, she knows you won't back up her story."

"The rumors you started are still circulating. Public opinion has Adain, if not condemned, at least still the main suspect in the murders. If something happened to McCray also, there could be a trial. It will do us little good if Adain is convicted and condemned before you have a chance to ensnare him into marriage."

With a feline smile, Therese turned and looked at her brother, noting with contempt the beads of sweat on his upper lip. "Trust me, Eddie. I have everything well in hand."

Chapter 6

Two minutes in the company of John Hexham told Robbie a great deal and he was suddenly glad Julia had been detained in the village by an offer to see the newborn babe of the cooper's wife. From a seat on a carved wooden chair, he glanced around the comfortable cottage, noting the fine quality of the draperies at the small windows and the elegant harpsichord in the corner. He said with deceptive casualness, "My wife told me a little about you, Hexham. How long were you at court?"

The young man was slim and fair, his face slightly flushed as he fiddled with a kettle, settling it over the glowing coals of a previous cooking fire. "Two years," he responded reluctantly.

"I've been there," Robbie commented neutrally. "Never have I seen such licentiousness and lack of morality. Music and poetry always seemed out of place in such a veritable pit of intrigue and openly flaunted vice. Tell me, who sponsored you?"

Hexham cleared his throat uncomfortably. "The Duke of Bonsford."

"Ah. We've met. I suppose that explains your apparent afflu-
ence. Bonsford is notoriously generous when he grows tired of
his . . . special friends."

His face tightening, the young man stood abruptly. "What are
you implying, sir?"

Robbie simply smiled lazily. "Nothing. I am a worldly man,
that's all."

A subtle defeat slumped Hexham's shoulders. "If you are here
to offer your censure and disapproval, sir, I want neither. I am not
hurting anyone and live a quiet, retired existence. A man like you
probably doesn't understand how desperately I value my anonym-
ity here."

One brow lifted, Robbie kept his expression bland. "I'm not
judging you, Hexham, so relax. And I'm certainly not going to say
anything to anyone. What you do and whom you choose to do it
with—man or woman—is your affair. I am simply trying to investigate the disappearance of my wife's brother. His close friendship
with you seems to throw a new light on things."

Almost warily, Hexham nodded in a brief tilt of his head. "We
had very similar . . . interests, if you will, for lack of a better way of
putting it. However, I don't think he quite realized just how similar.
It is a difficult conclusion to draw about yourself, believe me."

"I can imagine."

The young man's smile was a twist of open cynical amusement.
"I somehow doubt that, McCray. Your love of the *opposite* sex is
well-known. Anyway, Randal was drawn here time and again, but
he was . . . I don't know what would be the correct word, sir . . .
mortified, frightened, repelled, even, to discover our relationship
growing to be something he considered unnatural." Hexham paced

across the room, his face grim with recollection. The autumn breeze coming in the open window ruffled his fair hair, giving him an almost ethereal look. "I tried to explain to him that it isn't as unusual as he thought it was, that I'd met scores of men with his inclinations, but he was much too concerned with what his clan might think if his family discovered he was a . . . a—"

"You may spare yourself the nasty labels," Robbie said with sincerity, thoughtful over this new twist, "for while I don't quite understand your preference, I don't condemn it either. I doubt any man would choose it, but rather I believe it chose you. Tell me, would Randal have left because of all this? Did the two of you quarrel over it?"

Hexham gave a definitive shake of his fair head. "We never quarreled. Randal was confused, yes, but I have never thought he would leave without a word to me. That would be much like you leaving your wife and not looking back."

Which, in fact, was exactly what Julia wished Robbie to do in a few weeks. She wanted a house—her own—and enough money to live on. The recollection of their bargain startled him . . . and it sure as hell wasn't going to happen, he decided then and there with pure masculine arrogance.

He was becoming involved with his beautiful bride, he admitted to himself. He liked her spirit, her responsiveness in bed, but mostly there was just something about *her*. Something unique and fascinating in his experience—and he had quite a bit of experience. In many ways, they were kindred souls, and whether she realized it or not, he was beginning to see it. When she loved, she loved fiercely. The servants were fond of her because she was gracious and treated them liked family. She had pride, but not to an extent that she was haughty, and he had seen no evidence of vanity in his lovely wife.

Grief and confusion had sent her into his arms, but he intended that contentment and joy would keep her there.

And when the devil had *that* realization about their marriage happened? It might have even been the evening when she'd appeared out of the mist with an outrageous proposition—for he still was not completely sure why he'd agreed so quickly. The ships were tempting, but just for that he would never have tied himself for life to one woman. Her beauty was entrancing, but again, there was no shortage of lovely women in Scotland.

Infatuation at first sight? Oh, yes, he knew that was possible, but *love* at first sight?

Maybe.

"I wouldn't leave my wife," Robbie said curtly, "but then again, I am not in the midst of some moral dilemma over my own sexuality either. Randal was also faced with the heavy responsibilities of being laird, when he had no inclination for the job. It seems to me that leaving would have solved a lot of his problems."

"Randal is a lot of things, but not a coward. And he sincerely loves his family and would not willingly cause them pain."

There was a chilling conviction in that flat statement. Robbie glanced up, feeling some sympathy for the obvious strain on the young man's face. "So you think he has come to harm?"

"Look at what happened to his father. I cannot imagine any other scenario. Since I just declared I don't believe he would walk away without a word, what other choice is there but to suspect foul play?"

Unfortunately, Robbie had the same suspicions. But something felt not quite . . . right, and his gut was rarely wrong. "Did he ever discuss Therese Gibbons with you?" he asked, rubbing his jaw and gazing at his brother-in-law's lover. "I understand she expected a marriage proposal at any time. He wouldn't be the first man to marry to hide his less than socially acceptable inclinations."

Hexham shook his head. "Even if he were as drawn to women as you are, he wouldn't have married Therese. He disliked her intensely, though I know he kept the sentiment from his father and Julia, since both Lord Larkin and Lady Therese are practically family."

"I see. What was the source of this enmity?"

Frowning, the young man shook his head. "He never told me specifically, though I know Edward Gibbons had borrowed money from him time and again, especially this past year, since his father's death."

Now, *that* was interesting. Financial straits and murder often held hands and walked a primrose path together. Robbie got to his feet and gave John Hexham a straightforward look. "In the interest of finding out what happened to Randal, would you care to do me a favor?"

The other man said fervently, "For Randal? Anything."

Julia inhaled the acrid scent of burning leaves deeply as they rode along, finding the warm fall afternoon sheer pleasure for the senses. As she guided her horse around a hole in the road, she stole a covert glance at her husband. Tall and dark, he sat his mount with the ease of a born horseman, a faint frown furrowing his brow. Opening her mouth to ask exactly what it was that he had discovered, she barely registered the retort until she saw him jerk slightly.

Her question stuck in her throat as Robbie suddenly threw himself at her and tumbled her from her horse. She struck the ground with such force that she had the wind knocked from her lungs. Her husband rolled to the side and covered her body with his larger frame as her startled horse skittered to the side.

Stunned and bewildered, Julia lay sprawled underneath him in a pile of leaves next to the road, trying to take a struggling breath. When she could manage it, she squeaked furiously, "What are you doing, McCray? Get off me."

"Not until I find out if he is going to reload and fire again," her husband told her, his expression uncharacteristically grim. "Of course, lucky for us, the bastard has imperfect aim. For that I suppose I should be grateful. He just nicked me."

"You're shot?" Sure enough, even as she spoke Julia could feel an alarming warm wetness soaking her blouse from his encircling arm.

"Just a little."

"Dear God."

Gazing around, still holding her protectively as they lay on the hard ground together, Robbie murmured nonchalantly, "It's nothing. I've had headaches after a night of hard drinking that hurt worse. . . . Ah, where are you, my cowardly assassin? That copse of trees ahead is my guess. The cover is thick enough to conceal someone hiding, though if he is at all canny and saw he missed, he should be slipping away as we speak."

"Why would anyone shoot at you?" Julia was amazed at how distraught she felt. And how *safe* she felt pressed against him, even with an assailant in the woods intent on firing deadly bullets in their direction. There was something comforting in her husband's easy, bold confidence . . . and something undoubtedly sensual about lying beneath his tall form, whether on a road or in a bed. She could feel the lean, muscular hardness of his body and the protective embrace of his arms.

"Now that"—his dark gaze was amused and speculative as it shifted to her face—"is an interesting question, sweet Julia, isn't it? Who would have a motive to kill me?"

Looking into his eyes, she said slowly, "Adain seems a logical choice."

"Aye, I agree. Too logical, lass. You no longer trust him, I realize that, but do you think he's stupid?"

As she'd known her cousin all her life, Julia knew full well that Adain was intelligent—and what was more, a very good shot. Had he been aiming at them from such a short distance, she doubted he would miss. She shook her head. "Who else, then?"

"I don't know. But what would the rest of Scotland think if I had been shot dead, as surely was the intention?"

All that potent energy and sexual charm gone? Julia fought a stab of fear and sorrow at the thought of the vital and attractive Robbie McCray slain. Impulsively she reached up and touched his cheek. "I'm sure they would think my cousin the villain," she whispered.

"And that he shot me in a jealous rage over you." His statement was thoughtful, and Robbie eased off her, getting to his feet in one graceful, athletic movement. "Stay down for a moment or two while I make sure it is safe."

"Be careful," she said, rolling to watch him vault onto his horse, the big stallion shaking his head and whinnying. Robbie turned toward the woods, his dark hair gleaming in the afternoon sun, the beautiful day suddenly taking on an ominous cast as she thought of an unknown villain waiting and willing to kill. Her husband's white shirt was decidedly bloody, Julia saw as the horse plunged away, one sleeve streaked dark red, his jacket discarded earlier in deference to the warm afternoon.

When he returned a few minutes later, he slid from his horse and helped Julia to her feet. "There are fresh tracks behind the copse, but our friend is gone."

"Let me look at your arm." Julia felt a fresh wave of horror over what might have happened, her gaze riveted on the patch of scarlet wetness on his left sleeve.

"It'll keep until we get back to the house." Robbie shrugged dismissively and gave her one of his reckless, intoxicating grins. "There you can play nursemaid all you like, my sweet. In fact, I might need quite a bit of your . . . attention. My arm aside, there are certain parts of my anatomy that could use a little ministration from my beautiful wife."

Damn the man—is he always so devastatingly and inherently sexual, even when bleeding and wounded?

Julia muttered, "You're impossible."

"I assume you mean impossible to resist?"

She couldn't help it. A small laugh escaped her lips at his deliberately outrageous leer.

"I haven't tried yet, as it would infringe on our bargain."

Somehow that declaration made her handsome husband's smile fade, his dark eyes taking on a look she wasn't sure she'd seen before. Without warning, he pulled her close into the circle of his arms and kissed her deeply, his mouth insistent and seductive, his tongue plunging between her parted lips and taking possession.

For a moment, the lovely afternoon faded, the whisper of the breeze in the golden leaves did not exist . . . and all Julia could do was kiss him back, her hands clutching his broad shoulders and her body tightening in treacherous excitement.

When he lifted his head, he murmured roughly, "To hell with our bargain, Mrs. McCray."

Lifting her lashes, she asked in confusion, "What?"

"This is a *marriage*, not a . . . a negotiated arrangement." He sounded almost angry, his finely chiseled face showing no sign of his usual capricious charm.

Off balance, Julia reminded him sharply, "You married me for your ships, McCray."

"Perhaps."

"What the devil does that mean?" Julia stepped back, freeing herself from his embrace, tilting her chin up, afraid of the swirling emotions that were suddenly rising inside her. "Please don't try to tell me you were struck with passion that night back in Edinburgh or some such rot."

"All right," he said agreeably, turning toward her horse and catching the reins. "I won't tell you that."

It was unreasonable, it was foolish, but Julia remembered Scotland's wildest, most dashingly gorgeous bachelor admitting his romantic dream of a loving wife and a large family. Certainly they seemed compatible in bed, but surely any woman would melt to a puddle when faced with Robbie McCray's formidable skill in the boudoir. However, that did not mean they were falling in love.

Did it?

Hell, she thought violently, letting him help her mount her horse, the last thing she needed was to tumble head over heels for such an arrogantly good-looking, high-handed, wickedly sensual man as her husband.

Once upon a time, she had believed she loved Adain.

And look where that had gotten her. Betrayed, bereft, and disillusioned. No, it was better if she accepted the pleasure to be found in Robbie's arms but guarded her heart.

He'd had a splitting headache all day, which served him right. Grateful that Edward and Therese had left a little earlier, Adain nursed a cup of ale and stifled a low groan as his younger brother let out a shout of triumph and quickly pounced on one of the pieces on the chessboard.

"Your queen," Arthur declared, grinning. "Adain, you've lost your queen."

"I certainly have," he responded quietly, Julia's lovely face swimming up from his disloyal memory, her soft lips and long-lashed emerald eyes haunting him. She shouldn't belong to another man, but it was just harsh, hurtful reality that she did.

Sensitive always, even though he was young, Arthur seemed to catch the implications of his response, the gleeful smile fading from his face. "I'm sorry."

"So am I, but that doesn't seem to help ease this incessant ache." Getting to his feet, Adain paced across his study to stare out the window. "When you are older, Arthur, you will understand better the vulnerability a man experiences when he loves a woman. To think of her in McCray's bed—"

He broke off, watching the low breeze swirl a few leaves across the dying grass of the courtyard as the sunset poured bloodred across the horizon, staining the low roll of the hills.

His brother said awkwardly, "At least he isn't a bad fellow. She seems to like him well enough. I mean . . . they stare at each other a lot. . . . Oh, hell, I'm not helping, am I?"

"No, he doesn't seem to be a bad fellow." Adain turned and gave his brother the ghost of a smile. "I wish he were, damn him."

"Why do you suppose someone shot at him?"

A deep voice spoke from the doorway. "Probably because whoever killed your uncle isn't happy about my decision to stay on a few more days and ask a lot of questions."

The interruption wasn't a surprise. Adain had been expecting McCray to seek him out since his return, but Julia had dragged him off immediately to tend to his wound, and McCray hadn't exactly resisted. What man would? Adain acknowledged, for having a beautiful woman fussing over you had to be one of the joys of the world.

"How's the arm?" he asked, looking toward where McCray stood, more for politeness than anything, because chances were Julia's husband had been shot because of his openly declared desire to help Adain clear his name.

Looking at a glance none the worse for wear, McCray strolled in and helped himself to the whiskey decanter. "It's nothing. I went to see John Hexham this afternoon. He thinks Randal must have met up with our murderer, and Hexham wants to help us see justice done."

Adain frowned. "I also questioned him, but he was distant and unhelpful, telling me that he and Randal weren't really well acquainted."

McCray glanced at Arthur, and then, turning back, said neutrally, "I think Mr. Hexham values his privacy more than most of us and probably wished to be left out of any investigation. However, now that so many months have passed and Randal is still missing, he fears like the rest of us that his friend has met with foul play."

Though he doubted his younger brother caught the implication, Adain had no trouble reading the meaning in those carefully said words. He'd wondered himself a time or two over his cousin's sexual orientation, especially since they were of a similar age but so different in the way they reacted to women. Randal had never shown the slightest interest in the usual pursuits of randy young men, including losing one's virginity as soon as possible. But then again, he wasn't interested in drinking or gambling either, so Adain had assumed it was simply Randal's quiet, reclusive nature that made him so shy. He said with resignation, "I see. How is Hexham going to aid us?"

"By asking a few questions here and there . . . You and I are conspicuous, Cameron, but he is not. He also has friends in some high circles and is accustomed to secrets and intrigue. I'll be curious to hear if he finds out anything significant." Robbie sipped his drink, remarkably nonchalant for someone who had been the victim of a murderous attack just hours before. In truth, it was impossible to miss the fact that Julia's new husband had the air of a confident, fearless, *satisfied* man.

"And in the meanwhile?" Adain tempered his resentment by focusing on how he wanted Julia to be happy, and if McCray proved, surprisingly, to be the man who could give her that happiness, he would have to accept it. "We can hardly sit here and do nothing. That bullet might just as easily have hit Julia."

"Yes." McCray's expression darkened, a lethal gleam appearing in his dark eyes. His mouth twisted dangerously. "Our cowardly friend made a grievous error this afternoon. Before, I was only casually interested in your dilemma, but now it is personal."

"I think I get first crack at whoever has done his best to destroy my good name and rob me of my loved ones," Adain pointed out tersely.

For a moment, their gazes clashed, and then McCray said grudgingly, "I suppose you should be the one to kill him."

"Damn right I should be, McCray."

From his seat by the chessboard, Arthur grinned. "I wish the murderous bastard were here, listening to the two of you argue over which one gets to skewer him first. It would serve him right to have his blood run cold."

McCray lifted his glass and drained it, setting it aside with a definite click. "His blood will run, one way or the other, lad. In the meantime, I think Julia should stay in the house, where there are servants and family around her. Someone dangerous is out there, and I don't want her in the line of fire."

For the first time since he'd learned of it, Adain was able to feel a glimmer of amusement over McCray's being wed to his lovely, but undeniably headstrong cousin "I wish you luck with that," he said sardonically. "Julia won't like the notion of being confined to the indoors. Not one bit."

"Yes, that's the same conclusion I've come to myself," Robbie muttered, rubbing his lean jaw. "You've known her much longer. Any suggestions on how to approach this, Cameron?"

Adain found some small measure of satisfaction in being able to shake his head. "No. I'm afraid, McCray, that problem is *all* yours."

Chapter 7

Stacks of correspondence sat in disarray across the surface of the desk and spilled onto the floor in disreputable piles. Eyeing the mess with disdain, Therese Gibbons pulled the empty glass from her brother's lax hand and, in one swift motion, threw it across the room. It shattered against the hearth with a satisfyingly loud crack of breaking crystal.

Edward blinked, sitting up groggily, his red-rimmed eyes bleary, the clothes he'd been wearing since the day before sadly wrinkled and stained. "What the hell?"

"It's midafternoon, you little toad."

"I was sleeping," Edward muttered thickly. "Just a little nap . . . up late last night."

Disgusted by both his appearance and the rank odor of sour wine, Therese said, "Did you win?"

His eyes took on that shifty light she despised. "A little."

"Don't lie to me, Eddie."

As usual, he protested. "I never lie to you. Good God, Therese."

He *did* lie, though. And on the rare occasions he actually won money in those ill-fated gambling bouts he couldn't seem to avoid, he hid it from her like some sneaking tavern wench. Resisting the urge to slap his unshaven face, Therese snapped, "I've servants to pay. Hand it over. The cook is threatening to quit again. How do you think that will look? The exalted Earl of Larkin without means to put food on the table."

Sullenly, like a little boy, he said under his breath, "I don't give a bloody damn how it looks."

"You will when you are in the kitchen, trying to fry a piece of ham or cook a potato, you useless fool. Now give me the money at once and go upstairs to clean up. You smell like the bed of some cheap wharfside whore."

"Not a whore," he declared softly, defensive and triumphant. "Richmond's wife. She proved to be most . . . obliging."

It was unfortunate that Edward had been born both weak and good-looking, though Therese saw with a critical eye that his dissolute lifestyle was catching up with her brother. Tiny red veins threaded around his nose, and he was no longer quite so trim and athletically built. What the insipid Lady Richmond saw in him was a mystery, for he was usually so deep in his cups by evening that he couldn't be more than a fumbling buffoon in bed. "Can't you keep your cock in your breeches for one night?" she asked sharply. "It would serve you right if you found yourself in a duel over the non-existent honor of one of your sluts. Then what would I do?"

"Maybe you could kill off Julia and have the randy McCray and her inheritance," Edward suggested with a small, nasty sneer. "Since Adain doesn't seem to be coming up to snuff very easily."

Actually, the idea of killing off Julia Cameron had long held some appeal. The ungrateful wench was too lucky for her own good: beautiful, rich, and having enjoyed her handsome cousin fawning all over her ever since she was barely a woman. Even her impetuous marriage to the roguish Robbie McCray seemed to be touched with the same cursed good fortune, for by all accounts the two lovers spent an inordinate amount of time in the bedroom, and Julia seemed content enough with her devil's bargain. As Therese glanced around the disheveled mess of her brother's study, the once elegant furnishings starting to show the edge of shabbiness and neglect, she smiled coldly. Castle Cameron was a stately house, the grounds well kept, the servants trained and deferential. Being mistress there would be a pure pleasure. Adain was still a very promising prospect. "I might do just that," she murmured.

Pushing his rumpled hair off his brow, Edward said stupidly, "Do what?"

"Kill her."

"You cannot be serious." Her brother gaped, his mouth falling open unattractively.

"Adain can't forget her if the little bitch is still around."

Vigorously shaking his head, Edward said, "You're mad. The risk is too great, and she has McCray's sword to protect her." He contradicted himself in an ineffectual lie. "Adain will come around, Therese."

"One can," she observed coolly, "never have money soon enough, Edward, when one is in our dire circumstances."

Her brother looked a little pale. "Killing McCray was not a bad idea, not when you were going to vouch for Adain's innocence by telling everyone he was with you alone at the time of the shooting. That way he would have to marry you to protect your reputation, and undoubtedly to save his neck. It solves two problems, both put-ting an end to McCray's infernal inquisitiveness into the first two murders *and* snaring Adain very neatly in our trap."

"But you missed him, you incompetent idiot." Therese still felt furious over the lost opportunity. She'd managed to lure Adain into a walk in the gardens alone, and was going to claim they'd been *occupied* once Julia accused him of murdering her husband. She knew enough about her quarry to count on his sense of honor if she sacrificed her reputation to prove his innocence. Adain would have married her.

Edward's mouth tightened mutinously. "I am better at close range with a pistol."

"Let's hope that's true."

Suspiciously, her brother eyed her. "What do you mean by that?"

Therese elevated her brows. "Time is running short. Already rumors are leaking out about our shaky finances. It's time for a new plan, don't you think?"

The sky was a gorgeous blue, and out the window of her bedroom, Julia could see the water of the loch ripple in tiny frothy waves.

"Stop it." Half laughing, but also half irritated, she slapped her husband's hand away from the bodice of her chemise. He'd man-aged to untie it, she saw, the ribbon dangling and the material gap-ing open. She said firmly, "I am going to get dressed and go for a ride, McCray. It's a beautiful day and I need some fresh air."

"If it's a ride you want, lass, I'll gladly oblige." Ignoring her protests, her husband slid one of his long-fingered hands skillfully between the parted cloth and found her bare breast. His grin was both cheeky and unrepentant as he began to stroke and cup her flesh.

And damn him, she melted predictably, his sensual allure like a potent drug she'd become addicted to in the past days, her knees weakening. However, she'd come to suspect that not only did her handsome husband ardently enjoy making love to her for hours on end, but also that some of his amorous impulses, like at this moment, were conveniently designed to keep her from leaving the house. "Not that kind of ride," she muttered, finding his hand moving against her skin very distracting.

Lightly pinching her nipple, he leaned forward and whispered in her ear, "I promise I can be more fun than a cross-country gallop, lass. I'll even let you be on top and set the pace. Think of that movement, with me deep inside you."

Her resolve crumbled a little at the sensation of his warm breath against her sensitive skin. "We made love this morning," she said in weak protest, swaying a little as he brought her breast to full aching arousal.

"That was hours ago. . . . I need you again." Robbie slipped his other hand into her chemise, so both breasts were captive in his palms.

"The servants talk about us." It was an inane thing to say to the man whom most of Scotland whispered over as a sexual legend, and he chuckled.

"Good." His mouth caressed her cheek, and he kissed her lips with lingering pressure. "Tell me, what are they saying? Am I living up to their expectations?"

"As far as I can tell, you are *up* most of the time, McCray."

"I certainly am right now, sweet wife."

He was, she saw as her gaze traveled to the crotch of his breeches, that telltale bulge not a surprise. Though she hadn't ever known another man carnally, there seemed little doubt that Robbie's libido was proportionate to his reputation as a virile lover. In bed, he was tireless, and she was always the one who fell asleep first in contented exhaustion. One last time, she argued, "I don't want to waste this lovely afternoon."

He looked into her eyes then, his dark gaze so hot it made her catch her breath. "Now, there's a challenge if I've ever heard one, love."

He had her out of her newly donned chemise so fast she hardly realized what had happened, and in moments he also was magnificently nude, the toned muscle and sinew under his bronzed skin accented by the afternoon sunshine. Robbie kissed her with his usual audacious abandon, all invading, possessive tongue and firm lips, his hands outrageously roaming to every sensitive spot on her body. When his fingers slid into the cleft between her legs, it felt so decadently wonderful she gasped against his mouth.

"Wet and warm and ready, my love . . . here."

He tumbled her easily onto the bed, but instead of mounting her at once, he rolled to his back and smiled with a provocative invitation that could have seduced a nun. Long, elegant fingers went to his impressive erection, lightly stroking the hard length that pulsed against his flat stomach. "Sit on this," her husband suggested huskily, wiping the seeping tip. "Take it all the way inside you and ride it like a wild stallion."

Sit on it?

Not for the first time, Julia wondered if maybe she was too easily intrigued by his blatant sexuality and utterly masculine allure. His touch, his teasing smile, those seductively beautiful dark eyes . . . she was drawn into a spell that held her captive, unable to resist both his physical possession and his vibrant personality.

She'd thought she had loved Adain, but it had felt nothing like this unruly passion. This bothered her, for while she had sought out a husband for pragmatic reasons, it was something altogether different to fall in love with him.

How many women had succumbed to Robbie McCray's sensual charm? Probably too many to count, because aside from sexual prowess, he was infinitely likable. God help her, even Adain seemed to be warming up to the man.

Moving slowly, she eased up his long body, feeling his hands go to her hips as she rose above him and spread her legs to straddle his torso. Grasping the hardened length of his engorged shaft, Julia shut her eyes and exhaled in pleasure as she guided the tip to her throbbing entrance and slowly sank down.

Robbie made a sound, a purely male groan that indicated his enjoyment as his cock filled her inch by inch. When she was fully impaled, Julia followed the urging of his hands and began to move, lifting up to sink down, the motion actually reminiscent of a rolling canter on a fast horse. Hands braced on his broad shoulders, she rose and fell, finding the slide of his sex inside hers a revelation in pleasure. The delicious friction made her pant, her long hair swinging with each upward thrust and downward glide.

"That's it." Robbie's eyes were half-closed, thick, dark lashes a contrast to the angle of his cheekbones. "I love the way your gorgeous tits move when you are on top of me like this."

She could also feel her breasts sway as she rode his cock, the gentle bobbing motion somehow adding to the erotic enjoyment of what she was doing. Almost frantic as the pleasure built, Julia tightened her thighs and pushed up and down as fast as she could, a small sob of need escaping her throat. It felt wonderful, the wetness of her arousal coating his stiff cock, her body humming, it was so tight and ready for climax.

And when her husband slid his fingers between their melded bodies and stroked her, Julia cried out, the gentle manipulation exactly what she craved, her orgasm so intense she went completely still as her inner muscles clenched and tightened, rapturous joy taking away any rational thought. She was barely aware when Robbie rolled her over and began to move, thrusting hard twice into her before he groaned and the hot spill of his seed rushed inside her still quivering passage.

Damp, relaxed, and in each other's arms, they lay comfortably on the soft bed as their respiration returned to normal. Julia was discovering a world of sexual pleasure with her new husband, of that there was little doubt, but she was also awakening to the pure joy of tactile sensation. The slightly stubbled hardness of his jaw, the smoothness of his warm skin over the bulge of those impressive muscles, the satiny strength of his erect penis with that soft sac beneath. When they were still intertwined like they were at this moment, she could indulge her curiosity and let her fingers explore his body, and he quite often did the same thing with hers, stroking her skin, tangling his hands in her long tresses, his mouth caressing her temple and cheek. The intimacy of it was startling, but . . . wonderful.

Tracing a line down Robbie's broad chest, her head resting on his shoulder, Julia couldn't help but finally ask the question that had been plaguing her, even though she was fairly certain she wasn't going to like the answer. "Is it like this always?"

His eyes narrowed slightly, a purely male wariness invading his dark gaze. "Is what like what?"

Julia bit her lip, trying to stifle the pangs of jealousy and only mildly succeeding. "All the scores of women you've bedded, McCray, did you lie with them afterward and hold them close, whispering to them like you do to me? Did you make them feel . . ."

When she trailed off, not sure how to finish the sentence, Robbie's hand found her chin and cupped it, forcing her to look up at him. "Did I make them feel what?"

"Like you loved them." Almost defiantly, Julia met his gaze.

"Is that how I make you feel, lass?"

This turning of the tables was not precisely what she'd had in mind when she broached the subject. Julia sat up and pulled free in a flurry of dark, disheveled hair and said tartly, "I didn't say that."

Robbie reached over and hauled her back into his arms, sending her sprawling across his bare chest. "Don't leave now, my bewitching wife; this discussion is just getting interesting. So, let's make sure I understand you. You think I might be falling in love with you, is that it? It only seems fair that you should also feel that way about me. I think you do. There's fire between us, and it is starting to take hold and burn brightly."

He was impossibly arrogant, she thought with irritation, though the fear he might be right was a niggling suspicion she didn't care to acknowledge. "Let me go, McCray. It was a foolish thing to say, and that isn't what I meant at all."

"What if I told you that it's true, lass? I've never felt this way about any woman, whether I bedded her or not." He said the words in a quiet voice that was completely unlike his usual teasing tone.

Julia stopped struggling to break free and stared. His expression was serious and there was uncharacteristic vulnerability in the set of his beautiful mouth. "You like to fuck me," she said quickly, using the crude word he often said just to shock her.

Robbie laughed, his mouth curving wickedly. "Aye, I'll not deny that. I like to fuck you." His hands smoothed down her back, and he gently squeezed her naked buttocks. "But there's more to you than just your delectable body, Julia, and I'm discovering more every day. I never tire of your company. I admire your fire, the way you challenge me, the kind ways you have with the servants, your sassy mouth." His gaze dropped suggestively. "In truth, your mouth appeals to me in many ways. Kiss me, Julia, for I've just answered your question."

Was he sincere?

His power to charm and disarm was potent; she shouldn't forget that. But her arms slid around his neck, and she kissed him anyway, a lover's kiss, tender and soft. He responded in kind, cradling her close as he seduced her lips and tongue with skilled, ardent persuasion. And moments later, when he pressed her back onto the tumbled sheets and entered her, it was with slow and tantalizing long strokes, their bodies moving fluidly as they mated, gazes locked in sensual communion.

She'd never experienced such pleasure, such physical and emotional elation.

But then again, she'd never made love before.

The study door was ajar, the voices within subdued. Entering the room, Robbie closed the door behind him and said mildly, "Sorry I am late."

Adain Cameron glanced up, his face briefly tightening as he said caustically, "Glad you could spare a minute to join us, McCray. I sent someone up for you almost an hour ago."

"I must have missed their knock." Since he actually liked Julia's cousin upon closer acquaintance and knew the struggle Cameron had with his jealousy, Robbie didn't expound on why he had ignored the servant at the door. He nodded at John Hexham, noting how the young man looked both grim and triumphant. "I take it you found out something useful."

Still dressed for traveling, his boots dusty and his fair hair wind-tossed, Hexham nodded. "I found out plenty, sir; of that you can be sure. It is exactly as you suspected. The Earl of Larkin has markers from here to Edinburgh and back. His credit is no longer good almost anywhere in Scotland, and word is beginning to spread. The estate is heavily mortgaged, and matters only seem to be growing more dire each passing day."

Adain Cameron said stiffly, "I've known Edward my whole life, McCray. He has his weaknesses for wine and cards; it's no secret. But that doesn't make him a murderer."

"What about his sister?"

"She's a woman. The idea of Therese killing anyone is ludicrous."

"Is it?" Robbie asked, narrowing his gaze. It was getting dark, and the open study windows let in the soft sounds of birds as they gathered in the dusk. "She's a woman, aye. I've met her kind before. That particular brand of cold calculation makes me want to get on my horse and ride away as fast as possible. I know they were here when your uncle was murdered, but tell me, were by chance the Gibbonses here visiting also when Randal disappeared?"

Adain's mouth tightened. "Yes, they were. They stay often."

"It doesn't make you suspicious that every time someone comes to harm, your friend Edward and his sister are here?"

Cameron shoved himself to his feet and paced across the room. He muttered, "Before now, no. Why should it? The Gibbons family have been allies of the Camerons for literally centuries, the association starting generations ago. I don't remember not knowing Edward."

Hexham cleared his throat. "There's more, sir. A few years ago, an aunt, one who had a modest fortune that she intended to leave to Edward Gibbons, fell to her death from the balcony off her bedroom. No one could figure out how it could have happened, for the woman was healthy and in her right mind, and the railing was sound. Lady Therese happened to be visiting the aunt at the time. The money staved up the earl's failing fortunes for a while."

"Good God." Cameron stopped pacing, his expression growing disillusioned. "Therese?"

"She's a fair-sized woman," Robbie pointed out coolly. "Perfectly capable of tossing an old lady off a balcony, at a guess."

John Hexham stated flatly, "Randal told me she tried to seduce him." The young man's face reddened, but he went on doggedly, "He refused, naturally. . . . Even if he had been so inclined, I think he was beginning to guess at the same thing McCray suspects. He told me she came to his room, naked under her robe, and offered him her body. He certainly was not going to fall for such an open attempt to trap him into a marriage that had been suggested by her brother to his father many times but held no appeal for him. They had words and he wondered if she suspected his . . . secret. Not long afterward, he disappeared."

"She tried the same ploy with me a few nights ago," Adain admitted, looking faintly ill. "Luckily, I wasn't *that* drunk. Damnation . . . I don't like what you are saying, McCray, but you could be right."

"Didn't Edward conveniently find your uncle's body?"

"Bloody hell, yes, he did. My God," Adain rasped, "do they know what they've done? Two good men gone, all for their wicked greed. My life, also, ruined by the black whispers and suspicion."

Robbie gave him a direct look, the topic not comfortable for either of them but needing to be addressed. "Whatever convinced Julia that you murdered her father came from Therese Gibbons. My wife mentioned it but wouldn't elaborate."

"Therese has been particularly friendly toward Julia this past year. I thought it was just because she was trying to ease her loss and give comfort."

Robbie doubted that—more like she was trying to manipulate the situation to suit her plan. He said coolly, "My guess is that once she discovered Randal would never marry her, the lady was forced to adjust her focus, and you became her new target. The trouble was, you stood to inherit if your cousin also turned up dead, but you were already engaged to Julia. Therefore she needed to discredit you in the eyes of your fiancée, and she apparently succeeded very well. Whatever the evidence is, Julia will not say, at a guess because she holds enough affection for you still that she does not care to see you hang."

Shoving a shaking hand into his thick hair, Cameron snarled his response. "If what you say is true, I'll kill Therese with my bare hands."

"I doubt we have enough evidence for a magistrate to actually consider arresting either of them," Robbie mused, rubbing his jaw.

"Randal is still missing," Hexham said bitterly, his expression bleak. "If they killed him, I want to know where his body is to at least give him a decent burial."

"It would help Julia, also, to know what happened," Robbie agreed.

Adain said in terse decisiveness, "Maybe the best course is for me to talk to Edward. He is not an assertive man and will probably break under direct accusation, if done properly, with my sword at his throat."

John Hexham jumped to his feet. "I'll go with you."

If there was one thing Robbie preferred it was action over patience. "We'll all go. Let's not forget that one man is dead and another most likely murdered as well. If we want to intimidate the earl into a confession, the more of us the better."

Adain gave a brusque nod. "It will take us two hours. Let's ride."

Chapter 8

Julia picked at her meal, too restless to have an appetite. Her husband's impetuous departure with her cousin and Randal's friend was disturbing, since all three men had jumped on their horses and left without warning. It had been almost dark, which certainly seemed an odd time to leave, and Robbie had explained nothing beyond giving a quick promise that he would be back before dawn.

They'd been armed, and certainly not lighthearted.

What the devil is going on?

Toying with her wineglass, she frowned.

"That scowl does nothing for your pretty face." Mrs. Dunbar chuckled as she bustled into the dining room, shaking her head and clucking her tongue. "As a new bride I suppose you are allowed to miss your husband, but face it, lassie, it has only been a few hours."

"I don't miss him," Julia protested, biting her lower lip. "I'm just curious about where they all went in such a hurry."

"Robert McCray isn't a man to explain his actions, as far as I can tell. That bonny lad is a law unto himself."

The fond look in the older woman's eyes was inexplicably irritating. "You certainly seem to have fallen under his spell quickly enough," Julia muttered.

"I like a man who knows how to smile at a woman and look like he means it." The housekeeper gave Julia's uneaten food a knowing look. "And I'm not the only one under the spell of young Robbie. Whyever you went haring off to Edinburgh to marry a stranger, it's a fact that you didn't make a bad decision. Though Adain loves you, the truth is, he's not the right man for you. Ever since you were a little girl, there's been a taste for adventure in your nature. Robbie McCray will be an adventure your whole life. And not just in the bedroom," she added with a twinkle of amusement, "should the two of you ever choose to leave it for more than a few minutes."

Julia felt a blush climb up her neck to heat her cheeks. "That's his fault."

"Is it? A girl should have such troubles." Whisking away the full plate, Mrs. Dunbar left the room.

As she sipped her wine, Julia couldn't help but wonder if maybe it was true if tragedy had never struck and she had married Adain as planned, would she have been discontented?

"My lady? This just came for you."

She saw one of the maids holding a small folded piece of vellum. "Thank you, Cilla." Taking it, she cracked the plain seal and quickly read the contents.

A feeling of dread pooled in the pit of her stomach, making her glad she hadn't eaten her dinner. She got to her feet with alacrity, tossed aside her napkin, and told the waiting girl, "I'm going out for a short walk. Tell Mrs. Dunbar I'll be back in a little while."

Edward Gibbons wiped his nose with the back of his hand, his pale face beaded with sweat. Though he stank of cheap wine, he'd sobered up with remarkable haste when the three of them had burst into his house and interrupted his dinner—which looked decidedly unappetizing, Robbie decided sardonically, so perhaps they were doing him a favor.

The Earl of Larkin cowered in his chair and didn't even bother to ask them for an explanation for why they had barged into his house, a fact that was both damning and chilling. "It was Therese's idea," he said in a wobbly voice. "By God, Adain, you've known me all your life. I despise violence."

Both hands on the table, Robbie leaned forward deliberately. "I don't. So unless you want to test me, Gibbons, keep talking. Spilling your blood holds definite appeal at this moment. Why waste a magistrate's time when I could administer justice myself and save us all the trouble of a trial?"

Edward's watery eyes widened and he whined, "I have no quarrel with you, McCray."

Adain Cameron's silver eyes were bleak with betrayal. "How could you kill Rufus and Randal, Edward? They were fine men and your friends. By God, I defended you when McCray first suggested you and Therese could be involved!"

"I didn't kill Randal. *She* did." The protest was petulant, like a sullen child who was not actually repentant over the act, but more over being caught.

Robbie pulled Gibbons up by his stained shirtfront, half lifting him from the chair, not bothering to hide the disgust in his expression. "If you admit to strangling an old man, you sniveling bit of refuse, you aren't any better than your scheming, amoral sister."

"She made me!" Edward shrieked the words, squirming to get free. "She's insane . . . always babbling about Castle Cameron and how unfair it is that we were left this house and not something grander. She covets your fortune"—he shot Adain a desperate look—"and means to have it by fair means or foul. If Randal had just agreed to marry her, he would still be alive."

"You bastard." John Hexham said it without hiding his raw emotion, his thin face ashen. "What did she do to him? Where is he?"

When Edward didn't answer at once, Robbie gave him an encouraging shake.

Gibbons gasped. "McCray . . . you're half a head taller than me and stones heavier—"

"Don't forget damned furious and repulsed by being this close to you, you damnable coward." Robbie made his tone as lethal as possible. "I'd squash you like an insect and not blink an eye, Larkin, so answer the man's question. Now."

"The cliff!" Edward babbled out the confession. "She followed Randal to the cliff by the loch, where he liked to sit and write his wretched poetry. There she pushed him off, right onto the rocks below. The water must have taken his body, because I went the next day and it was gone."

"No." John Hexham said the word as a single protest of pain.

"Damn you to hell, Edward." Adain also looked sick at heart, his face reflecting sorrow and lost hope. "He never hurt anyone in his life. Why didn't you stop her?"

"I couldn't. . . . She's out of control. Anyone with an ounce of sense is afraid to cross her; ask the servants." A low sob escaped the earl's throat, tears beginning to stream down his unshaven cheeks. "It's getting worse. . . . Now she wants to kill Julia. I pleaded with her to abandon the notion, knowing we would eventually be suspected if she follows this mad course, but she is determined."

Robbie felt as if someone had slapped him across the face. "What?" he hissed, tightening his grip and lifting Gibbons completely free of the chair. "Kill Julia? Why?"

"She's envious and afraid Adain will not forget her easily. If Julia is out of the way, she speculates it will be easier to capture his attention."

Adain shared Robbie's sudden fear. It was evident in his voice when he asked hoarsely, "Where is she, Edward? Where's Therese now?"

"The cliff." Dangling helplessly in Robbie's grip, the earl sniffled. "It worked so well with Randal, she said she was going to lure Julia to the cliff."

Thin moonlight helped illuminate the grassy slope, giving the landscape a surreal feel. The night was warm for the time of year, which was pleasant, but that special tang that came only in autumn filled the air. Julia walked with purpose, finding that her heart beat rapidly in both excitement and apprehension.

Meet me at Loch Cam in an hour and tell no one about this. I'm frightened for you—you may be in danger. You do not know whom you can trust. I know what happened to your brother.

It was foolish, perhaps, to go meet the mysterious person who had written the note, but since both Adain and Robbie were gone, she had little choice, she reminded herself. If she ignored it, and ignored the warning to keep it to herself, would she lose the only opportunity that had surfaced in the past year to learn about Randal's disappearance?

Casting an uneasy glance at the shadowed woods to her left, Julia skirted a small knoll and started up the path to the top, where there was a glorious view of the water.

Randal had loved it here. He had been a friend as well as a brother, and she missed him terribly.

The breeze was soft as she neared the rocky summit over the lake, tugging at her hair.

"You came." The voice from nearby made Julia nearly trip over her own feet.

Casting around, she stopped, and felt sudden relief as Therese stepped into view from a shadowed niche between two boulders. Julia's hand went to her heart and she gasped. "Good heavens, you scared me nigh unto death. What are you doing here? Did you also get a note?"

Clad in a dark cloak, her friend incongruously carried a pistol, which she extended in front of her body. Therese said coolly, "Get a note? Like the one I sent you?"

Julia shook her head, staring in disbelief at the gun pointed at her chest. "What do you mean? You . . . you sent a note?"

"Not a note, *the* note. The one you just received. Getting you alone was a definite challenge, but I decided if I offered up information on Randal's death, you'd come running along without your attentive husband. His departure earlier was a boon."

In the pale illumination, Therese's face looked foreign and

frightening, her teeth bared in a sneer that made Julia stare. "What's wrong with you?"

"Do you want the information or not?"

"You have information on what happened to Randal?" Julia was almost lightheaded from confusion and fear. "If so, why haven't you told me before?"

"Because I suspected that if you knew I killed him, you wouldn't exactly be ecstatic to hear it."

Thoroughly shocked at the open confession, Julia took a wobbly step backward. "What?" she asked her friend incredulously. "*You* killed my brother?"

"He was never going to marry me." Therese followed, the weapon in her hand extended in a way that left little doubt she would use it. "In case you didn't know, women are not his preference."

That remark was mystifying enough that Julia's mind simply rejected it. "Where is he?" she cried, starting to tremble, backing toward where the lip of the promontory stuck out over the rippling water. "What did you do?"

Therese gestured carelessly with the gun toward the loch. "He's there, I suppose."

"Or maybe not."

The sound of the male voice made them both freeze. Julia felt the slide of the familiar cadence along her skin like a touch, while Therese's face went rigid. As she watched, the woman she'd thought to be her friend stared at something behind her, turning as white in the pouring moonlight as bleached bone. Therese gasped. "No."

Whirling around, Julia saw her brother standing there, thin and ethereal, his eyes like dark holes in a pale face. She wasn't one to believe in ghosts, but at this moment . . .

She whispered, "Randal?"

"Julia . . . move away."

Not certain whether she was dreaming, she stumbled a few feet to the side. Her brother looked the same, tall and dark haired, but there was a ferocity in his expression that was frightening. He said slowly, "You killed me, Therese. Pushed me off"—his hand lifted and slowly pointed—"there."

"Yes . . . yes, I killed you." Therese seemed to have trouble keeping hold of the gun, and it wobbled. "You're . . . dead. Dead. Go away."

"I don't think you can kill me twice." Slowly, he began an inexorable walk forward. "Don't even try."

Backing up, clumsy and tripping, Therese tried to both keep the gun trained on Randal's advancing form and control her obvious fear. Frantically, her gaze swung to the rocks behind her, and then back to what she clearly thought was a ghostly apparition.

Now that the first shock had passed, Julia wasn't quite so sure. He was thinner than she remembered, and dressed differently, in plain clothes suited to someone shorter and broader. Would a specter change his clothes in the afterlife?

Would a ghost also bother to wrestle away a gun from a potential assailant? Even as she watched, her brother caught Therese's arm and twisted, eliciting a low cry of pain accompanied by the clattering of the weapon falling on the stones of the cliff. Though it was difficult to feel sorry for her, Therese's eerie screams rang out with increasing volume and the two of them staggered toward the edge.

Then all sounds stopped except for a faint, distant splash and only one figure stood there.

Heart pounding, Julia sank down on the path, no longer able to stand, not able to make herself follow and investigate. She closed her eyes and tears seeped between her lids, and she could not stop shaking. What kind of bizarre dream was this?

Then someone loomed over her, knelt, and a familiar voice said, "Julia?"

A very real pair of arms went around her as she shuddered, her face pressed against a solid shoulder that both comforted and brought tears to her eyes. "Randal?"

Her brother said in a matter-of-fact tone, "In the flesh."

Four hours in the saddle, half a bottle of whiskey, and a generous dose of Cameron drama, and all Robbie wanted was to go up and fall into bed and sleep. . . .

Well, perhaps not *just* sleep.

Julia sat next to him, her dark head on his shoulder, her lashes lowered slightly over her pale cheeks. Now and again, she opened her eyes to look at her brother in wonder, her remarkable green eyes soft with affectionate regard.

He knew what it was like to lose someone you loved, and her tangible happiness made *him* happy.

"So you knew Therese and Edward had killed your father," Robbie asked Randal, refraining from stroking his wife's lustrous hair by sheer will. "Didn't it make you wary? How did she catch you out by the cliff?"

Randal shook his head. "No, I didn't know they'd killed him. I knew she and Edward were in financial trouble. How bad it was exactly, I didn't guess. When she followed me that day, it didn't occur to me she would attack me. I didn't even try to defend my-self, I was so taken off guard." Color burned into the other man's cheeks in splotches, his fine bone structure reminiscent of his lovely sister's.

"I was only half conscious when she pushed me off the cliff and I hit the water below," Randal Cameron elaborated, "and I don't really remember anything after that. I think I must have washed onto shore, for when I woke, I was in the sheepherder's cottage."

Adain sat, drinking ale and watching his cousin with narrowed eyes, though his expression was more relaxed than Robbie had yet seen it. "Why didn't you contact us? We were looking for you. For that matter, I am sure we came by there, asking if you'd been seen. That cottage isn't ten miles from here. The old man said nothing about you."

Julia's brother shifted a little. "I healed very slowly. By the time I realized where and who I was, weeks had passed, maybe months. The sheepherder was kind, but also elderly and deaf, and I'm sure he didn't understand your questions. He died about a month ago, very peacefully in his sleep." Randal's gaze slid briefly to where John Hexham sat quietly in the corner. "I needed some time to sort things out, and when I discovered I was presumed dead, I took advantage of it. I went up to the cliff often to sit and think, though the walk was long. It's private there and close to home. I was never far away."

Hexham said quietly, as if they were the only two people in the room, "I can understand that, Ran."

"Can you?"

"I can't. How could you?" Julia stirred, straightening enough that Robbie snaked his arm around her waist to support her. Her mouth trembled. "We were frantic. Adain is right. You should have let us know right away."

"I'm sorry you were worried." Julia's brother looked contrite. "But please realize I took a severe blow to the head, and it took me a while to recover. For weeks, maybe months, I couldn't even see. As my vision returned and I realized where I was, I contemplated my return but, I confess, put it off. I knew Adain had things well in hand, probably better than I would ever manage. Believe me, if I had remembered sooner that Therese had been the one to push me off the cliff, I would have come home. As it was, I recalled flashes only. None of it was clear until tonight, when I saw her standing there, and I remembered all of it. I was on one of my late-night pilgrimages to the cliff and as I took the path from the opposite direction, I heard Julia's voice, and then Therese threatening her."

"Thanks be to God you were there," Robbie said fervently, looking down at his wife with his heart tightening. She looked fragile and exhausted.

And so very beautiful.

"Yes," Adain agreed, his expression somber. "I've sent men to inform the magistrate about all that has happened and to look for Therese's body. If she survived the fall, she'll hang."

Julia turned a little, her face poignantly unhappy as she stared at her cousin. "I owe you an apology, Adain. How . . . how do you say you are sorry you suspected a man of murder? The only thing in my defense is that Therese had evidence, for she claimed that Edward found the pin I gave you near my father's body. She had been such a supportive friend, so sympathetic, and I had no cause to think she would lie to me. With all the other ugly whispers, I am afraid I lost faith."

Adain's expression was bleak, but he forced a smile. "You were grieving. . . . We all were, but none as much. I wish you had come to me and told me about her accusation, but there is no way to rewrite what happened. I am also at fault because I didn't wish to tell you I'd lost the pin. It never occurred to me it might have been stolen, because it was unique, and if anyone else wore it they would be exposed as the thief. Therese was a ruthless and clever woman, and we were all taken in." He lifted a brow and glanced at Robbie. "If you hadn't brought McCray here, who knows, I might have ended up trapped into marrying her eventually."

That was going to be as close to a thanks, Robbie guessed wryly, as he would ever get from Adain Cameron for helping clear his name, but it would do. Standing in one fluid motion, he lifted Julia in his arms without regard for the gathered audience, making Mrs. Dunbar chuckle. Robbie said meaningfully, "If you will please excuse us, it has been an eventful evening and I think Julia needs to go to bed."

"She needs some sleep, young Robbie," the housekeeper said pointedly.

He grinned and winked. "Eventually."

Julia protested in an indignant hiss as she clutched his shoulders when they left the room. "Must you always be so . . . so impetuous!"

"Yes, lass, I must when it comes to you." A deliberate, devilishly suggestive smile curved his mouth as he headed for the stairs. When they got to Julia's room, he shouldered his way through the door and deposited her on the bed. Leaning down with his arms on either side of her body, he looked into her eyes, feeling as if his soul were caught in those shimmering emerald depths. "So what happens now?" he asked softly.

Her hand came up and her fingertips lightly traced his mouth in a tender gesture that made his heart skip a beat. "I imagine we're going to take our clothes off and you'll demonstrate once again why you are so notorious."

"That sounds like a reasonable prediction." His erection swelled, there was no doubt about it, but why wouldn't it, when Julia lay amid a tumble of silken skirts and ebony tresses, her eyes half-shut and her soft pink lips slightly parted? But his need aside, he was plagued with important, life-altering questions. He asked with honest raw emotion, "I meant now that your brother is safe. It changes everything, lass."

Her mouth trembled a little. "Randal is still alive, but it doesn't affect my inheritance. I still get half, since I married, so you'll get what you were promised."

"Damn the stupid ships."

"But—"

"Don't." His mouth came down hard, crushing hers, the kiss wild, yet tender. When he lifted his head, he said thickly, "Let's talk about the rest of our bargain. I am not releasing you from our arrangement. And since this is over, I'm leaving in the morning; what say you to that?"

"You are?" Her tongue swept out and licked her lower lip.

"Indeed. And you're going with me."

"Am I, now?"

Of course, it was just his luck to fall in love finally with a stubborn, raven-haired lass who would challenge him at every turn, he thought wryly. Served him right, most would say, as penance for his licentious past. "I want you to go with me," he amended.

"Why?"

How had he known she would ask that? Damn all, she was going to make him say it. "Because," he hedged, "if you don't, who will provide me with ghosts, murderous neighbors, and hostile former lovers? I might perish from boredom."

"I am merely entertainment to you, then?"

Why was it that women had such an infernal sense of how to wring the truth from a man? "No," he said, his throat tight. "You are my wife. I ask you humbly to share my life, Julia, and if you wish my heart, I pledge it to you."

Julia swallowed and blinked, her eyes filled suddenly with tears. After a small pause, she whispered, "I promised you children, I believe, McCray. There is only one way to get them, as far as I understand the process. Don't I have to go with you so that part of our bargain is fulfilled? Are you implying I'd go back on my word?"

Relief and desire flooded through him at the teasing tone of her voice and the open emotion shining in her green eyes. "Never, but you'll have to prove it."

He brushed a kiss across her mouth, whispering wickedly against her lips, "I won't fuck you unless you call me by my given name, beautiful Julia."

Breathlessly, she sighed. "Please . . . Robbie."

Book Three

Seducing Adain

Chapter 1

I t was a mere scythe, a pale crescent that barely illuminated the road. The kind of moon they called a traitor's moon, because it could hide any manner of ill deeds.

Adain Cameron put his booted heels to his horse, making the animal surge forward despite the encroaching darkness. The shots had been followed by a definitely female scream. The sound had come from up ahead, and as he rode around a bend in the road, he saw both the source and the reason for it.

A carriage sat in the middle of the road. He could see three men, one on horseback, two others in the act of dragging a young woman out of the vehicle. She screamed again as one of them lifted her free, her frantic struggles having little effect on her much larger assailants. A body lay on the ground, undoubtedly that of the hapless coachman.

Perfect, Adain thought.

If the truth be told, he was spoiling for a fight.

"Halt," he called harshly as he pulled his sword free. "What goes here?"

The man on horseback held the leads of his companions' horses, but he let them go as Adain charged up, reaching instead for the pistol jammed into his belt. Without hesitation, he leveled and fired, but Adain was on a moving horse and the shot luckily did no more than graze his sleeve.

With the slightest tug of the reins, his horse swerved, his sword flashed, and the bandit—for Adain had a fair idea of what was happening—uttered a low cry and pitched from the saddle.

That was one down. Not a bad start.

He pulled up his stallion and slid off, bloody sword in hand, and stood in front of the other two men. There was no mistaking the menace in his stance. "The lady seems to take issue with being removed from her conveyance. Let her go."

Lawlessness was the order of the day in the Borders, and the two other robbers looked the part: unkempt, unshaven, but well armed, for like their fallen companion they both carried pistols and dirks. One of them let go of the young woman's arm, shoving her at his companion. "I'll take care o' this gallant," he said in a low growl as he drew his sword.

"You are welcome to try, of course." Adain felt an unholy delight as he parried the first thrust and easily blocked another.

The man was an oaf, and Adain experienced little triumph as he ran him through. With a groan, the would-be assassin crumpled, clutching his belly, and pitched onto the muddy road. Adain turned purposefully, but the fight was enough for the third man, who released the girl and grabbed one of the loose horses, jumping on, and departed with almost comical speed.

Not much of a damned battle after all.

What a disappointment. Adain wasn't even breathing hard.

He turned to the young woman, who now leaned weakly against the side of the carriage, her eyes wide in the faint light. Tendrils of soft fair hair had escaped her chignon and curled against the slender length of her neck, framing her delicate features.

"Are you hurt, lass?" he asked her, jabbing his sword back into the scabbard to hide the dripping blade.

"No . . . no." She took in a shuddering breath. "Thank you."

"You're English." He frowned at her accent, even those few words giving away her origins. With tensions running so high right now between Scotland and her nemesis, most of the English stayed south of the border. "Good God, where's your escort? No one should travel these roads without a guard," he stated bluntly, taking in her fashionable rose-colored gown and the quality of the carriage. He knelt by the slumped figure of the driver, but unfortunately the man was dead, shot through the chest.

"Yes, I'm English." The girl watched him, her voice unsteady as she answered, "And as for guards, we haven't any."

Adain stood and stared at her. "That's ill-advised enough during the day, but what are you doing traveling into the night? It's beyond foolishness and onto madness."

"My uncle said we could not afford to hire one. Nor to stop at an inn when it began to grow dark. We hoped to be in Hawick by now, but he's been ill the whole journey."

Her uncle's tight purse and lack of foresight would have cost her some very unpleasant moments had the highwaymen dragged her off, but she already looked ghostly pale, and Adain didn't pursue the subject. Instead, he peered in the open door of the carriage, wondering why her uncle, ill or not, had not even done so much as lift a finger to protect his niece.

The man appeared to be sleeping, but how he could manage that through both gunfire and the brief but bloody fight was a mystery.

The answer was obvious enough upon a closer look.

As if there were not already enough dead bodies littering the road. When Adain clambered inside and pulled the old man's neck cloth aside, he could feel no pulse.

Blood and thunder.

He climbed back out and wondered how in the devil he was going to break this bit of news to a young woman who had already been through a hellish, frightening experience. As gently as possible, he said, "I think your uncle was more ill than he realized. Perhaps if he had agreed to stop and summon a physician, he could have been saved."

Even in the thin moonlight, he could see her tremble. "What?"

"I am sorry."

"He's . . . dead?"

"Aye, it seems so, lass."

For a moment, she seemed unable to speak, and then she whispered, "I wondered whether he was getting worse, but he wouldn't listen to anything I had to say. I could hear him struggling to breathe. I thought he was finally falling asleep, but perhaps he was slipping away."

Comforting suddenly bereaved young ladies who had just been the near victim of an unexpected attack was not his forte. Adain murmured, feeling inadequate, "Perhaps the excitement of the attempted robbery stopped his heart. Perhaps it was inevitable anyway. Who knows."

She swayed slightly, and he stepped forward to catch her by the waist, alarmed that she might swoon. "This is a nightmare," she said, collapsing against his chest, her slim form shaking. "Surely I will wake soon."

Though Adain sympathized with her shocked sensibilities, he hadn't lied earlier; the road was a dangerous place to be. Risking it himself was one thing, but she needed to get to safety as soon as possible. Those disreputable three were hardly the only predators on the prowl. The local magistrate could take care of what should be done with their bodies.

Why does she have to be a bloody English lass? he thought with wry cynicism as he felt the light, delicious weight of her body against him, a soft floral fragrance drifting from her pale hair. He despised her country as much as any good Scot, but she was stranded and alone, no matter her nationality.

He'd much rather rescue a bonny Scottish girl.

"I will help you in any way I can, but at the risk of sounding callous, we should ride on. At the next village, we can make arrangements for your uncle and coachman to be buried. You need rest and shelter. It grows later with each passing moment."

She said nothing. Then he felt her straighten her spine and heard her inhale a deep breath as if composing herself. "You are right. And very generous, sir. Thank you for your aid, and for your offer. I feel I have been a great deal of trouble already, and I do not even know your name."

"Adain Cameron, at your service."

"I am Lady Gillian Lorin."

He almost smiled at the formal tone of her voice despite the grim and tumultuous circumstances of their meeting, and released her waist. "A pleasure, Lady Gillian. Now, let us go."

*   *   *

Gillian sat across a pair of muscular thighs and felt the night wind caress her face. The events of the past hour had left her dazed. The ride had a surreal feel to it—except for the man next to her, guiding his horse with an expert hand down the dark, gloomy road. The one who wielded a sword as if it were part of his body, so smooth, graceful and yet deadly; he had made the entire fight look effortless. He felt solid, hard, strong, and very male as they rode along.

Was she safe with this man? There was no doubt she was entirely at his mercy, but what choice did she have? Adain Cameron seemed kind.

Could a man who had cut down those two ruffians without blinking an eye still be kind? Well, she supposed so, because he'd acted in her defense and they weren't even acquainted. Even now, he was helping her and had no obligation to do so. Her plight was dire, but not his affair.

Through her lashes, she dared an unobtrusive look at his face. It was handsome, she thought, though the light wasn't good. Dark hair brushed his shoulders, framing features that had clean, masculine lines: straight nose, square chin, and downy dark brows. His eyes were a light gleaming color, and she had a feeling that if he ever smiled, he would be very appealing.

But there was something somber about him that made her wonder if laughter were not a stranger in his life.

"There is an inn a few miles up ahead," he said in his clear, brusque voice. "We'll stop there and hope there is available space and something hot to eat. It's getting late."

She didn't exactly have an appetite after the evening's events, but he was right; they could do nothing for her uncle now.

At least her future was settled, and Cameron had found the betrothal papers and brought them along.

Practical and efficient, he had emptied her uncle's pockets and made her retrieve any small valuables she carried lest more criminals come upon the abandoned carriage. It had been on the tip of her tongue to mention her fiancé as she saw him fold the documents and tuck them in a small bag, but she had refrained. Complicated explanations were beyond her at the moment. She felt numb all over.

The minute Aunt Eugenia had died, her world had shifted, and now it was shifting again. She was entirely dependent on an utter stranger, and the feeling wasn't new.

She didn't like it, even though it was becoming disturbingly familiar.

Her rescuer trotted his big horse into the yard of the inn and slid off in one lithe, athletic movement. With ease, he lifted her from her sideways perch in the saddle and set her down. There were still lights in the windows, she saw with gratitude, and both fatigue and a lack of food made her feel light-headed. He led the way, escorting her inside.

In moments, she was in some sort of private parlor, her shivering eased by a crackling fire and a glass of warmed wine in her hand. Abstractly, she could hear Mr. Cameron explaining to the innkeeper what had happened and offering coin for someone to retrieve the carriage and the bodies. Her mind didn't seem to function properly, trying to absorb this latest catastrophe in a life that had been less than settled as of late.

"Drink some of the wine; it will warm and ease you. I've ordered food and secured you a room, lass."

She glanced up at the sound of the quiet words. Her savior was very tall, and the flickering firelight threw his shadow across the small room. "I am grateful to you for everything," she said truthfully, lifting her cup obediently and taking a sip.

"I understand your grief, as I lost a beloved uncle not that long ago. If you would prefer to be alone, I can take my meal in the taproom."

"He was not beloved to me in any way," Gillian said firmly, the glass in her hand wobbling a bit. Maybe she shouldn't tell this to a stranger, but the words spilled out before she could stop them. "Though I certainly did not wish him dead, I did not even know my uncle until a few weeks ago. When he became my guardian on the death of my mother's sister, he made it quite clear he did not want me or the responsibility. I am shocked, but not grieving."

Cameron's dark brows shot up. "I see."

"I suppose it sounds unfeeling of me, but I was more contemplating my situation. He was the last of my family."

In better light, she could see Adain Cameron had gray eyes, the color almost pure silver. There was something about them that made him seem vividly alive—a distinct gleam of intelligence and purpose, perhaps. At the moment, they held sympathy and an awareness of what exactly she was saying. "Is there no one who will take you in?"

"That depends. My uncle had arranged a marriage to one of your countrymen. I am betrothed . . . or, well, almost betrothed, I suppose. We were traveling to my intended's estate near Hawick.

I believe the marriage will take place only if he approves of my appearance."

"I somehow doubt that will be a problem." The words were said neutrally, but there was a subtle undertone in the voice of the tall man leaning so casually against the fireplace mantel that made her cheeks flush suddenly. "You are lovely. He won't refuse you."

The compliment flustered her, but it also brought up some unsettling doubts about her future.

"My uncle didn't think so either," she admitted, doing her best to hide her bitterness, for it was hardly an uncommon practice—most young women did not get to choose their husbands—and it made her seem ungrateful. "He was quite cheered at the idea of relieving himself of any responsibility and acquiring a substantial marriage settlement at the same time."

In short, she'd been sold.

Cameron reached for the bottle on the small table between them and refilled his glass, the splash of the wine low against the comfortable crackle of the fire. "Hawick is not far from here. If I can escort you there, I would be happy to offer my assistance."

Considering all he'd done already, it was a most generous offer. "I am sure Lord Kleiss would be in your debt, though I confess I know little about him."

"Lord Kleiss?" Cameron stopped in the act of taking a drink, the glass arrested inches from his mouth. "The Earl of Kleiss?"

Gillian wasn't sure she liked his reaction. "Yes. Do you know him?"

Darkness . . .

She'd sensed it all along in her uncle's evasiveness about her fiancé, in how he'd put aside her questions.

Cameron said, "Personally, we have never met. I know *of* the earl, however."

From the grim expression on the tall Scotsman's face, she deduced that her day—horrible enough already—was about to get worse. The warm little room with the cheerful fire felt suddenly cold. "What you have heard is not to his credit, I take it," she said in dismal resignation, her fingers tightening on her wineglass. "I see it in your expression."

He didn't answer for a moment, and then shook his dark head. "I am afraid not. The least of it is that he is old enough to be your grandfather and has buried four wives already."

That wasn't completely surprising, for she had guessed he wasn't young if he was a contemporary of her uncle. It made her feel sick to contemplate lying with an old man, but she wasn't given a choice in the matter, so she had tried not to think about it.

"If that is the least of it," Gillian asked hollowly, not certain she even wanted to know, "what is the worst of it?"

"Not for your ears," Adain Cameron informed her curtly. "And I withdraw my offer. I'll not take you to him."

Chapter 2

The table was sticky with spilled ale, and the sound of drunken laughter echoed in the huge space as his men drank freely and traded bawdy jokes, the meal long since finished. Thomas Graham, Earl of Kleiss, sat in his usual spot at the head, in a massive chair his ancestors had brought from Italy two centuries before. Once, it had been a work of art, but now it was scarred from careless use, the legs scratched by booted feet with spurs, the armrests nicked and worn.

He did not mind the battered appearance, for he liked his possessions to be well used.

Except his women.

If Baron Lorin had told the truth about his English niece . . . Well, he felt a rush of dark pleasure at just the thought of deflowering the pretty young bitch. As his wife, she'd learn her place soon enough. He didn't want someone to run his household. He had perfectly competent servants for that. If they *were* incompetent in any way, they were punished with prompt and inventive viciousness, which made for a very efficient staff.

Neither did he need to breed more children, for he had three sons already, all of them brawny and capable.

No, what he needed was someone to service him like a whore at his bidding, and who better than a pale Englishwoman? With Scotland's increasingly urgent bid for independence, the feelings against the English were running high, and though he eschewed politics normally, he hated the arrogant bastards south of the border.

Not that he really cared about her nationality except in an off-hand way. She was the same as any other woman, a convenient receptacle for his lust, with all the right places for his cock.

A young man strode into the hall, his booted feet thudding on the hard floor, and his expression apprehensive. He stopped and gave a brief bow. "My lord."

"Well?" Thomas growled.

"There is still no sign of them, and as the hour is late—"

He eyed the young trooper murderously and reached for his ale. "Are you complaining about your duties?"

"No, my lord." The young man paled.

"I should hope not." Irritated, because patience was not at all in his blood, Thomas swore violently. He had need of her at once and a priest standing by. As long as she was everything he'd been told, she could have warmed his bed this very night, but Lorin, the weak fool, was damnably late.

"Ride back out," he instructed. "I don't care if you have to go all the way to Northumberland. They are a full day late. Find her."

*   *   *

Adain felt regret for his vehemence. He had further shocked Lady Gillian on a night when she hardly needed more disheartening news, but it couldn't be helped.

Did the woman really think he'd hand her over to a monster like the Earl of Kleiss, English or not? It was obvious her uncle was not an admirable man in any way, but to bargain his lovely niece into an arrangement with one of the most notoriously ruthless and violent men in Scotland was downright cruel.

And she *was* lovely.

Even pale and understandably distraught, she had a delicate beauty that would please any man, especially a lustful bastard of Kleiss's reputation. The fragile bone structure of her face, coupled with large, long-lashed blue eyes and a soft rose mouth, gave an impression of feminine grace, as did the slenderness of her body. She was young, but, from the full curve of her breasts, not too young to be wedded and bedded. At his guess certainly no more than eighteen. Now that he could see her better, he realized her gown was finely made but not new, and the cloak she'd worn against the chill of their ride was mended in several places.

"You withdraw the offer?" She stared at him, clutching the wineglass so tightly her knuckles were white. "Sir, you must tell me why. I beg you."

Adain rubbed his jaw, wondering darkly what to say. How the bloody hell had he gotten in this predicament anyway? It was actually none of his affair, but the girl was suddenly alone and unprotected, and apparently also penniless. Her uncle hadn't carried more than a few coins, not even enough to pay for her room for the night. No wonder the old greedy rat had refused to stop. It hadn't been an option.

"Let me put it this way," Adain explained with reluctant honesty. "You'd be better off as a plaything for those three bandits, shared between them until they had their fill and let you go. Marriage to Kleiss is a sentence of rape and degradation until the day you die, which, if you are anything like his other four wives, you will do quickly."

Even her lips had gone white now, she was so pale. "He is that awful?"

"Aye, lass," Adain confirmed in a gentler tone, "and I'd not deliver any woman into his hands."

Lady Gillian sat very still in the plain chair near the fire, the leaping flames lending hollows to her beautiful face and gilding her pale hair. Slowly, she said, "I am glad you told me, but I am unsure now what I am supposed to do. He is expecting me. That aside, I truly have no place to go, or if I did, no means to get there. The carriage is his, sent by Lord Kleiss to bring me to him."

It was one hell of a dilemma, that was for certain, and Adain didn't have an easy solution for her. "I am surprised he didn't send an armed escort along with the carriage to protect his future bride."

"He sent money to hire one." Her soft mouth twisted. "However, my uncle spent it at once. He had an ungovernable penchant for wine and cards, Mr. Cameron. It had ruined him. The small amount my aunt left me on her death he appropriated to appease his creditors into giving him more time. From the moment I arrived on his doorstep not even a month ago, he started to arrange this marriage, his pressing debts an issue."

"One look at you, and I suppose he knew he'd get a tidy sum from the right man." Adain didn't bother to hide his disgust for the beautiful Lady Gillian's deceased relative. "No doubt he described you in detail to Kleiss when he wrote him and offered you, counting on his lordship's lecherous tendencies and rich purse. It is a despicable exchange, flesh for coin."

The indirect compliment on her looks brought a little color into her cheeks. Gillian said, with admirable calm given her circumstances, "But then again, that is your opinion, and you are a good man, or certainly seem to be, and my uncle was not. I did not wish him dead, but will not miss his acrimonious nature. I was hoping my new husband would be an improvement."

"He wouldn't be; take my word."

His conviction obviously shook her. "Mr. Cameron, since his lordship has already gone to some trouble and expense, do you think he will want the contract honored if he finds me suitable?"

Suitable? That didn't do her justice in the least. Moreover, at least on short acquaintance, she seemed to be not only alluring physically, but intelligent, and certainly had remarkable courage. Most females he knew would have gone into a fit of hysterics if accosted on the road, dragged summarily from their carriage, and then witnessed a bloody—all too short, in his opinion—fight. Add in her uncle's unfortunate demise on top of the mix, being stranded in a foreign country . . . and aye, the girl was resilient, even after getting the news about her intended's true nature.

Julia had those same characteristics. He thought it with a flash of the old familiar pain that didn't seem to ease. The woman he had once been engaged to marry would probably have reacted in a similar brave way as Lady Gillian: with an uplifted chin and squared shoulders.

Julia. No, he couldn't think about her. He'd done that too much already. She was another man's bride and out of his reach. He needed to move forward, not stay mired in regrets of what could have been.

In fact, he needed a distraction.

Lady Gillian might serve nicely.

He may have just met her, but Adain knew there was no way he was going to allow this beautiful girl to marry the deviant earl just because she felt she had nowhere to turn. Surely, with her looks and shapely form, she could easily find another man to wed. One who needed a wife, who would respect and care for her, rather than regard her as property and use her body for his depraved pleasures. With some assistance to escape her situation, she could make a good marriage.

"Kleiss isn't going to have you," Adain said firmly, the statement both so authoritative and presumptuous it startled him. "Yes, I agree you need the protection of a man, but not a lawless, immoral blackguard. I won't allow it."

She also seemed disconcerted at his proprietary declaration. Her fine arched brows, a darker shade than her shining honey-colored hair, lifted a fraction at his brash statement. "Sir—"

"I am offering mine temporarily. In the morning, we'll ride on to Castle Cameron. Once safely there, you can review your options, my lady. They exist, believe me."

Her gaze was luminous suddenly, as if unshed tears threatened to spill over her long lashes. "You do not know me and I am English. Why would you go to such trouble on my behalf? You said yourself the earl was ruthless. What if he takes exception to the fact that I never arrive? Eventually he is bound to find out about the events of this evening and that I left with you."

He looked into her eyes and responded softly, "You do not know me and I'm a Scot. Why would you travel with me willingly to my home and trust yourself into my care? The answer is because it is the best thing for you. And as for the earl, I will deal with him if need be. In fact, I invite him to try to claim you."

Evidently, she remembered his eager rush into the fight on the road, for a small frown furrowed her smooth brow.

No, he thought, *do not ask me about the demons that currently occupy my soul.*

Do not ask.

The arrival of a serving maid with their food fortunately prevented her from saying anything.

Good, because the last thing he wanted to admit was that his motives were not entirely based on chivalry when he made his offer.

It had been a long time since he'd felt even a stirring of interest in a woman besides Julia.

The madness of the day continued, compounded by something she had never felt before.

Clad in only her shift, her body so weary she ached, Gillian slipped under the blankets and closed her eyes. Unfortunately, as tired as she was physically, her emotional state left her mind in turmoil. She knew sleep would be elusive this eve.

Though he seemed a much better alternative than Kleiss, it was a shocking notion to agree to ride off with the young man who had suddenly taken charge of her. Adain Cameron carried an air of command so easily. It seemed as effortless as the way he wielded his sword. She sensed in him goodness and compassion, but also something more.

Though she tried always to stifle it, her intuition was a part of her, as natural as breathing. She was not sure why, but she could feel the thoughts of others, sometimes with such an accuracy that it was uncomfortable.

This eve, she'd learned a great deal about Adain Cameron.

She had to admit he fascinated her.

He might be brave and valiant enough to ride boldly to rescue a woman he did not even know, but he was wounded inside. His heart bled. She had felt it in small bursts during their conversation. A turn of his head, a twitch of his sinewy hand as he looked away, the ferocity with which he had rushed to her rescue . . . not to mention the bleakness in his unusual silver eyes.

This man had a past, of that she was certain, and she would venture to guess there was heartache involved and he suffered still. Gillian couldn't help but wonder what woman would choose another over him. Not only was he a skillful warrior; he was undeniably handsome and, from the quality of his horse and clothes, affluent. He'd paid the innkeeper in gold. The way he spoke indicated he was well educated too.

Restively, she rolled over.

His room was next to hers and she knew he did not sleep either. At first she could hear him pace, those restless footsteps muffled but still audible. Now and then he threw more wood on the fire. When the pacing ceased she could imagine him as he sat sprawled in a chair next to the hearth, his long legs extended, still drinking as he stared into the embers. Cameron had ordered whiskey and taken the bottle with him when they retired, and every so often

Seducing Adain 237

came the clink of glass on glass as he poured himself another measure. Gillian had the feeling he often sought to numb himself in such a way.

The ache of his frustration and loss came through with amazing clarity, even though he appeared so self-possessed and confident.

There was no chance of her finding slumber unless she talked to him.

About what? she asked herself wryly. She didn't know what was amiss with her attractive rescuer, and whatever kept him from sleep was not her concern, except she owed him a very great debt.

The least she could do was to offer him some company, if he wished it. She had lost her parents when she was twelve to a virulent fever that had ravaged the countryside. Never would she forget the awful, overwhelming sense of loneliness as she had adjusted to her orphaned state, even though her aunt had taken her in and had been a caring, wonderful woman.

Adain Cameron was *alone*.

Gillian slid out of the bed and donned her rumpled gown again. It was now well past midnight and the inn was quiet, the hallway deserted as she cracked the door and peered out. She didn't bother with her stockings and shoes, and the bare floor was chilly.

As she lifted her hand to rap lightly on his door, she wondered if he would turn her away. She'd had a sheltered upbringing but knew enough about masculine pride to realize men viewed emotional turmoil as a weakness. Her widowed aunt had often discussed her deceased husband, relating not just his positive attributes with fondness but his foibles also.

Gillian knocked.

She heard the creak of the chair as he stood, and the slight unsteadiness of his footsteps as he approached the door. It was jerked open, and he frowned when he saw her standing there. "Is something wrong, lass?"

"No, not precisely." She offered him a tentative smile. "May I come in?"

Those silver eyes narrowed as he registered her bare feet peeking out from under the hem of her dress, and the loose tumble of her hair to her waist. "Mayhap I should take you back to your room, Lady Gillian."

"I do not wish to go back to my room. Please, may I just come in? It is rather chilly here in the hallway."

Adain Cameron hesitated a moment, but then stepped back to allow her to enter his room, his expression inscrutable. She guessed that if their circumstances weren't so unusual he would be more concerned with propriety. She had no chaperone and was in his care. Her reputation was probably ruined anyway, but from what he'd told her earlier, it was better than marrying the nefarious earl.

"Now, what is so urgent? You have had a trying day, lass, and it is very late." He had discarded his coat and wore only a white, full-sleeved shirt, half-unbuttoned, doeskin breeches that hugged his muscular thighs, and fitted boots. She could smell the whiskey on his breath, and also his unique scent, a tang that reminded her of pinewoods or an autumn afternoon.

"Neither of us is asleep," she said quietly. "I thought maybe we could . . . well . . . pass the time together."

There was a short silence, loaded and powerful. He hesitated to speak, and then exhaled raggedly. "How did you know I wasn't asleep?"

Gillian looked into the silver depths of his eyes. "I just knew. I am restless myself."

That seemed to leave him at a loss, which she guessed didn't happen often. His gaze wandered downward for one betraying moment, over the bodice of her gown, lingering briefly on the curve of her breasts before jerking back upward. Earlier, he'd called her beautiful, and Gillian fought a blush, reminding herself the whiskey bottle by the hearth was half-empty.

To her surprise, she felt a flicker of purely female triumph over how she affected him. What was more, she couldn't help but notice she could see his muscled chest through the gap in his unfastened shirt. It looked hard and wide, and intriguingly male.

"May I sit down?" she asked, unsettled by her reaction to this man, but not enough to prudently return to her room. He'd risked his life for her, and then concerned himself with her future. If she could help him, she wished to do so.

He lifted his brows. "If you desire, though I warn you I am not the best of company at the moment. You'd do better to go back to bed."

She ignored the warning and took the other shabby chair by the fire, lifting her skirts enough that she could warm her bare feet. "Is sleeplessness a normal affliction for you?"

"For the past several years, aye." He didn't sit but went to lean against the mantel, his gaze steady, the amber liquid in his glass shimmering in the flickering firelight.

"It happens to me also sometimes," she admitted.

"I doubt somehow an innocent lass like yourself has my demons to keep her awake," he said sardonically, lifting the whiskey glass to his mouth.

Carefully, she considered him. "What demons in particular?"

For a moment she thought he wouldn't answer, but then he laughed without mirth. "Are you always so direct?"

"Usually. My aunt always told me I am insatiably curious. I suppose it is true."

She was curious about *him*; that was for certain, and in a way she hadn't anticipated. Her aunt had been a remarkable woman with many facets to her personality, and one of them was her forthright approach to life. When Gillian was old enough to comprehend the subject, Aunt Eugenia had described matters between men and women in very frank terms. There was pleasure in the joining, she'd been told, if the male in question knew what he was doing and took care with his partner.

From under the fringe of her lashes Gillian studied the curve of Adain Cameron's finely molded mouth, the strong column of his neck, the fascinating width of his shoulders. She was drawn to this man, and it wasn't all because of his timely, gallant rescue.

Yes, she was *definitely* curious.

"Let me just say I lost something precious to me, and I still wonder, as I look back, what I might have done differently."

"A woman." Gillian did not phrase it as a question, for she somehow knew the answer already.

"Aye." He stared at his whiskey glass, his expression bleak.

"What a fool she must be."

"Not at all." He said the words with fateful resignation. "She had her reasons to distrust me and she married another. *I* am the fool who cannot seem to forget her."

"Can I help?" Almost beyond her will, her heart beginning to pound, Gillian rose and closed the short distance between them.

"After all, I am here . . . and she is not." As she'd been wanting to do since the moment she'd walked into the room, she reached out and touched his bare chest between the parted cloth of his open shirt. His skin felt hot under her fingertips.

"Don't." He said the one word in a clipped tone, but he didn't move, and his lean body gave a small quiver of reaction.

"Is there some reason I shouldn't touch you?" She asked the question softly, not understanding herself why she was doing what she was doing. But she was compelled just the same. Maybe it was the nature of his suffering, which aroused in her both compassion and an inexplicable need to give something back. This evening, he had saved at the least her virtue, and also her life, if what he knew of Lord Kleiss was true.

If she was honest with herself, he was also a very attractive man, and she had experienced a fateful thrill the first time she had looked into his remarkable eyes.

She wanted to ease his pain.

She also *wanted* him, and it was a very exciting sensation.

Adain's heart pounded under her splayed fingers. "Yes," he said unevenly, "quite a few reasons. You are a lady and, if I am any judge at all, a virgin. I am not a knave who takes advantage of innocent young women, Scottish or English. I'm foxed, but not that far gone."

The words were said with conviction, but his gaze strayed again to the swell of her breasts underneath the thin material of her gown.

She tilted her head back, aware her nipples tingled, the unfamiliar excitement intriguing. "If I give myself freely, you are not taking advantage, sir."

Long fingers curved around her wrist, but he still didn't pull her hand away.

"Your gratitude does not have to take this form," Adain told her almost roughly. "When I offered my protection, it was done honorably."

Gillian smiled tremulously. "I know. If you tried to exact a payment for what you have done for me, I would have resisted you. Can you not see I wish to be here with you?"

"Your maidenhead should be taken in your marriage bed, lass." His voice had a husky timbre.

She arched a brow and said wryly, "That is an entirely male sentiment. I prefer it be given as I wish to a man of my choosing. It is mine, after all. Do you not want me?"

His eyes glittered suddenly. "I am breathing, last I knew. Yes, you are very desirable, and I want you. But defiling you because I cannot control my lust is hardly admirable."

"If you take me to bed, I will be defiled?" Gillian gave him what she hoped was a provocative smile. "I think just the opposite. If I didn't, I would not be here."

To emphasize her words, she boldly reached up and touched his mouth, running her fingertips along the curve of his lower lip. She couldn't believe she had the nerve, and was a little embarrassed, but also exhilarated.

Adain Cameron gave an audible inward hiss of breath as he stared at her, his eyes going the color of a winter sky.

At that moment, she won the debate and he abruptly swept her into his arms.

*   *   *

The small, shabby room felt overwarm, but that was probably just the raging need spiking straight to his groin. Adain strode toward the bed, the delectable—and infinitely persuasive—Lady Gillian cradled against him, and he no longer cared about the dishonor of his actions.

From that first moment on the road, he'd wanted what her uncle had sold to Kleiss, which might make him not the better man. He wanted her wet and willing underneath him. He needed to feel his cock sink deep into her inviting softness, and to lose himself in pleasure and desire.

Except, he vowed as he held her slender body in his arms, he would take care with her. Not just take pleasure, but also give it.

He *needed* to go slowly. She was untried. One look in her eyes had told him that the moment they met, and seducing her was bad enough. He didn't want the experience to be painful for her.

Actually, he had the feeling *he* was the one being seduced.

The sensation of her small hand, so dainty and smooth, pressed against his chest would stay imprinted in his mind forever. The image of her standing just outside his door—silken hair in a loose pale tumble of gold around her ivory shoulders, and her eyes dark with an emotion he couldn't quite comprehend—would not be easily lost either.

He might be a thrice-damned fool for doing it, but he was going to bed her anyway. This night, he would lose himself in her arms, her scent, the silky feel of her mouth and skin, and forget, even if it were temporary, about what he had lost.

The consequences could be addressed in the morning.

For an untried maid, she didn't seem so much nervous as a little shy, and when he laid her on the bed and removed her gown, she blushed but still held his gaze. Her shift was disposed of just as promptly, and he found the perfection of her body was just as he had waywardly imagined all evening: beautiful firm breasts, a narrow waist, slim hips, and long legs. Her blond thatch gleamed in the meager firelight that was the only illumination, the delicate triangle concealing her sex.

He sat down on the edge of the bed to tug off his boots. "You're lovely, lass. Lovelier than any I have seen."

Lovelier than Julia? He didn't know, for he had never seen his intended bride nude, though he had certainly imagined it a thousand times before an ill-fated misunderstanding caused her to break their engagement and marry another man.

She is Robbie McCray's now. The matter is done.

Gillian gazed at him with a soft look he did not quite understand on her face. "I am glad I please you. You are also very . . . appealing to me."

By the gods, he was rock-hard already, his erection painfully stiff as he shrugged out of his shirt and unfastened his breeches. His cock rose high, drawing his testicles into a tight sac, the engorged tip beaded with semen. As he slid in beside the woman lying so compliant and expectant in his bed, his erection brushed her smooth hip. He stifled a groan, wondering how long, after months of self-imposed abstinence, he would even last.

Gazing into her eyes, he lightly touched her cheek and said with raw honesty, "Soon it will be too late to change your mind. All men have limits of self-control, and mine is weakened by drink. If you wish to dress and leave now, we can pretend you never came into my room or my bed. Once I touch you, I may not be able to stop."

Blond hair, so gloriously soft and shining, moved against the linens as she shook her head. "I am not going to change my mind, Adain. I want to give you pleasure."

He liked the way she said his given name, her soft English accent endearing. It was arousing, and he was already aroused as hell anyway. "So be it."

His hand glided over her smooth shoulder and down to her hip, cupping the satiny curve and pulling her close so her pelvis nestled against his groin. As he lowered his mouth to claim hers, he could feel the pulse of his erection where it lay like a sword between them, pressed hotly against the softness of her belly.

It had been too long since he'd felt the fierce rush of such desire, since he'd wanted to find satisfaction in a woman's body and hear her cries of enjoyment as he took her.

There was little doubt of Gillian's physical innocence, for though she rested willingly beneath him, he discovered quickly that she had never even been so much as kissed before. Gently, he forced her lips to part so he could taste her mouth, and she was obviously startled at the first brush of his tongue against hers.

The kiss was long, and as leisurely as he could make it with his rock-hard cock clamoring for an invasion of a more carnal kind. Innocent she might be, but also responsive, for she slipped her arms around his neck and pressed closer, the enticing softness of her full breasts pliant against his chest. A part of him was astonished at her lack of fear, but he'd downed enough whiskey to not be capable of deep analysis, especially when his hungry body held control over his mind.

"Ah . . . lass." He nuzzled her neck, kissing the small hollow beneath her ear. "You smell sweet, like a Scottish summer meadow."

"Do I?" Her hands slid down his back and she sounded breathless. "And you feel very large and hard, like the warrior you are, yet your touch is gentle, as I knew it would be."

"I would that you enjoy this as much as I do." Adain meant it, his voice husky. "Let me ready you to accept me, Gillian. Lie back and trust me in what I ask."

"If I did not trust you, I would not be here," she pointed out with a charming candor he was coming to recognize was part of her personality. Obligingly, she rolled to her back, an expectant light in her long-lashed eyes. Her mouth was damp from his kiss, and her nipples already tightened to small pink buds.

There was no doubt he enjoyed and admired every part of the female anatomy, but he was particularly enamored of women's breasts. Hers were spectacular, the fullness almost a surprise, because otherwise, she was girlishly slim. Ivory skin showed the faint blue threads of the veins beneath, and her nipples were perfectly shaped and delicately tinted a soft rose color. He cupped one breast in his hand just as he lowered his mouth to take the other nipple into his mouth.

She gasped, a small sound as he began to suckle, and her hands clutched his upper arms tightly. "Oh."

Earlier, he'd tried to drink himself into oblivion to escape his personal hell, and now he was in heaven. How had it happened so quickly?

He lavished attention on first one breast and then the other, licking, kissing, stroking as he savored the swelling soft flesh, gratified at her growing restlessness as she arched and moved in response. When his hand slid lower, he briefly caressed her hip and whispered, "Spread your legs, my sweet."

The moment of virginal hesitation did not surprise him, and he gave her a wickedly persuasive smile. "You'll like it, lass."

Gillian's cheeks flushed a deeper pink, but she complied, parting her thighs so he could touch her cleft. It was damp, sleek, and beautifully warm, telling him she was almost ready for penetration. He stroked, finding the small bud he knew evoked the most sensation for any woman, and circled it.

A small moan came from between her parted lips.

"That's it, lass," he said in encouragement as her legs fell farther apart. "Feel the pleasure. Let it come to you."

Before long, his fingers were coated in the fluids of her desire and she arched impatiently against the persuasive pressure of his hand. As her orgasm rose and built, her slender body began to quiver uncontrollably, and she let out a keening cry. Adain continued the stimulation, keeping her on that peak, taking pleasure in her abandoned enjoyment.

When she went limp, he withdrew his hand and moved upward, pushing her legs apart even farther so he could position himself between them. His hard cock found her small opening, well lubricated and soft from her climax, and he began to ease inside her passage.

Gillian's lashes lifted at the pressure of his entrance. There was a look in the blue depths of her eyes that spoke of her awakened awareness of sexual release.

Go slow; give her it inch by inch. Do not selfishly rush this because your eager cock rules your head. . . .

Even though he was taut with need, he said hoarsely, "I will be as gentle as I can."

A smile curved her mouth and she whispered with humbling conviction, "I know."

*   *   *

The muscled power of his body should probably frighten her, Gillian thought, still feeling a little dazed from the wondrous thing that had just happened to her. Braced on his arms, Adain Cameron's powerful body dwarfed hers as he hovered over her, his lean hips wedging her legs wide-open. She could feel the hard strength of his shoulders under the grasp of her hands, and most certainly the size of that part of him that made him male was imposing. How her body was supposed to accept it, she wasn't sure, but she *was* completely sure of one thing.

Drunk or sober—or in his current in-between state—he would never hurt her purposely. While it was sometimes uncomfortable to be sensitive to the emotions of others, it was certainly to her advantage when it came to judging their character.

The slow progress of his cock as he pushed it into her passage was only a little uncomfortable, and balanced by the unique coil of excitement in the pit of her stomach. Handsome face flushed, he advanced until he was arrested by the barrier he had to breach. The nudge of the tip of his engorged shaft against it was not enough to break through, and he leaned down to kiss her, his mouth warm and persuasive. "I am sorry, lass, for there is no other way past. You are so small and delicate. I don't wish to hurt you."

"A little pain is inevitable," Gillian told him, recalling Aunt Eugenia's no-nonsense recital. Moved by his care for her, her voice was unsteady. "Do what you must."

Still, he hesitated. "It is only this first time. Once your maidenhead is gone, you can take a man with pleasure."

"I am resigned to the pain, and then you may show me the

pleasure." She said it breathlessly as she waited, open and almost impaled.

One ebony brow arched and he chuckled, his face lighting magically. "That sounds like a challenge, Lady Gillian."

He didn't laugh often. *That* she knew about him already.

"Call it what you will, but please move." It was probably audacious for her to be so impatient, but she was anyway.

He did so, a hard thrust that suddenly sheathed him fully and impossibly deep inside her. The pain was brief, and not at all the ordeal she expected, and Gillian barely noticed it in contrast to the sensation of being so filled and possessed. "Adain." She gasped.

"I'm sorry." His voice sounded thick. "But the deed is done."

"Do not be sorry. It was nigh to nothing. . . . What happens now? Surely there's more."

"Aye, lass." Silver eyes gleamed. "Much, much more."

As he began to withdraw, she tightened her hands in protest, rewarded when he sank back in with a smooth forward movement that tore a moan from somewhere deep inside her. He did it again and she arched into that seductive, sinful forward glide, wanting—needing—his cock buried as far as it could go. "Yes."

"That's it. Move with me," he murmured, eyes half-closed as he slid in and out between her open legs. "Lift your hips, my sweet. Ah . . . yes, exactly that way. It's good . . . so damned good. . . ."

His words were a background to her pleasure, a running dialogue of heated masculine desire, and she undulated to his rhythm and took him over and over as tension built and she felt that incredible rising need for blissful release. Panting and nearly wild, she clung to the man possessing her body. When she finally shattered from the sheer pleasure of it, he seemed to come apart too, the inner tremor of her muscles igniting a reaction. Adain stiffened and groaned, the flex of his sex spilling a warm, sudden flood as he forcefully released his seed.

The full weight of his body took her breath away for a moment, but he quickly rolled to his side, dragging her with him, his embrace comfortable and intimate. Sprawled across his damp chest, hearing his rapid breathing in the aftermath, Gillian smiled in deep contentment.

Long fingers sifted through her hair, moving softly, and his arms felt strong and secure. "It has been too long," he said softly, as if talking to himself.

"I agree," she murmured sleepily against his heated skin.

She could feel a laugh rumble from his chest. "As you were a virgin, that's an odd sentiment to hold."

"I meant for you."

He peered down into her face, his eyes narrowed.

"You needed to love someone," she explained, then added, "and I am glad I was the one."

The hand stroking her hair stilled. Adain's whisper was barely audible. "Have you always been so insightful, lass?"

Gillian was too tired to answer. Instead, she surrendered to a deep, contented sleep.

Chapter 3

The afternoon was as wet as the bottom of the River Tweed, a cold drizzle falling from steely skies and a chill wind whistling by. His men already looked miserable on their stamping horses, and the Earl of Kleiss didn't care in the least.

He'd woken with a foul taste in his mouth from too much drink, and an even fouler mood blackening his temper. Thomas tugged on his gauntlets with impatience and fought the urge to smash his fist into someone's face just to brighten his day.

His oldest son, Malcolm, eyed him warily, the younger man well aware of his own availability as a potential target. Even though at nearly forty years of age Malcolm was thick-bodied and a seasoned fighter, he obviously had a healthy respect for his father's temper, and that was just exactly how Thomas wanted it. More than once he'd caught a hint of rebellion in his oldest son's eyes, and he wasn't about to stand for it. As earl, he ran his holdings, his men—and his family—with an iron fist, and all who knew him held his legendary wrath in deference.

He liked it that way.

Malcolm said in a curt tone, "I'll have Simon bring another woman. A little sport should ease your need, Father, and bedding her should pass the time until Lady Gillian arrives and can take her place."

"I don't like whores; you know that." He snarled the words, motioning for his horse to be saddled. "Their well-used bodies and willingness disgust me."

It was true, though occasionally he did use them, if the mood struck him. He knew Malcolm would be too prudent to remind him.

"I itch for English blood on my sheets," he said, his voice heavy with menacing conviction. "And I shall have Lorin's golden-haired niece beneath me this night, if I have to ride into England to get her. Now mount up. If our incompetent men cannot follow a simple road and find an old man and a girl traveling in a carriage, by the gods, I can do it myself."

It was true. Travel stained and weary, the men he sent to investigate the delay in the arrival of his future bride had come back empty-handed.

He had gone from impatient and eager to furious.

"They tried, Father," Malcolm protested, grabbing the reins of his own mount and swinging into the saddle. "Dammit to hell, we lost two horses, they pushed them so hard. There was no sign of the girl. Perhaps the baron changed his mind about the marriage."

Thomas narrowed his eyes to slits. "If he has, he will wish he had never entered into his pathetic existence on this earth. Besides, he has too many debts and no affection for the girl, for she was raised by an elderly relative. Why would he change his mind? She needs a husband and I offered good coin. I was even willing to overlook her black English blood, by damn, so he should be crawling on his hands and knees at the opportunity to wed her to an earl."

"Why would he change his mind?" Malcolm repeated deliberately. "Perhaps, in retrospect, even for a damned Englishman, he's found himself a conscience and considered your reputation."

He'd thought his son was too experienced and cautious to mention the less than savory repute that made it almost impossible for Thomas to now find a Scottish wife. It was not his fault his brides—all four of them—were in their graves. He had simply used them as women should be used, but now even the most callous of fathers this side of the border did not bargain their daughters. It was something that enraged him, but the promise of the English lass had soothed his anger somewhat.

"Are you arguing with me, you loutish idiot?" he asked in a raspy voice.

"If she is as beautiful as he says, mayhap he got another offer." Malcolm continued to prod him in the same taunting voice, holding his restive horse with an easy hand.

For a moment, Thomas saw red at that possibility, and the man leading his horse to him halted abruptly, his face blanching. "The papers have been signed and the girl is mine," he said through his teeth, striding to jerk the reins of his mount from the cowering servant. "I will kill anyone who says otherwise as I would step on an insect. Now let's ride."

At least they were out of the damnable weather and tomorrow would be at Castle Cameron. Adain brooded at the rain-lashed window, his hand cradling a brandy snifter. Dry clothes, hot food, and a stiff drink made all the difference in the level of his physical comfort, but his mental state was decidedly unsettled.

". . . Scottish flouting of the navigation acts has Westminster fuming, and our Parliament . . . Are you listening to me, Cameron? I seem to be having a decidedly one-sided conversation."

Adain turned, blank for a moment. "What? I'm sorry. I admit my mind was elsewhere."

"Ah, the girl and your damned impulsive rescue."

He said coolly, "What would you have done, Harry, in my place?"

His host, Harold McFerran, lounged in a wing chair by the crackling fire in his study, long legs carelessly extended, and elevated his brows. "Probably the same thing."

"Only 'probably'?"

The other man ran his hand through his short red curls and sighed. "No, you're right. Yes, I would have done the same thing." The same age as Adain, with russet hair and an easy, charming grin most women found irresistible, Harry was more than an old friend, and he and Adain were as close as brothers in many ways. Even though it made the journey a little longer, Adain had chosen to stop at the McFerran country house for overnight shelter, to give both Gillian and his horse some rest. After all, it had been very late when she finally drifted to sleep in his arms the night before.

Harry said in a noncommittal tone, "She's lovely."

Adain turned restlessly, downing a gulp of brandy. "I know. But even if that weren't the case, I would help any stranded woman in such circumstances."

"Maybe so, but you wouldn't look at her the same way, I'd venture to guess, my friend." Harry's lean face wore an expression of amusement.

"Is that so? And how do I look at the lovely Gillian?"

"Like a wolfhound eyes a bone. Possessively. And with a good deal of hunger."

It was true. He couldn't get the previous night out of his head, and their journey hadn't helped either. She had ridden in front of him, cradled in his arms and huddled against his chest, her cloak pulled up against the weather. The soft feel of her had evoked every step of the way impressions of the intimate carnal pleasure they had shared, and he had been hard for almost the entire trip.

"It's lust," Adain said defensively.

"Did I imply it wasn't?" Harry grinned. "No argument here." His smile slowly faded and his gaze was very direct. "However, there is one problem. . . . No, let me correct myself: There is one very *large* problem ahead. If the abominable Kleiss realizes where she is, he just might come for her. He isn't a leader who inspires loyalty, but fear can work just as well, and I am sure he can summon hundreds of men within hours if you refuse to relinquish her peacefully. On the other hand, the man is such a callous brute he might not care if his intended bride has disappeared and will just pick some other hapless lass to take her place. God help her."

"I've weighed both options myself." Adain crossed to drop into an opposite chair, his turbulent unrest making it hard for him to sit quietly. "Gillian had no idea of his true nature. Her uncle had kept all of it from her. I tried to gloss over how truly bad his reputation for cruelty and lawless force actually is, for I believed she was too innocent to understand. However, obviously I got my point across, for she agreed to come with me, even though she does not know me."

"Doesn't she?" Harry's mouth quirked. "I got the opposite impression at dinner. The lady acted as if she might know you quite well."

It was a little disturbing, but true, Adain pondered, not sure how he felt about the situation. It was almost as if she just *knew* him. How he thought, how his demons haunted him, maybe even how to heal him . . .

Not really comfortable with his inner speculation on the matter, he switched the subject back. "If Kleiss thinks I've appropriated something of value and decides to come for her, the Cameron clan will rally to my side. If he can raise hundreds, rest assured, I can raise a thousand in less than a day."

"A Scottish battle for an English girl?"

"A Scottish battle for the principle against sacrificing her to someone I know will treat her cruelly."

"I suppose I concede that point." Harry nodded briskly. "I just wondered if the Camerons would fight for her."

"They will fight for *me*, if I ask. Randal inherited the title, but I am laird now in their eyes." His cousin might have been officially in line, but Randal had no stomach for leadership, and the responsibility had fallen to Adain some time ago. His clan looked to him and, in turn, would take arms against anyone at his bidding. "Especially against Kleiss, since Scotland would be well rid of that odious blackguard," he added in a steely tone. "And I could probably count on the McCrays' support as well."

There was a short silence in which the rain pelted the window and the wind wailed eerily. Harry finally asked, "You would ask Robbie McCray for a favor?"

If things had to be as they were, at least Adain could answer that hesitant question honestly. "We are friends, believe it or not. He did not seduce Julia away from me; the choice was hers. He might have a reputation as a wild rogue, but he is also honorable and genuinely cares for her, as far as I can tell." He swallowed hard, the next words difficult. "She seems to return the sentiment. I would have her happy, so I am indebted to him in that way."

Harry didn't comment, which was just as well, but instead expressed his sympathy by refilling Adain's glass. "You may call the McFerran clan up also, if you have need of their swords."

It was a generous and moving offer, indicative of their long friendship. Adain took a drink and grinned. "I was hoping you might say that."

"You would do the same for me, so how could you doubt it?" His friend looked bland. "However, fight or no, tell me—what are you going to do with your beautiful maiden in distress? If, as you tell me, she is truly alone and without means to live, once Kleiss is thwarted, you cannot simply send her on her way."

"I know." Adain had pondered the matter all day. Though he had to admit, with Gillian in his arms, thinking was a bit difficult.

Harry was anything but a fool. "You should marry her, Adain. She is a lady, and both charming and well mannered. Since you admit you desire her, why not? Yes, she's English, but as far as I can tell, that is her only flaw, and there is the irrefutable point that you spent the night together at an inn. Even if you didn't as much as touch her hand, people will assume the worst."

Since their assumption would be entirely correct, it was difficult to argue. He'd touched a hell of a lot more than her hand. In fact, he had explored every inch of her delectable body. Adain muttered, "If you assume that hasn't occurred to me, think again. What choice did I have but to find her shelter? It was late, and she was both shocked and upset over the attack and her uncle's death. Her reputation seemed the last thing either of us should worry over."

But, yes, it *had* occurred to him the moment he'd opened his door to her knock and she'd asked to come in that there might be consequences if he agreed.

Yet he hadn't done the right thing, the prudent thing, but instead invited her inside and proceeded to take her virginity. It wasn't like him, but it was what it was, and he now needed to repair the damage done.

"Finding a husband for a woman of her obvious appeal should be simple enough under other circumstances. However, finding a husband for a ruined English girl with no dowry is another matter."

"What makes you think she's ruined?" Adain asked irritably, even though he was guilty as sin.

And astonishingly not all that repentant about the matter.

"Lady Gillian looks at you the way a woman looks at her lover." Harry's face wore a shrewd expression. "At least, that is what my wife tells me. And I have already mentioned how you look at her. I, for one, do not blame you in the least. She needed comfort, at a guess, and you offered it in your bed."

Actually, that was not correct, Adain thought with ironic insight. *He* had been the one who needed comfort, and she had offered it to him. With a sigh, he admitted, "My head was not in charge, but a very different part of my anatomy controlled my actions. However, I was not planning to wed anytime soon."

"What do you mean? You are five and twenty. Bloody hell, Adain, you would be married to Julia right now if things had not gone awry."

"That is my very point," he shot back. "I still love Julia. Maybe I will always love her. It is an injustice to marry anyone when my heart lies elsewhere."

"The injustice," Harry countered, unfazed, "is that you are not moving forward. It is a step toward curing yourself of your melancholy to take a woman into your life. Breed children, Adain, and enjoy Lady Gillian's soft, willing body beside you each night. She is not Julia, I concede it, but surely it is possible to develop affection for another? Lust is an acceptable place to start. Perhaps love will come with it. Either way, you will no longer be alone and bereft."

Adain gave his old friend an exasperated look. "You are as romantic as an old woman, Harry."

McFerran shook his head. "I am not. I am trying to explain that something good can perhaps come from your snatching away Kleiss's betrothed and risking your fool neck to protect her. If you marry her right away, even if the coldhearted bastard does discover where she is, he will have no legitimate claim."

"There was a marriage agreement, signed and legal," Adain argued—but a voice in his head said Harry was right. If he married Gillian, it would be a greater stumbling block if the earl took issue with her presence at Castle Cameron. Besides, honorably, he did need to do the right thing. Even now, she could carry his child.

"Do it so it can't be revoked in court. I can have a clergyman here in an hour. You will have to pay a fine, but you're rich enough that hardly matters. My wife and I can be the witnesses. I've a lot of influence in this area; by God, I own half of it. If I testify to the marriage, the matter is done, from the point of view of the courts."

By Scottish law, if there were two witnesses to not just the wedding, but the bedding, it could not be contested legally. Adain had his own reservations over having an audience to what should be an entirely private matter, but Harry was right: Kleiss would have no recourse except to acknowledge Gillian was out of his filthy reach.

Adain was a little surprised he wasn't more opposed to the idea. He'd spoken the truth before: He did still ache for Julia with a persistent need he feared would never go away. It felt unfair to marry Gillian, considering his feelings for another woman, but she was most definitely better off marrying him than a rapacious, murdering bully who reputedly beat his servants, browbeat his family, and terrorized his tenants. Rumor had it the earl's last wife had died after he'd punished her for some slight, and the details of what he'd done would sicken even a hardened warrior.

He thought of the vulnerability of Gillian's satin-smooth skin, the slender grace of her body, the beauty of her deep blue eyes.

Adain shoved himself to his feet. "Send for the clergyman."

Would he come to her?

Gillian wasn't sure how these things worked, since she had never had a liaison before, and most certainly had no idea how to be someone's mistress.

Was that what she was now?

She wasn't sure. Adain Cameron had bedded her most thoroughly, but perhaps that was all there was to it. One shared and entirely memorable night of passion in which they sought solace together against her ill-fated engagement and his shattered heart. The trouble was, she didn't want it to be left that way. An offer of protection could mean many things, and if letting him bed her made her a whore, so be it. She'd live with the label if it was what he wished of her. What she'd heard about Kleiss was bad enough, and by her lover's own admission, he was sparing her the more gruesome details. She was much better off in Adain's arms and bed, even without the benefit of honest marriage.

Besides, an inner voice reminded her in droll observation, it wasn't like she hadn't thoroughly enjoyed every moment of their lovemaking. Aunt Eugenia had been right: If done properly, it was quite an enlightening experience.

With restless anticipation, she paced across the room she'd been given. It was very fine, with velvet hangings on the bed, carved heavy furniture, and tall windows that still whispered with the persistent rain.

A sharp knock sounded and a deep voice called her name.

Gillian froze midstep as she realized Adain was just outside. A small curl of excitement spiraled through her body. Was it wanton to be so eager for his touch? She didn't care. Impulsively, she crossed the room to open the door.

His gaze ran over her thin nightdress and loose hair. "I see you are still awake, my lady."

"I've been waiting," Gillian confessed, feeling her face warm in a blush. "I hoped you would come to me."

That was shameless enough, wasn't it?

His silver eyes glimmered and his well-shaped mouth looked a little tight. "I need to talk to you."

The intense expression on his face made her heart sink a little. "I . . . see." She faltered. "Of course." She stood aside and watched him enter the room. He didn't look at all like the tender lover of the night before, or even the solicitous escort of their journey. Instead, he stalked restlessly across the room to look out the window for a moment before he turned his gaze to her. Dark hair, a little tousled, curled against the strong column of his neck, and his gray eyes were very direct.

Without preamble, he said, "We need to marry. Tonight. The arrangements are being made."

She blinked, not expecting that statement in the least. "What?"

"Will you accept me? If so, it will keep you safe from ever having to marry Kleiss."

Gillian was so off balance she wasn't sure what to say, so she just stared at him for a long moment.

When she said nothing, his expression changed. "I . . . see, lass. If you don't wish this—"

His reaction registered and Gillian quickly shook her head, knowing he'd been rejected before, her hands clenching in the filmy material of her sleeping gown. "It isn't that I don't wish it, Adain. I am simply surprised. We do not know each other."

He crossed his arms over his broad chest. "You were promised to Kleiss and you have never even met him. And besides, lest you forget, we know each other in the most intimate way a man and woman can."

Gillian flushed. "That's true," she agreed faintly, aware of the vulnerability he tried to hide. She was just flustered over this unexpected proposal. "I simply meant that two people cannot decide to wed within a day of their acquaintance."

"Yes, they can, if you agree. I would never force you against your will, but I do think this is best." He added quietly, "You could carry my babe even now. I will not see you shamed, or my child born a bastard, and I will never allow Kleiss to claim you either, so my solution is logical, is it not?"

"I . . . I suppose so." She felt a little giddy, and for the first time since her peaceful, sheltered existence with Aunt Eugenia was shattered by the tragedy of her beloved relative's death, a glimmer of hope came for the future. What she had prayed for with Lord Kleiss was at best a kind husband who would treat her decently. Never had she dreamed she would be able to marry a handsome young man, who—even if he had a wounded heart—would seek to protect her at such cost.

"Your answer is yes, then?"

The intensity of his expression took her breath away and she simply nodded, unable to speak.

"Very well." He made no move to take her in his arms but instead glanced at the small, ornate clock on top of the mantel. "Harry swears to me he can have the necessary parties here in just a short time."

She didn't have an extensive wardrobe by any means, but her trunk had not been something they carried on his horse, which meant she had next to nothing appropriate for such a momentous event. She had selected only a set of clean clothes for their journey and the simple sleeping gown she had on now. Gillian said in dismay, "I have nothing to wear."

"What you have on is fine." His gaze dropped briefly to where her breasts swelled beneath the thin material, and for the first time he seemed to relax a little. "Actually, it is perfect."

"My nightdress?"

"The ceremony will be here, in this bedroom." He glanced at

EMMA WILDES

the bed, neatly turned down by one of the McFerran maids. Don't worry. It will all be very quick."

Gillian felt a little weak-kneed suddenly, and she stared at the bed for a moment, then gave him an outraged look. "You wish to marry me in a bed? I didn't realize *that* was a Scottish custom."

One dark brow edged up, and he smiled with a hint of masculine amusement. "Haven't you been taught from the cradle we're all barbarians, Lady Gillian?"

He looked the furthest thing from a barbarian in a fitted coat of dark claret-colored velvet, his neck cloth pristine, tailored breeches clinging to his hard thighs. As always, his unusual eyes had a slightly guarded look. She said, "No. My aunt and I lived a simple life, and the politics on either side of the border did not interest her. She taught me that people are simply people, no matter their heritage. Some are good; some are not."

"She sounds very wise. At any rate, if we are already in bed, it makes it easier for the witnessing of the consummation. We can get married more formally in the chapel at Castle Cameron later, if you like."

She'd heard of witnesses being used, of course, but certainly it was not a common practice except among royalty. "Is it strictly necessary?" she asked faintly, a little shocked at the prospect.

"The consummation? Oh, yes, from my point of view, definitely necessary." There was meaningful suggestion in his soft tone.

"The witnesses," she clarified, feeling mortified over the notion. "Which I have a feeling you know well was what I meant."

"It will make the union bound in iron, from a legal standpoint."

How he could sound unconcerned over doing something so intimate with people *watching* was beyond her comprehension, but she supposed if they were going to do this rash thing, it was best to make sure it couldn't be contested. "I wish I could summon your casual attitude over this," she muttered.

Her future husband simply looked bland. "They will not stay for the entire thing; don't worry."

Remembering her unrestrained enjoyment of the night before, she blushed again at the idea of anyone hearing her unladylike moans of pleasure. "I certainly hope not."

Chapter 4

*D*id the fool honestly think Thomas would not be able to extract the truth?

The crack rang through the room and the inn-keeper fell to his knees, clutching his face. Blood poured from his nose, and the stupid man fairly sobbed for mercy.

Fortunately, the Earl of Kleiss was not familiar with that concept. Mercy was for weak idiots, and Thomas was neither an imbecile nor a spineless woman. Had the proprietor properly considered the repercussions of his lies, he might have saved himself a beating.

"If her uncle died, did this man kill him?"

"There was not a mark on his body and he was frail and ill. No, milord, he killed the men who tried to rob them, but not the old man."

"Once again, I would have his name." Thomas glared, not un-aware his son had turned away, looking as if he disapproved of his method of questioning.

"He did not tell me," the terrified man said again, his voice muffled. "I can describe him for you, but that is it. He paid in gold, and took the girl with him when he left, mounted on a great black horse."

"He abducted her?" Thomas felt his teeth grind together. The innocent Lady Gillian was *his*. How could this happen?

"She went willingly, milord. At least as far as I could tell."

"Why would she do that?" Thomas spat, the reek of the stale ale spilled on the floor of the taproom making him more irritated than ever. "He must have forced her, for she knew she was coming to me, to be my bride."

For a moment, it looked like the idiot, bleeding and beaten as he was, might actually argue, but instead he said meekly, "I am sure you are right, Lord Kleiss."

Malcolm, for once, was slightly useful. "Describe him, then, and tell us what direction they took. That's all we want and we will be on our way."

Apparently not willing to risk getting back to his feet, the inn-keeper crouched on the floor and nodded. "He was tall, dark haired, with a slightly dangerous look about him. After all, he dispatched the highwaymen without trouble, didn't he? Oh, yes, he had silver eyes; I noticed that. In the morn, he took the lass and rode east."

Thomas looked into the innkeeper's eyes and saw fear, but also defiance. Men had tried to deceive him before and not lived to regret the effort. He said with a cruel smile, "We'll ride west, for I think you are trying to misdirect us. Malcolm, dispose of this inef-fectual liar."

His son's normally ruddy face paled slightly. "He's told us what he knows. He's an old man, not a threat to us."

Thomas lifted his brows. "Do it."

"Father, I—"

"Do it, you blithering coward, or do I have to teach you again the measure of obedience?"

For a moment he thought Malcolm would argue further. Thomas stared him down, though his son was of a height. "You take after your mother a wee bit too much," he said with vicious emphasis. "She was weak and good for one purpose only. I let you cling to her skirts far too long. Let's face it—you're soft, boy."

Malcolm's hand dropped to the hilt of his sword and he looked like he might actually draw it and challenge him. The fool always had been too attached to his mother, and had blamed him for her death. Thomas had beaten it out of him, but now and then the resentment resurfaced.

Over a woman. It was laughable.

"If you pull your weapon," Thomas said coldly, "I advise you to use it to dispatch this stupid old man."

Then he swung on his heel and exited the shabby inn, shouting to his men to mount up and head west.

The ceremony was brief—blessedly so, because he was more than ready for what came next.

It seemed his worries over performing for an audience were unfounded, Adain thought with self-mocking amusement. Only moments after he shed his clothes and slipped into the giant four-poster bed beside his lovely bride-to-be, he'd had an erection. With the sheet and blankets drawn to his waist, it was not visible to the man who performed the brief ceremony, or to their obliging host and hostess, but it was damned disconcerting to be so aroused so easily. Maybe his long abstinence had taken its toll and his hungry cock now knew it was permanently over. After Julia had married another, he hadn't had the heart to engage in a casual dalliance.

He still didn't, apparently, for this wasn't casual at all.

Her smooth cheeks were tinted a rosy hue in embarrassment over the unorthodox setting for their nuptials, and Gillian's slender fingers trembled just slightly as he clasped her hand. However, she recited her vows with quiet dignity, and signed the papers afterward in a clear hand.

And it was done.

He had married an Englishwoman he'd known for only a day. It sounded insane, but with the warmth of her tempting slender body beside him, it did not feel that way.

If the plump, cheerful man of God Harry had dragged away from his warm fire disapproved of the bedroom setting, he did not show it. Instead, he warmly congratulated them, put the correct seals on the documents, and gave an indulgent chuckle over Gillian's scarlet face before he left. At a guess, it was not the first time he'd been summoned to perform a hasty wedding for two impatient lovers.

Harry, standing at the foot of the bed, also looked amused. His pretty wife, Anne, who was notoriously outspoken, gave Adain a look of grudging approval. "I'm glad you did the right thing, Adain Cameron, for I could tell by the way the two of you looked at each other at the dinner table, Lady Gillian would not be sleeping alone this eve."

Next to him, Gillian made a small, muffled sound of what he guessed was mortification. Mildly, he responded, "I am not an irresponsible rogue, Annie. You know me better than that."

"I know *all* men can be rogues." She gave her husband a stern glance, but her tone was teasing. "Don't try to look innocent, Harry McFerran."

"Me? Never." He slipped his arm around her waist and looked at Adain. He said quietly, "Whenever you are ready. We needn't stay for more than a few minutes. Just long enough so I could give my word before a judge, if it came to that. Kleiss has enough influence in the courts that we need to be careful."

Adain was certainly ready, but his bride probably wasn't. He turned and gazed at her. Propped against the pillows, Gillian still wore her nightdress and looked young with her gold hair tumbled over her slim shoulders and her blue eyes demurely downcast.

Gently, he caught her chin and lifted her face so they looked at each other. He whispered, "If I did not think this was necessary, they would not be here. They can't actually see us because we are under the blankets, and you can keep your gown on until they leave. Just relax, my sweet."

"I'll try," she said, and her mouth curved into a small, bewitching smile.

God, you are so beautiful. . . .

Gillian reached up and touched his mouth, a featherlight brush of her fingertips. "You are beautiful, Adain," she said so quietly only he could hear it.

Had he spoken out loud? He wasn't sure, because just from that simple touch, his body ignited, and though she was obviously uncomfortable with the notion of the McFerrans being in the room, she did not protest when he leaned over and kissed her.

Her mouth was warm, silky, and she tasted like heaven.

It was his intention to lure her to arousal with tender caresses and soft words, but almost against his will, passion took over instead. His tongue slid into her mouth time and again, rubbing hers suggestively, teasing every corner. In sweet response, Gillian twined her arms around his neck and pressed passionately against him.

The last thing he needed was that kind of artless encouragement. Not when his throbbing cock ached to be buried inside her. Through the material of her nightdress his hand skimmed her body, feeling the enticing curves beneath the cloth. Slowly, he inched the hem upward until the material was bunched around her waist, all the while kissing her mouth, her neck, and the delicate line of her jaw.

Caressing her hip first to get her used to the notion of his touch, he slipped his fingers between her legs.

And found to his surprise, despite her nervous shyness, his gorgeous new wife was already wet. Sleek, hot, and definitely well on her way to arousal even with the witnesses in the room. She might look like an innocent angel, all golden hair, ivory skin, and blue eyes, but beneath it, she was a sensual woman. When he slid a finger deep into her vaginal passage, she made a small sound he knew was involuntary because of her trepidation, and her hips lifted in a movement he found impossibly erotic.

Silken softness, warmth, acceptance . . .

Very well, if she was ready, he certainly was more than eager. Shifting, he moved so he was braced over her, using his knees to part her legs. With his hand, he guided his stiff cock to her entrance and, with as much care as possible, sheathed himself deeply inside her.

Gillian caught his shoulders and arched into his penetration with an audible gasp.

Dimly, in the haze of pleasure, he heard the door close.

They were alone.

Raggedly, he said, "They're gone."

"Thank heavens," she said on another audible swift intake of breath. "Oh, Adain."

"My sentiments exactly." He slid backward in a movement as controlled as he could make it, and surged forward.

The delicious friction almost sent him over the edge in just one thrust. "You're so tight," he managed to say through his teeth. "God help me, lass, I hope I can wait for you."

Beneath him, Gillian smiled, her eyes shimmering suddenly. "If you cannot, don't worry. We have the rest of our lives, remember? I imagine we will do this again."

For a moment, he stilled, though it took every bit of his control. "I remember," he said, his inner amazement over how it did not frighten him a revelation. He added with dark, sinful promise, "And, yes, we will do it many, many times, my sweet wife."

The warm suction made Gillian's eyes open, her lashes lifting in a languid movement. Adain's dark head was bent over her breast, his mouth closed over the crest of the nipple, his tongue working magic with the sensitive tip. Small tingles of pleasure rippled through her body, centering between her legs in a seductive pulse.

It was very late, for the fire had burned down to almost nothing, the only illumination coming from the thin moonlight filtered by the draperies at the windows.

She could sleep another time, Gillian thought in a haze of rapturous enjoyment, her fingers sliding through her husband's thick hair as he ministered to the other breast. This was her wedding night, and it certainly seemed Adain was determined to make the most of it. He'd taken her twice already, but it was more than obvious he was ready again.

"I could play with these all night," he murmured against her skin, lightly licking into the valley between the mounded flesh in his hands. "So beautiful and female. Like all of you."

And he was entirely male, with his hard, muscular body and imposing height, even the softness of his hair, masculine against the tensile strength of his neck. Gillian had to acknowledge a fascination with the part of him that lengthened and grew in evidence of his desire for her. At the moment, she felt the hardness against her hip, and she experienced a shiver of anticipation over what she knew was to come.

"I like it when you touch me," she admitted, clasping him closer. "I know I am ignorant yet, so tell me, do women also touch men . . . well, I mean . . . *there?*"

He lifted his head, and the heat in his gaze was palpable, brushing her like a licking flame. "Aye, lass, they do, *if* they wish it."

"I want to touch you." It sounded like a brazen thing to say, but it was the truth. He had touched her everywhere, and even had those long, skillful fingers deep up inside her. The most she had done during their lovemaking was touch his shoulders and back and neck, but the memory of how his hard chest had felt beneath her palm the night before was intriguing. Though the man she had just married was decidedly working on her education, she was still avidly inquisitive.

"It would be my pleasure," he said huskily, and rolled to his back. Arms crossed behind his head, gloriously nude and aroused, he gave her a lazy smile that made his face more compellingly handsome than ever. "Do what you like, my sweet wife. I am at your disposal."

Gillian rose up to her knees and shyly ran her hands over his broad chest, marveling at how sculpted and defined it was, not an ounce of fat on his lean body. There were a few scars, the silvery healed flesh indicative of a man who had seen a battle or two. His nipples were small and flat, but actually hardened slightly as she brushed them with her exploring fingers.

"I like that," Adain said in a husky tone, lounging nude and unself-conscious against the pillows. His cock jutted upward, rigid against his flat stomach, a light dusting of dark hair trailing from his navel to his groin.

Tentatively, she touched his erection.

It was hot, magnificently hard, and so long she could not quite believe it would fit completely inside her. At the tip, there was a small opening, and as she ran her fingers up the velvety skin of his rigid sex, it leaked a few drops of a sticky clear fluid. At the base, there was a soft sac and she cupped it, feeling the soft weight with wonder.

Her tall husband made a sound, like a low groan. She glanced at his face and saw he watched her fondle his cock with glittering half-closed eyes, and his chest lifted rapidly. It pleased Gillian to think she had his complete attention, for she felt a small, irrational jealousy that he had loved the woman who had broken his heart so completely.

And maybe still loved her.

However, there was no question he was pleasured and distracted from dwelling on what he'd lost when they were intimately together. If she could do nothing else, she could offer him whatever he wished in bed. After all, he had just married her to protect her.

Aunt Eugenia's words drifted back, and while Gillian had been shocked at the time, she was now glad her progressive-thinking guardian had been so explicit.

Adain just might be glad also.

Leaning forward, she slowly took the swollen tip of her husband's cock in her mouth, her lips sliding over the engorged crest. It felt both alive and silky smooth.

Adain's intake of breath was an audible hiss of both surprise and—she didn't have to guess—enjoyment.

It was certainly not possible to take the entire thing, so she slid down as far as she could, tasting the salty essence, brushing the swollen tip with her tongue.

"Lass, what are you doing?" His voice was raspy, and long fingers slid into her hair, tangling in the strands.

It was a little difficult to answer with his shaft in her mouth, and she sucked gently, much as he liked to do at her breasts. It was immensely wonderful when he did it to her, and she had no doubt at all that he liked this equally well, because his breathing changed and from under the veil of her lashes, as she peered up, she saw his eyes drift shut.

Delighted to have such a dramatic effect on him, she continued, not certain of what she was doing exactly, but he seemed pleased enough, and that had been her goal. Before she and her uncle had departed on their fateful journey, she had been given a stern lecture on being a dutiful wife.

This, she supposed, was being very dutiful indeed, but she highly doubted it was what her uncle had meant.

"Gillian, stop. I need you now." With urgency, her husband pulled his swollen shaft from her mouth and moved over her in one lithe, fluid motion.

She parted her legs and his hips wedged them open wide as he thrust deeply inside her. Their joining was so wonderful she couldn't help but moan out loud as he began to move in long, powerful strokes, unlike the tender care he'd taken with her earlier.

In moments, she felt that telltale rise, the escalation incredible and out of her control. If Queen Anne herself had walked into the room, she could not have stopped the inarticulate sounds she made with each delicious pumping motion of Adain's lower body. He shared her wild hunger, for while she was much too distracted to concentrate on anything but her own pleasure, she knew their goal was the same.

When it burst, it was like a shower of sparks, the flame exploding in a maelstrom of physical joy that left her gasping and shaking. Her release triggered his climax as well, and Gillian could feel the rushing pulse as he filled her passage with his seed.

Heart pounding, her arms still wrapped around him, she was beautifully content and acutely replete in a physical sense.

If a man was honorable, brave, devastatingly attractive, and a wonderful, considerate lover, was it wrong to fall in love with him in less than two days?

Probably, she reminded herself with an inner shiver of dismay, if he was still in love with someone else.

Chapter 5

Malcolm Graham stared at the captain of his father's troops in unconcealed dismay. "The devil you say, William."

The other man, bearded and thickset, with the shoulders of a bull and a ferocious will to fight to match, nodded grimly. "By all accounts, the girl is with Adain Cameron. They stopped to rest and refresh themselves in a small village, and the stable boy who tended his horse knows him. He recognized him from the description, and apparently the young lady is quite memorable too, and as beautiful as Lorin promised. The keeper of the inn confirmed it when pressed and given a few coins."

"Fucking hell, this will not please my father."

"That," William said with a humorless smile, "is why *you* can tell him. I decline the honor, sir."

Malcolm paced across the courtyard and then back. "Tell me, what do you know about Cameron?"

"Good with a sword and cool in battle. An able leader since his uncle's death, also. He was suspected for a while to have had a hand in Laird Cameron's murder, but those rumors were proven false. He must be an honorable man, for though all the evidence pointed to him, most did not believe it, and he was never charged. Other than that, what I know is that taking on the Camerons will not be an easy task. He has a loyal clan and, if we go after the English lass, also the advantage of being on his own land."

"Damnation, he must have taken her on purpose, for surely she told him about the betrothal!"

"No doubt she did, and he was moved to intervene by either her beauty or your father's black reputation. Both the boy and innkeeper said she did not seem forced, quite the contrary. Without intent to offend, sir, who could blame her? Cameron is young and handsome, and rescued her once already. What young woman wouldn't prefer him to an old man she has never met?"

"Since when has my father cared what anyone else prefers?" Malcolm could feel the bitterness over his bleak childhood rise like bile in his throat. Though she had never said so, he'd known his mother despised her heartless husband, and when she died, Malcolm had the solace of knowing she went to a life without suffering. He too had endured countless beatings as he was honed into the kind of warrior his father believed he should be. Had he not learned a long time ago to conform and not resist, he had no doubt he would also be dead, heir or not. What his father saw as weakness in him was more a sense of survival hard-learned early in childhood. With two younger brothers, Malcolm was expendable.

"I doubt we are going to have a choice but to try to take her." Malcolm rubbed his gloved hand over his face roughly. "My father is obsessed with the notion of bedding the English girl. He has always been ruthless, but lately, I worry his reason is slipping."

William stayed silent, but the expression on his broad face showed he agreed.

"If we do manage to retrieve Lady Gillian, she had better still be untouched, for her sake." He knew his father, and Malcolm shuddered to think of what he would do if he found out she had given herself to another man first. He added somberly, "I doubt she would survive the night."

"Cameron is not just going to hand her over. If he wanted to do that, he'd have simply found her an escort here."

"I am sure you are right," Malcolm agreed reluctantly, finding the notion of men dying over his father's lustful greed unpalatable. "Yes, there is going to be blood spilled."

Adain had an unsettling suspicion.

His new wife, so lovely, so innocent and ladylike—and also so generous and sensual in bed—was unusual in a way that had nothing to do with her entrancing blond beauty.

In fact, he was starting to come to the incredible conclusion that she could actually guess with fair accuracy what he was thinking. He'd never thought of himself as transparent to others, and he still didn't. It was more that she listened and observed. Often enough he'd caught her watching him with a faint smile, or been the recipient of a thoughtful gesture that mirrored something he wanted or needed.

They had been married for a week now, and he had to say she had settled very well into the life at Castle Cameron. Even the housekeeper, Mrs. Dunbar, who had been there for decades and had a well-known aversion to both change of any kind and the despised English, grudgingly admitted that Lady Gillian was a pleasant addition to the household. His appearance with a new, unexpected bride in tow had certainly stunned his family, but they accepted her with a cautious politesse that was already thawing into liking.

He liked her himself.

Quite a lot.

Especially at moments like this.

A warm tongue licked his neck playfully, and Gillian's lissome naked body rested on top of him, her bare breasts soft against his chest. Though it was midmorning, they were still in bed, and he knew he should have gotten up hours ago. "Adain," she murmured, "that was wonderful."

"For the fourth time," he agreed, smiling, running his fingers down the graceful curve of her spine to gently cup one firm buttock and give a small squeeze. "You bewitch me, lass."

She stiffened slightly. "I am not a witch. Don't say that." She shook her head firmly, blond curls moving across her slim shoulders.

"Gillian," he said softly, the sudden fear in her blue eyes giving him true pause. "I did not mean to insult you. I was jesting, of course."

The way she stared at him told him he was exactly correct about frightening her. She whispered, "You know what happened to my aunt, don't you?"

Adain felt her tremble, their naked bodies so entwined it was impossible to miss. Puzzled, he couldn't help but stare at her now ashen face. "No, I do not."

Gillian scrambled off him, clutching the sheet to her chest. She knelt next to him, her eyes dark and her bare shoulders gleaming. There were tears gathered on her lashes like crystalline drops, and she turned her head away.

"Gillian," he said gently, resisting reaching for her only by sheer will. "I meant nothing except that I find you entrancing to an unsettling degree. What's wrong?"

"They accused her."

The light dawned and Adain sat up straighter. He said carefully, "Are you telling me they accused your aunt of being a witch?"

Face averted, she nodded. "She was nothing of the kind." Her voice was thin and reedy. "She was simply gentle hearted and she liked . . . people. She always told me that you could tell what a person was thinking if you watched their actions. The way someone holds their body, their posture, their gestures . . . Aunt Eugenia always said there were all types of people in this world, the bright lights and the quiet shadows."

"She sounds quite wise." Adain knew ridiculous charges of witchcraft were still brought up often enough, especially in the countryside. "What happened?"

His wife shrugged, but it was feigned nonchalance; he could tell by the unhappy set of her mouth. "She died before they brought formal charges. Some even said that was a sign of her dark powers, but in truth, she'd been having pains in her chest off and on for some time. I am glad she was spared the humiliation of a trial on such false allegations."

"I'm very sorry, lass."

"Then my uncle on my father's side came for me. I suppose I was naive to think he'd exhibit the same gentle nature."

Adain leaned forward then and caught a single tear on his fingertip from the corner of her eye. "I understand how it feels when people disappoint you."

"Yes, I know you do." All tumbled blond hair and enticing curves, she nodded, faint color coming back into her face. "From the moment we met, I could sense your pain, but it had nothing to do with magic. I simply felt . . . connected to your soul."

Connected to his soul. It was possible. Certainly he'd never seduced a woman so quickly, and then there was the indisputable leap to marriage the very next day. Perhaps their souls *were* connected.

An interesting thought.

She correctly read his expression in her usual disconcerting way.

"Can a woman not also feel desire?" Gillian demanded, lifting her chin. "Yes, I felt your pain, but it alone did not bring me to your bed, Adain. I am sorry you are hurt and feel betrayed by what happened in your past, but it is the least of why I went to you or why I married you."

More than her words, the charmingly defiant tilt of her chin replaced his chagrin with relief and inner amusement. For such a dainty, feminine creature, his young wife had spirit, and he admired it as much as or more than her tempting physical appearance. He was twice her size, yet from the sudden light of battle in her eyes, he wondered if he wasn't going to lose most of the arguments that were an inevitable part of any marriage.

Especially if she could practically read his damned mind.

"I see. All right, I'll stand corrected if you demonstrate exactly how it is you do feel when you are in my arms." He reached out and tugged at the sheet she still clutched to her chest, covering her nudity.

"I have been doing that for most of this morning," Gillian argued tartly, but she released the sheet, and the set of her mouth softened.

She was so lovely. He found it inexplicably arousing to see the evidence of their earlier lovemaking on her pale thighs, the iridescent smears of his seed mingled with her sexual fluids.

He looked into her eyes and was even more moved by what he saw there. His entire life he had assumed he would marry Julia, and when the expectation was shattered, he had been devastated.

However, Gillian had changed that in a remarkably short amount of time.

I want you. Adain smiled, gazing at his wife with undisguised longing.

"You have me," she promised, and slipped her arms around his neck as he rolled her to her back. As always, she accepted him eagerly, spreading her legs wide for his penetration, pressing into each thrust with equal fervor, and when she shuddered in climax, the way she gasped his name touched his soul.

Maybe, he thought, drowning in delicious sensation, everything had worked out for the best after all.

Arms askew, hands on her hips, the housekeeper gave her a stubborn look of refusal, but Gillian refused to be intimidated. "Please, Mrs. Dunbar, I think I need to know what happened."

"I'll not be telling tales behind his back, lassie. 'Tis not my place."

As a gesture of truce, Gillian offered a small glass of wine. She was at the main table in the dining hall, and though there were servants moving around the castle, no one was near enough to hear their conversation. "I do not want idle gossip, which I believe you know. I think I need to understand exactly why Julia Cameron declined to marry Adain and eloped with someone else instead. He told me that much, but nothing more. It still pains him, so I don't want to make my husband talk about it, but I admit I am very curious. Adain is a wonderful man, so why would she choose another?"

The older woman lifted her brows. "Aye, he must be wonderful at something," she muttered, "for the two of you to stay in bed half the day. Ye have the look of a well-satisfied lass. He has quite a smile on his face as well, which I haven't seen in some time."

Gillian blushed to the roots of her hair, not certain how to respond. With as much dignity as possible, she said, "I know you are fond of him, so can you fault me for also holding him in high regard? Please, there is no one else I'd dream of asking about this."

Grudgingly, the housekeeper sat down. She eyed the glass of wine for a moment and then chuckled. "Trying to loosen my tongue? That must be a sly English trick. I warn you, my lady, I can hold my liquor."

"If it is a trick, I've never used it before." Gillian spoke mildly. "My aunt didn't believe in strong drink of any kind." She glanced around, the interior of the huge baronial-style house as foreign as the country she now called home. "I am doing my best to adjust to Castle Cameron and make Adain a good wife."

Now that she had capitulated, Mrs. Dunbar didn't seem to hold her earlier reservations over a small chat. "For a Sassenach, you do not seem to be totally unacceptable," she conceded, as if it pained her greatly, "and you are a bonny lass; that is certain. However, Adain would never have married you just for your pretty face. He is too practical for that. He makes a fine laird, even if the position isn't rightly his."

"Where is Randal Cameron?" From the bits she'd gleaned here and there, Gillian had already discerned that Julia's older brother was in direct line for the position of leading his kinsmen, but he was conspicuous by his absence in what must be his own home.

"France." The housekeeper fiddled with the stem of her glass for a moment and then took a quick sip. "He and a friend chose to leave Scotland. 'Tis probably best."

Gillian looked at her expectantly, not sure how much she could ask. There was certainly more to the story.

Upright in her chair, the housekeeper looked back. She said gruffly, "Adain is a leader, but Randal is not. It's best this way, and everyone knows it. There was a time of doubt, but that's all over."

"If everyone admires Adain so, why did Julia choose someone else?"

"She thought he'd murdered her father in cold blood for an inheritance."

Gillian blinked, stunned and horrified as everything fell into place. "Adain? He never would do such a thing."

Finally, she saw a gleam of approval in the other woman's eyes. "You've known him only a short time. Are you sure?"

Was she? Yes. Absolutely.

"I'm sure," Gillian said firmly. "Why wasn't *she* sure, when Julia had known him her entire life?"

"Grief can take a person in many ways, my lady." Mrs. Dunbar pursed her mouth. "Julia is like my daughter, but she wasn't thinking straight when she ran off and married that charming hellion Robbie McCray. However, let me tell you it was for the best; take my word. Adain is too steady for her, too responsible and settled. She was always a daring lass and needed a mate who would give her adventure."

That anyone would find the very idea of being with her new husband unexciting was astonishing to Gillian. "Adain is not dull," she spoke defensively. "You should have seen him as he defended me from those horrible ruffians. He married to save me from ever having to wed Lord Kleiss, and it is the most unselfish thing I have ever heard!"

"I never said he was a coward, my lady—or selfish, for that matter. Don't bristle up so. He's a fine man, and every bit as handsome as the devilish McCray in his own way. You are not the first lassie to get moon-eyed over him, but before you, he never looked at anyone but Julia."

Suddenly, Gillian realized she was being teased a little. She took great interest in her wine for a moment, and then sighed. "It is obvious to you I am in love with him, is it not?"

"That is the only reason I sit here now, neglecting my duties." Mrs. Dunbar's usually dour face was softened by a smile.

There was one more thing she needed to know about her husband's failed engagement. "I know he loved her. You know him well. . . . Tell me, do you think he will ever get over his sense of loss?"

"Aye, child, indeed I do." The housekeeper shook her gray head, her shrewd eyes narrowed. "You are so young to think he would be heartbroken forever." She gave a small, derisive snort.

"He has a beautiful lass in his arms and bed, which, since he is a man, will make up for a great deal. Satisfy his body and his heart will follow."

With reluctance, Gillian asked haltingly, "What will happen if the earl decides he's been slighted? I've asked Adain, but I can tell he doesn't want me to worry over it. He just brushes my concerns aside."

Mrs. Dunbar got to her feet in her brisk, no-nonsense way and smoothed her hands on her pristine apron, signaling the end of their conversation. "Make no mistake, he'll fight to keep ye, and so will any he calls up to stand beside him. You're his wife, and a Cameron now. You belong to us."

Chapter 6

Malcolm reined in his mount with an inner curse at the cold wind. His face streamed moisture, and the horses blew breath from their nostrils in white puffs. Giving the signal, he brought the company to a halt and surveyed the Cameron defense.

It was strong, of course. That was why the castle still stood after centuries of legendary bloody battles that comprised the history of the area. The fortified towers were obviously part of an older structure that had been modernized by wings and gave the house a sprawling effect. It stood on a rise, with a small loch to the south and a forested area to the north.

"I doubt," he told his father, "our approach has gone unnoticed. Unless Cameron is a fool, he has guardsmen posted somewhere to alert him of anyone crossing his land."

In answer, his father stared at the imposing house with fanatical anger, his thin-lipped mouth twisted in a snarl. In his sixties, he was no longer as heavily built as he once was, and his clipped beard and long hair were entirely gray. His weathered features had been handsome years ago, but harsh lines were deeply incised beside his mouth and nose, and his forehead was permanently furrowed. He said with the arrogant, decisive conviction of a man who was used to getting his own way, "He'll know we are here soon enough when we attack."

"Let me at least ride in ahead as your emissary and ask for Lady Gillian's return." Malcolm had argued all along that they send an official communication first, though he knew the request would be met with refusal.

"No, I want Cameron dead. He took my property without provocation."

The lass was not property in Malcolm's mind, but his father thought differently. Scotland was too small a country for the rumors over his father's infamously volatile and unreasonable temper not to reach every corner. Malcolm knew it was probably provocation enough if Cameron had decided to play the role of protector over the woman in question.

"It's been two weeks now," he pointed out with reckless disregard for his own health, since his father already had his sword drawn. "By all accounts, he married her, even if it is just a rumor and we have no proof of it. She is no longer the innocent maid you bargained for; rest assured of it. Choose another bride and forget her. Besides, to kill Cameron," he pointed out, "will bring the wrath of the entire Cameron clan down on us. They might not care to lose lives over an English girl, but they will be incensed if Adain Cameron is killed."

"My men do not care to fight over a traitorous slut either, but they will. When I get hold of her, she will grovel at my feet like the whore she is."

Malcolm doubted the girl was a slut or a whore in any way, but his father's view of women was, as always, simple and straightforward. They existed to spread their legs for men and give birth to their children. Otherwise, they were weaker creatures, and the Earl of Kleiss delighted in terrorizing anything that could not fairly fight back. He had treated Malcolm's mother like chattel, and it had broken her. Malcolm had been young, but he still had realized her desire to live had simply ceased when her health began to fail.

It was hard to decide where cruelty ended and madness began. There were times, more often than not lately, when he hated his overbearing parent with a vengeance.

This obsession with Lady Gillian might be fatal to them all. Cameron was by all accounts perfectly capable of defending himself, and certainly if he had taken the girl to wife, he had a vested interest in keeping her safe. "It may not be easy to do," Malcolm pointed out with grim asperity. "Look."

Sure enough, over a rise came a party of men hundreds strong. They wheeled their horses and stopped in a defensive position between the castle itself and the forces under the Earl of Kleiss.

Yes, they were definitely expected.

So that was Kleiss, a hulking form on a pale charger, his jutting beard and ramrod posture speaking of arrogance and the iron will that made him so infamously feared and despised.

Well, Adain was absolutely *not* afraid.

He was furious.

He nudged his horse forward, his hand resting on the hilt of his sword, heedless of the inclement weather. The minute his sentries had reported a large force on the move from the east, he'd sent out to raise as many loyal Camerons as possible, and it looked like they were in the majority.

Those were odds he liked. More men, familiar territory, and a conviction that he was entirely in the right. He'd taken pleasure in burning Gillian's marriage documents, watching the pages curl and disintegrate. They were in essence meaningless anyway, since the marriage had never been sanctioned by the Church or consummated.

No, Gillian was his. All of her, from her remarkable mind to her soft and sensually willing body, and he intended to keep her.

For the first time since he'd heard of Julia's marriage, he dared to think happiness lay in his grasp.

Next to him, Duncan Montague, his first cousin, said coolly, "No flag of parley, I see. The old bastard thinks to take us on. Who is that next to him, his son?"

"As alike as twin babes, so I'd guess so," Adain agreed. "It appears they are arguing."

"It looks like it to me. I'd guess the son is losing."

"The old man's insane," Adain muttered, "to try to approach us this way. Does he think I left the castle itself unguarded? With McCray arriving this morning and surrounding the house, Gillian is safe. There is no way Kleiss can win this fight."

"Insane might just describe him. At least, most of Scotland thinks so." Duncan unsheathed his sword in a supple, skilled movement. "The question is this: Will his men stand behind him?"

"I suppose we'll find out." Adain also drew his weapon, adrenaline surging in his veins. "Lord Kleiss," he shouted, urging his mount forward a few paces. "Go back home. You are trespassing, and should you advance any farther, we will cut you down like mown hay. I've two hundred McCray clansmen waiting at the castle if you should break through. It's hopeless. Go home, and save your men."

At the mention of the extra ranks, the earl's son said something and vehemently motioned with his hands, but the older man violently shook his head. Kleiss made a restive movement with his sword, jabbing it in the air. He responded, "You have something I want back, Cameron, bought with gold. Give me the English harlot and we will leave without staining the soil red with Cameron blood."

Adain's hands tightened on the reins, and it was all he could do to keep from charging forward in a headlong attack at the insult to Gillian. Duncan, who was by his side, shot his hand out and grabbed his arm in restraint. "Don't rush in and get yourself killed over a petty slur that no one believes. Keep a cool head. It isn't like you to be impulsive."

It was sound advice, but he was angry. Adain called back in cold, gritty challenge, "I'll see you dead, Kleiss, for that."

The old earl smiled evilly, the flash of his bared teeth showing even in the gloom of the rain-soaked afternoon. "Better men than you, Cameron, have tried and failed for decades before you were even born. Now, let's see how an impudent thief such as yourself fares in battle against our clan. You will not be so cocky with my sword through your throat."

"I welcome the opportunity to correct the failures of your past opponents." Adain smiled back with intentional insolence. Normally self-possessed in all situations, he fought to regain his calm for the sake of his wife. Even though he was certain the men guarding her would keep Gillian safe, he knew it would cause her pain should he come to any harm, even if it was not fatal.

She had whispered she loved him that very morning.

How had she penetrated his cold shell so quickly? All he knew was that when he looked into her soft blue eyes and heard the words, he felt suddenly free of the invisible chains of disappointment and hurt that had held him captive since the moment he realized Julia believed him capable of murder.

The most fortunate moment of his life was when he rode around the bend that fateful night only weeks ago and saw Gillian being dragged from that carriage. With a joyful future in reach, he wasn't about to relinquish it.

Turning in the saddle, he lifted his sword to signal his waiting men for the charge.

"Adain, wait!"

The urgency in Duncan's voice gave him pause, and he glanced back.

"Look."

In disbelief, Adain saw that the two men in front of the opposing troops were still in obvious dissention. The earl's son seemed to be against the fight, and his father insanely adamant. To his surprise, he saw Kleiss swing his sword viciously at his own son. The younger man managed to dodge the blow, and his sword slithered free of his scabbard. Kleiss roared in fury, taking another swipe, and the clang of metal came through the dreary afternoon.

No one interfered, and Adain wasn't sure who was more astonished at the outbreak of discord, the earl's forces or his own men.

"I hope he kills the old bastard," Duncan commented gleefully. "The earl—may his black soul rot in Hades—is trying to kill his own flesh and blood. His son is just defending himself, but the old man is in earnest."

It was true. Malcolm Graham was getting the worst of it, and his father's maniacal temper was unquestionably out of control.

"Good God," Adain muttered as the earl forced his horse closer and the fight became more intense. "Surely Kleiss's son understands he has to kill him to save himself."

Apparently so, for as swords flashed and blood was drawn, suddenly the younger man said something and feinted in with an effective slash across his father's right leg. There was a howl of pain and Kleiss reeled in the saddle.

It gave the earl's heir a chance to gain his inheritance, for he plunged his weapon deeply into his father's chest.

Both sides were silent as the old man slowly toppled over and slid to the ground, the sword sliding free as he fell.

Into the hush, Duncan murmured, "Well, I admit, that's not something you see every day, now, is it?"

"No," Adain admitted, watching as the victor of the unexpected battle stared for a moment at his father's fallen body. He was bleeding from a host of wounds, but did not seem to notice. Instead, he looked up at where hundreds of Cameron troops sat in disbelieving audience to what had happened. Then he urged his horse forward, galloping all alone the short distance that separated them. He halted in front of Adain and Duncan and gave them a brief salute with his bloody sword. "I am Malcolm Graham. As you can see, Cameron, I disagreed with this quarrel in the first place. There will be no fight unless you wish one."

"I am never interested in useless bloodshed."

Graham smiled grimly, blood trickling down his chin from a

gash on his cheek. "Neither am I. I will take my men and go. I wish you joy with your new bride."

He turned and rode back to the front; then the entire company whirled their horses and headed east.

It was over that easily, and no Cameron blood stained the grass.

The Earl of Kleiss was left behind. His body was splayed on the wet ground, sightless eyes staring at the gloomy sky.

Duncan said with a grin, "Well, that's a lesson learned, isn't it, lad? His own kin didn't even take him home for a decent burial. Now we're left with the refuse. What do you want us to do with him?"

"Toss him somewhere to rot, for all I care."

"My pleasure. Let the worms have him, I say."

Robbie McCray wasn't at all what she expected.

Well, that wasn't true, Gillian thought, watching him casually drink ale from a mug and chat with his men. He was tall and compellingly handsome, with dark hair and eyes, and a wickedly sensual smile. However, the wild border rogue had been polite and respectful upon their introduction, congratulating her on her marriage with obvious sincerity.

That Adain would call him to come join a fight he had no party to was a little surprising. So was the fact that he had come without hesitation.

It made her very nervous, for the sheer volume of men her husband had summoned told her he expected a very real battle.

Over her.

Well, no. Over Lord Kleiss's sense of insane outrage. He'd never even seen her.

Still, she felt guilty.

Afraid *and* guilty. For she had the suspicion that if harm came to Adain, she would feel as if her life had ended. Pensively, she sat and stared across the room with unseeing eyes, sick to her stomach at the thought of what could be happening. Her hands were clasped so tightly in her lap her fingers ached unmercifully.

"Don't fret, lass."

She glanced up. McCray sank into a chair next to her and gently lifted her entwined hands and pried them apart. He lightly rubbed her fingers and palms. "I could see you worrying from across the room." He flashed that charming smile. "There is naught to concern yourself over, for Adain can handle Kleiss. I am here only because he is overprotective of his new bride. I can understand it completely."

She attempted a smile, but her lips trembled. "If he is harmed, I would be . . . I am not sure how to even express it. I know we have been married only a short while, but I am—"

McCray laughed and shook his dark head, interrupting her. "You do not need to try to explain, my lady. I knew Julia a scarce three days before we wed, and I was captivated at once." His dark eyes showed a glint of devilish amusement. "I still am, in fact, even now, when she is breeding and a bit on the shrewish side. She claims her ill temper is entirely my fault."

Gillian lifted her brows, his levity and confidence easing some of her discomfort. "I believe it could be, Mr. McCray."

"Well, I suppose I had a thing or two to do with it." He winked and cocked his head to the side. "It is nice to see you smile. Adain is a lucky man, and I am glad for you both. I once loved a bonny English lass, and you remind me of her. Instead, I married a fiery Scottish girl with dark hair and a sharp tongue." He gave a theatrical grimace.

The door swung open and a young man came in, his gaze raking the room and settling on the two of them. The arrival came over and said breathlessly, "Riders coming, Robbie. It could be the Camerons returning, but they are riding fast and with a purpose."

Instantly, McCray changed from charming courtier to decisive leader. He released her hand from his comforting grip and stood, swiftly moving across the room with long strides. Her heart pounding, Gillian could hear him give staccato orders on what to do in case it actually was the earl's attacking forces.

Luckily, it was not.

There was a great commotion outside as hundreds of horses thundered up, and moments later Adain strode through the door. He crossed the room and smiled at her, the curve of his mouth nothing at all like the teasing smile McCray seemed to produce at will, but instead something intense and real. Before he could even speak, Gillian jumped up and threw herself into his arms, twining her arms around his neck and burying her face against his chest. She gave a small sob of relief and inhaled the smell of fresh rain and his own male scent, the one she knew so intimately.

"'Tis over," he said, his fingers gently caressing her back. "Without one drop of blood shed except that which needed to be spilled a long time ago. You can rest easy and so can I, for you are mine."

"Forever," she promised in a muffled voice against his chest. It was wet, but she did not care.

Adain laughed then, a low rumble of amusement. His voice dropped a notch in timbre. "Yes, forever sounds very appealing."

Men poured into the main hall of the big house and he gently freed himself from her embrace. "I have to speak to Robbie and Mrs. Dunbar, for McCray will wish to hear what happened, and all these men need to be fed."

"I'll help all I can." She nodded and wiped at her wet cheeks, the moisture not just from his sodden clothes.

"That will endear you to her, though she seems to have accepted you well enough for an Englishwoman."

She lifted her skirts a little and started across the room.

"Gillian."

The sound of her name, said in such a husky tone, made her pause and look back.

Her husband's beautiful silver eyes glimmered. "I do not embrace violence, but I warn you, the fire of battle is in my blood and was never satisfied. Tonight, will you assuage it in another, much more pleasurable way?"

I want you. . . .

She could read the desire in those eyes she loved so well.

"I look forward to it," she said truthfully, with a blush.

McCray poured himself another drink and grumbled, "I anticipated at least some sort of combat. Damn Malcolm Graham—he should have done that long ago and saved us all this trouble. I got my hopes up for naught."

"It was not a pretty sight," Adain admitted, sprawled in the chair behind his desk in his study. "Father against son. Entirely unnatural."

"Yes, but history shows it has happened before this day." Robbie's gaze was direct. "Though I cannot imagine it. You have heard Julia is expecting our first child?"

"She wrote to me," Adain acknowledged, inclining his head. "Congratulations."

Congratulations. He could say it and, what was more, mean it. Gillian had healed him that much.

"As always, my wife and I disagree, for while I insist that a girl would please me, she wants a boy." The other man ran a lean hand through his dark hair and grimaced. "You know how she is, stubborn to a fault. I want an heir, naturally, but a bonny girl would suit me just as well. A healthy child and safe birth are all I ask."

"I will drink to both." Adain had to wonder at how little rancor he had over this news, which just weeks ago would have blackened his life even further. He felt joy for his cousin and her husband, not sorrow for himself.

Why should he begrudge anyone happiness and glad news when he knew Gillian waited for him upstairs?

McCray lifted a dark brow. "Somehow I feel certain you will follow in our footsteps soon enough. Your bride is lovely, Cameron. And as sweet as a summer's breeze across Loch Cray. The thieving renegades who tried to rob her uncle's carriage did you a favor, my friend."

"I think so too. And you are a true friend, McCray, despite the hard feelings that at first fell between us. I appreciate your coming at once."

"Don't thank me." Julia's husband grinned. "I attract trouble in an uncanny way. How I see it, you now owe me assistance if the McCrays are rallied against at any time."

"You have it." Adain frowned. "We'll be fighting our enemy soon enough, from the sound of things. This is where the Sassenachs come first when they invade. It has been that way forever. The Borders get the brunt of it each time. We are the gateway for English wars."

"We'll send our wives north to Ian if we hear word of another invasion over our independence. They'll be safe with my cousin in the Highlands, and he will protect them as none other could."

"Agreed." Adain hoped it wouldn't come to it, but he knew that at least some fighting would break out, if not now, then within the next few years. The struggle for Scottish independence went on, as it had for centuries.

"This is not the time to worry over that." McCray shoved himself to his feet, his lazy grin all-knowing. "I think it is getting late. I know what *I'd* be doing if I were wed to such a winsome lass and she waited in my bed."

"There is no question of that," Adain replied dryly. "We've all heard of your reputation."

The other man looked uncharacteristically sober for a moment. "Go to her, for there were tears in her beautiful eyes this afternoon as she worried over your safety."

"That is a very sound idea."

McCray sighed. "I get to sleep with my men and horses this wet, cold eve. Maybe you can think of this as retribution of some kind as you enjoy her charms."

Adain replied quietly, "I no longer need retribution."

Not when he had love.

*   *   *

Gillian lay expectantly in the big bed, wondering if it was truly shameless of her to be entirely naked beneath the coverlet.

Probably, but she just didn't care.

Adain *had* said he wanted her, after all, and certainly she wanted him.

Surely she was just sparing him the trouble of immediately removing her nightdress.

The latch lifted and the slight sound made her heart suddenly pound. Tall and dark, he stepped into the room. When he saw her bared shoulders above the drawn-up blanket, he gave her a heated look of entirely male approval. His hands went to unlace his shirt.

"I see you read my mind." His grin was a flash of white teeth in the dim room.

"Hardly," she countered. "You made your wishes clear enough earlier. No insight was involved or needed."

"So you are obedient, then?" He pulled off his shirt. "I've heard Englishwomen can be difficult. Perhaps you seek to disprove the notion."

He was teasing her, and she loved the slow warmth of his smile. She loved *him*.

Well, two could play that game. Very slowly, she eased the sheets downward and first exposed her breasts, already tight with desire, her nipples hard as jewels. She arched her back slightly, thrusting them upward. He made a small sound as he stared, and his shirt flew carelessly across the room as he tossed it away.

The sheets slid down her rib cage and stomach, and then past her hips as her pubic hair was exposed. Gillian wiggled a little as she bared her body, and finally the entirety of the bedclothes were pushed toward the foot of the bed.

Her husband sat down to tug off his boots with a rough impatience that fired her overwhelming need.

She spread her legs apart, letting him see the most intimate part of her body, exposing her wet, soft sex.

"Perfect," he murmured. "Show me more."

It was a decadent request, but she felt quite decadent. Decadently happy, decadent in complete sexual need.

Her thighs parted as far as she could open them.

"I'll be right there, my lovely wife."

There was little doubt he was as ready as she was, if not more. He jerked down his breeches and exposed his erection, the springing magnificent length of it a promise of pleasure and completion. Nude, beautiful, with an almost ferocious expression on his handsome face, he joined her on the bed and at once moved over her, rubbing between her labia with the tip of his cock, smearing the crest with the fluids of her arousal.

His entrance was a forceful thrust, and she absorbed his entire length gladly, the sensation exactly what she needed. They mated, absorbed in each other and the glorious union of their bodies, his need as primitive as he had warned her it would be. Gillian found completion twice before he climaxed, his powerful body shuddering over and into her, the forceful spurt of his seed accompanied by his groan of satisfaction.

Afterward, they floated together, arms locked around each other, and she felt grateful and triumphant that her life had taken such an unexpected turn.

Her husband finally lifted his head and tenderly skimmed her cheek with the backs of his fingers. "That was a little impetuous. I hope I didn't hurt you."

"You would never hurt me."

"That shows a great deal of faith."

She looked at him from under the veil of her lashes. "Not so much. You are a good man. I knew it the minute I saw you. Besides, you are remarkably easy to read."

"Am I?" He nuzzled her neck with his warm mouth, and she shivered in enjoyment. "What am I thinking now?"

I love you.

Dared she hope he would say the words? He'd been wounded before, and all scars, even when a person healed, remained.

"That you think I am not too much of a bad bargain for an English waif you had to rescue on a deserted road."

"Ah, you are not as insightful as you think you are." Adain kissed her gently and looked into her eyes. "Try again, lass."

Gillian responded in a hushed voice of pure joy, "Perhaps . . . something very wonderful?"

"Such as?"

"Adain," she finally said reproachfully, "if you wish to say something, say it yourself."

"It's difficult," he admitted after a moment, still stroking her back. "The last time I felt this way about a woman, I lost her."

"*I* am here to stay." Gillian touched his cheek and added teasingly, "Unless, of course, you tire of me and wish for me to—"

"Never," he said in a growl. "I love you and you are mine, wife."

Never sounded perfect, Gillian thought in joyous contentment as she rested in his possessive embrace.

Photo by Jon McMahel

Emma Wildes grew up loving books, so turning to writing seemed a natural course. She has been a #1 bestselling author at Fictionwise, a WisRWA winner in historical romance, a Lories winner, a Passionate Plume winner, and a first-place Eppie winner for best erotic historical romance. She lives in rural Indiana with her husband, three children, and a menagerie of pets. You can keep tabs on Emma at www.emmawildes.com.